BADD ASS

A BADD BROTHERS NOVEL

Jasinda Wilder

BADD ASS

ONE

Mara

IT TOOK ME A FEW MOMENTS OF BLINKING IN THE DARKNESS to pull my thoughts together and figure out where I was. I stared around me, my breath coming hard and fast, my chest heaving, sweat dripping down the small of my back. The walls seemed close and the ceiling low. Out of the small window I could see moonlight reflected off the rippling water...Alaska.

Right. Alaska.

Shit...why was I in Alaska again? And where was I, exactly? Think, Mara, think.

Wait...why was I naked?

I twisted in the bed and hung my feet off the side, touching the floor—the carpeting was thin with a tight pile. I heard a noise behind me and turned to peer over my shoulder at the bed—and nearly screamed.

A man.

Big. *Huge.* Massive. And fucking *gorgeous*. He was on his back, an arm thrown over his forehead. Buzzed brown hair that showed signs of being allowed to grow out from a standard military high-and-tight. Muscles upon muscles, and more muscles, lean and hard and shredded, as in maybe eight or ten percent body fat at the most on a six-foot frame...and the muscles he was packing put him at two hundred pounds easily, if not two-ten or two-fifteen.

He was sleeping, but somehow I just knew he had a pair of brown eyes that looked like shards of polished mahogany. I'd tossed aside the blankets upon waking, so they were bunched down over his thighs, and the moonlight in the bedroom was bright enough that I could clearly make out every inch of him, and *Jeeeeee-sus*, there were a lot of inches. The man was hung like a horse, and this was when he was limp as a wet noodle. Hard? My throat tightened and my stomach flipped, and my hoo-ha ached, because erect he'd be jutting a monster cock so big he could be a porn star.

Come to think of it, I was achy and sore down there, and I was naked in this guy's bed, and he was naked in his bed...two plus two equals four, Mara. Ding ding ding! You slept with another stranger, you hopeless slut.

How shocking...not.

My head ached, and my mouth was dry, which explained my difficulty in remembering things. I'd gotten hammered.

So, think.

Remember.

I remembered his eyes. Somehow, those were seared into my memory, mainly because I could remember his eyes searing into me as he moved above me. Oh, yep, here we go. The memories were bubbling up—guess all I had to do was think about fucking this gorgeous god of a man and the details would come back all by themselves.

I remembered the way he'd picked me up in the kitchen, carried me in here as easily as if I were a rag doll, and then tossed me onto this bed. And then... he'd shoved my legs open, spread my pussy apart with a pair of big, callused, but gentle thumbs and his tongue had performed some kind of sorcery on me, bringing me to a thrashing orgasm so fast he had to have made a deal with the Devil to acquire oral skills like that. Within seconds I was biting back screams.

And he'd just gotten started. He'd licked and sucked and fingered me to orgasm three more times, and then he'd crawled up to kneel over me, reached into the drawer of his nightstand and produced a condom. Rolling it on, he gave me a look that had asked me if I was ready, or if I wanted to back out. I'd taken a long gander at his cock, and had almost backed out, because yeah, goddamn, that thing was a fucking club.

Just kidding. I hadn't almost backed out. A man as gorgeous as Zane? With a body like his, a face like his, and a cock like his? You don't back out of that, even if you are a little scared of what his Godzilla dong might do to your poor little lady bits.

There had been no need to be scared, though, because he was clearly no novice at making sure he didn't hurt me. He'd gone slowly, easing in gradually, and his mouth had been doing exciting things to my nipples, and I was all loose from the multiple orgasms, so it almost hadn't hurt at all. Then he'd pushed all the way in, and the ache and the burn as I stretched to accommodate him had turned to rapture, the like of which I'd never felt before—and then he'd started moving, and rapture had turned into something else so crazy hot I had no descriptor for it. Like, literally, he'd fucked me so good I didn't have adjectives for how good it felt, and I'm pretty decent with my words.

Just then I remembered his name: Zane Badd.

I scrubbed my face with both hands, letting out a soft sigh as more details flooded back. God, he'd been incredible in bed. Normally after a one-night stand, I was gone the moment I woke up. I've made an art out of sneaking out of men's beds, and it's not a walk of shame if you don't feel shame, right?

Yeah, who am I kidding? Not myself, that's for damn sure. I was going to do the walk of shame in about three minutes. My record time for going from waking up to out the front door is ninety seconds, and I'd only managed that because I'd stuffed my bra and underwear into my purse and run out the door wearing my LBD, purse in one hand and shoes in the other. The guy I'd slept with hadn't been entirely honest about his relationship status, it had turned out, which had gotten him a black eye, his girlfriend a sincere apology from me, and myself a month-long case of self-recrimination, and a feeble attempt to answer the question: what the hell is wrong with me?

Today's walk of shame is brought to you by the letter D, for *damn, do I wish I could stay and ride his D one more time.*

But no. I don't dare. I remember very clearly the conversation we'd had, how I'd been the one to insist this was a one-and-done. I hadn't missed the stubborn look in his eyes, though, which meant I had to make myself scarce before he charmed, flattered, flirted, and seduced me into sticking around for another round of mind-blowing sex. Which, no, didn't sound bad at all. If I was honest with myself, I was kind of longing for some sober sex, especially with a Don Juan of this guy's abilities. The part that sounded like hell was the sure-to-come fallout, the part where he'd turn out to be a complete ass-bag, and I'd get attached and then end up with a broken heart.

I cast another long, appreciative glance at Zane, at his acres of lovely man muscle, and his California Redwood of a penis.

Still asleep, thankfully, both the man and his dong. I mean, if he'd gotten morning wood, it might have been—ahem—*harder*…for me to leave.

Chicks can make dick jokes, too, you know.

I slid carefully out of bed, scrounging on the floor for my bra and underwear. I stepped into the underwear and tugged them up, hooked the bra in front, slid it around to shrug into the straps and into the cups. The jeans were tricky, because those bitches were *tight*, necessitating me doing the tight pants shimmy until my big ass finally squeezed into the skin-tight denim. Shirt, shoes, purse, and done.

Now the hard part: leaving without looking back. It was an especially challenging operation this time, because Zane Badd was the most gorgeous man I'd ever laid eyes on, and he had, by far, the most talented mouth I'd ever felt, and the most perfectly sized, well-proportioned and aesthetically pleasing cock I'd ever had the pleasure of being pleasured by.

Stop thinking about his dick, Amarantha Quinn, I scolded myself.

Sigh.

Fine. Time to go.

The doorknob didn't squeak when I turned it, which was helpful, and nor did the hinges. A few quiet, careful, tiptoed steps and I was out of his bedroom without looking back or getting sucked back in by his goddamn ridiculous body and face and dick.

Damn it, damn it, damn it—stop thinking about his penis!

That was hard, though, because his dick was just so damn pretty. And that penis pun was unintentional, FYI.

I literally palm-slapped my forehead in a futile attempt to dislodge all thoughts, puns, and images of Zane's cock, hard or otherwise.

The living room was empty, as was the kitchen. Coming from the kitchen, however, was an aroma that made it nearly impossible to keep walking: the smell of brewing coffee.

Damn it. Don't stop to steal a cup; don't stop to

steal even a sniff.

I paused at the door, which would lead me down into the bar, longingly inhaling the scent of coffee.

"Thought you could just sneak out, huh?" a deep, gruff, sleepy voice murmured behind me.

I was proud of myself for not jumping, even though he'd come up behind me without so much as a sound. "Yeah, that was the general idea."

"What about a goodbye kiss?"

I refused to turn around. "Not a chance."

"Goodbye fuck?"

"Nope." Steady on, Mara—stick to your guns.

"How about a goodbye blow job?" His voice was close to my ear, buzzing, rumbling, amused. Teasing, mostly, but also partially hopeful—you know how guys are about that, laughingly suggesting a BJ as a joke, but also hoping just maybe it'd actually happen.

"Let me think…no." I twisted the knob. "Bye, Zane. It was amazing."

"You know what was amazing?" he asked, his hands settling on my hips. "Watching you trying to get into those jeans."

I whirled, pressing my back to the door in an attempt to get away from the heat and thrill of his proximity. "You were watching?"

"Navy SEAL, remember? I sleep light and wake easy." He gestured at the coffee pot on the counter a few feet away, behind us. "Plus, I wake at four regardless."

"I wondered about the coffee," I said.

Fuck, fuck, fuck me. He was naked. And *hard*. Like, hard enough to hammer nails.

He saw me looking, and smirked. "So. We've ruled out goodbye kisses, fucks, and BJs...how about some goodbye coffee?"

"Will you be wearing pants?"

"Probably not. I like forcing you to look at what you're walking away from."

"Then no goodbye coffee." I frowned at him. "And you have a pretty high opinion of your cock—and my attraction to it—don't you?"

He shrugged. "Can you tell me it's misplaced?"

I couldn't, actually, but I'd be damned if I'd admit that. "Bye, Zane." I turned back to the door, my hand on the knob.

He sighed in irritation, and let me get the door pulled open before he grabbed me by the wrist, yanked me back, spun me around, kicked the door closed, and pressed me back up against it.

His face was right in mine, his breath on my lips, his hands on my hips.

"Um...Zane?"

He nipped at my lower lip with his teeth. "Hmmm?"

"I thought we agreed we wouldn't make this awkward?"

"You're telling me this is awkward?" He whispered into my ear, his hands descending to cup my ass, and then his mouth was on my neck, and I was having trouble breathing.

I was paralyzed; head tipped back, breath caught in my chest, feeling his mouth descending from the side of my neck to my jaw and then to the dip of my clavicle. Shit, shit, shit, this is exactly what I was afraid of.

Because now his mouth was on my skin, and my brain was going doolally—as my dear Irish Gran would say—and I was having trouble remembering why I was supposed to walk away.

Wait…what were my hands doing? Where were my hands?

Goddammit! The stupid, traitorous wrist appendages were drifting up and settling between our bodies, and then I felt his cock in my hands, sliding through my fists, because apparently I couldn't be this close to that magical organ of his without putting my hands on it.

"Um." This was a young-sounding male voice, from behind us. "You know, they have these really cool inventions we kids like to call bedrooms. They have doors you can actually close, too. Just…you know…saying."

I gasped in surprise, peering around Zane.

Eighteen at most, he was tall and rangy, hair in a messy undercut, the sides shaved to the scalp, the top long and curly and deep brown, almost black. He was wearing a pair of Stanford sweatpants, the cuffs tugged up above his calves, and his torso was bare, displaying lean muscles and tattoos on his forearms, a bunch of interlocking, interwoven geometric shapes and higher math symbols. He looked enough like Zane that I was fairly sure this was one of the seven brothers I vaguely remembered Zane mentioning.

"Oh, hey, Xavier, didn't know you were awake." Zane backed away from me and turned around to face his brother.

The younger brother cringed away. "Holy shit, Zane! Do you go around clubbing baby seals with that thing? Jesus! Put it away, man!"

Zane laughed. "Baby seals? No. Who would want to club those cute little things? I have been known to club…other things, though." He lurched toward his brother, waggling his hips to make his dick sway back and forth. "Like you, for example. I could club you with it."

Xavier scrambled away from Zane with alacrity,

hurling himself over the back of the couch and toss-
ing a throw pillow at his brother, shouting "NO CLUB
ME! NO CLUB ME!" in a faux accent.

I couldn't help cackling, because Zane was still
jumping around, buck ass naked, chasing his brother, his massively erect dick bobbing and swaying back
and forth like the mast of a sailboat in choppy water.

"Prepare for a clubbin', kid!" Zane said in voice
even deeper and gruffer than his own natural rough
bass, climbing onto the couch after his brother, taunt-
ing him.

"I swear to god, if you don't get that fucking
monster out of my face I'll make you a Grindr account and give all the horny gay boys your phone
number," Xavier threatened.

That worked.

Zane hopped backward off the couch, holding
the pillow over his anaconda. "You wouldn't."

Xavier scraped a hand through his messy mop of
curls, brushing it back out of his eyes. "Try me, com-
mando-boy. You'll be drowning in gays faster than
you can say power bottom."

This was as good a chance as any to make my es-
cape, I realized, since Zane was facing off with his kid
brother. I snuck out the door while Zane was count-
er-threatening Xavier. I tiptoed down the stairs and
into the darkened bar.

I made it to the dead-bolted entrance of the bar before Zane noticed my absence. "Goddammit! She's getting away."

"What is she, a prisoner?" I heard Xavier ask.

There was no verbal response from Zane, but I heard his footsteps on the stairs as I flipped the dead bolt. "Mara, wait!"

I didn't wait, because if I did, I'd end up with my hands around that cock again, and then I'd never leave.

Something important to note about Navy SEALs: they, by definition, don't have a give-up-easily setting. I was outside, and a good twenty steps down the street, shuffling through piles of discarded red Solo cups, bags of trash, overturned folding tables, carts full of folded chairs, a garbage bin full of empty beer bottles...all the detritus of a hell of a party. They'd cordoned off the entire block around their bar and were planning on cleaning up this morning. Although, as hammered as some of Zane's brothers had been, it'd probably be several hours yet before the street was back to normal. Not to mention the fact that they needed to deal with the brother who had gotten injured last night—Baxter I think his name was. Someone had taken him to the hospital to get stitches in his leg after he and Zane had fallen on some glass. As far as I knew, Zane was none the worse for wear 'cause he sure hadn't complained when we were having sex last night.

I made it to the Ketchikan Public Works barrier when Zane caught up with me—wearing a pair of basketball shorts, thankfully. They didn't really do much good, though, because he was still sporting a hard-on big enough to tent the shorts, although it did seem to be subsiding a tiny bit.

He hopped over the barrier and put his hands on my shoulders to stop me. "Why are you in such a hurry to leave?"

"Why are you so determined to make me stay?" I demanded. "It was great sex, Zane, but…" I trailed off with a shrug, hoping he'd accept that as a non-verbal explanation.

"But what?" He demanded.

So…no, he wasn't going to accept it.

I sighed. "But I'm leaving. It's what I do."

"What if I just flat out asked you to stay a few days?" There was no guile in his dark eyes, no hint of any kind of nascent assholery.

But then, in my experience, the asshole tended to crop up when you least expected it, often without warning, and it wasn't until you had the benefit of 20/20 hindsight that you finally noticed the warning signs you should have seen before. Thus, I leave before the assholery has a chance to emerge.

I ducked under the barrier, being too short to be able to step over like he'd done. "Nope."

He growled in frustration. "You're difficult."

"You have no idea," I said, still walking.

"Maybe I'd like to have an idea."

"No, you wouldn't. My brand of difficult is... not something I'd let anyone sign up for." I kept walking, ignoring Zane as he kept pace with me, barefoot, shirtless, and too fucking sexy in the pre-dawn moonlight for anyone's good, least of all mine.

"You know," he said, finally stopping, "people accuse me of being arrogant, and now I think I'm finally getting a taste of what they mean."

I halted in my tracks, whirling on him. "*I'm* arrogant? *Really*? You're a jackass."

"Yeah, maybe." He used my pause to close the space between us. "But at least I'm honest."

"And I'm not?"

"Nope." He tapped my nose. "You lyin', baby girl."

"To who? About what?" I huffed and spun on my heel. "And why can't you just let me make my walk of shame in peace?"

"To both of us about why you're walking away and, no, because I don't want you to make the walk of shame."

"Yeah, well, then I'm lying. Fine by me. But I

said last night this was going to be one night only, no strings attached, no weirdness in the morning." I gestured between us. "This? This is weirdness. A lot of weirdness. I thought you were down for a hook-up, and now you're making it all…awkward."

He quirked an eyebrow at me. "You are really hung up on things being awkward, you know that?" He crossed his arms over his chest. "And for the record, I *am* down for a hook-up, I just…want more than *one* hook-up."

"Zane, that's not—"

He cut in over me. "But since you're so intent on leaving, I'll let you leave, no more weirdness."

"Really?" I quirked an eyebrow back at him. "Just like that?"

He shrugged. "Just like that."

Temptation, you're a nasty bitch.

But, I'm a strong woman, and I've faced temptation before. Been burned by it, too, so…yeah. I walked away.

"Nice to have met you, Zane Badd."

"Same here, Mara."

I walked, my head throbbing and my stomach churning with a raging hangover, following the docks, the water on my left, unsure of where I was going, because I still couldn't remember why I'd come to Ketchikan in the first damn place. It was hard to make my exit look purposeful when I had no idea where I going, but I gave it my best, dammit.

A block, two blocks, three...I kept expecting him to appear behind me with that sexy, gruff voice of his, but he never did. He actually let me just walk away.

The bastard.

It wasn't until I was walking past a docked cruise ship that I remembered why I was here: my best friend Claire was on a cruise that was docking here tomorrow morning—this morning, now, I suppose— and I'd come to Ketchikan to surprise her. Claire had recently taken a job in Seattle, leaving me behind in San Francisco. The bitch, she'd broken up the Gruesome Twosome. I hadn't seen Claire in person in something like six months, although we spoke on the phone, texted, and emailed each other constantly. But digital communication just isn't...the same.

Claire and I had been nurses together in the Army, assigned to the same unit right out of Basic. Our efficiency together as a team had earned us the nickname Gruesome Twosome, and we'd just kept using it. It was funny, too. Or well, ironic maybe, because we were both these short, good-looking blonde chicks, so the nickname seemed somewhat misplaced, unless you'd seen us in action, up to the elbows in gore.

Then, when we both took our papers at the same time, it just made sense for us to live together. And we had for several years. She'd found work in the tech industry doing something fancy with computers, because even though she was an experienced nurse she had no desire to keep doing it once she got out of the Army. I worked in the tech industry, too, although my job was in an HR department rather then working with the actual machines.

We had each other, we had our awesome apartment in the heart of downtown San Fran, we had our favorite bars…it was great.

And then Claire got the offer of a lifetime, doing what she'd been doing only getting paid double…in Seattle. Of course she had to take it, and I as her best friend had to support and encourage her decision to go to Seattle. Didn't mean I had to like it, though.

My new roommate, who had taken over Claire's bedroom,…sucked. Loud, annoying, she watched the stupidest shit on TV and she didn't even like *The Walking Dead*, for fuck's sake—and to top it off she was a shitty wing girl at the bar. She brought home annoying guys, too: grunty, weird, the kind who'd walk around naked making dicks jokes while I was getting ready for work. She ate my food and didn't replace it, left her garbage everywhere, and made these stupid, obnoxious, yelping noises during sex.

She sounded like a damn zebra.

So, when Claire forwarded her cruise itinerary—rubbing in my face that she could *afford* a cruise—I'd decided it was high time I got some girl time with my bestie. I used my vacation days, packed some shit, and booked a flight to Ketchikan. I had a room at a B&B, and I'd checked in and left my stuff there last night before deciding to explore the city on foot.

Those explorations had led me to an awesome outdoor party, a wedding reception open to the public and put on by a local bar owner...which had led to a few drinks while people watching...which had led to someone shouting *medic*. It's ingrained, at this point. Once a combat medic, always a combat medic. You hear that word...your training kicks in and you just go where you're needed.

I'd found myself face to face with a mesmerizing pair of deep mahogany eyes, framed in the sexiest, handsomest face I'd ever seen. Which had turned out to be connected to the most amazing body I'd ever seen, and the most amazing cock I'd ever seen, which had led to the most amazing sex I'd ever had...

And walked away from.

It was for the best, though, I told myself when I finally I reached my B&B. He was clingy, following me out onto the street, practically begging me to come back for more sex.

I didn't do clingy.

I hosed off in the shower when I got to my room and passed out, still naked and wet, on the bed, telling myself not to have any dirty dreams about Zane Badd.

You can guess how well that worked.

TWO

Zane

I CLOSED AND LOCKED THE DOOR TO THE BAR BEHIND ME and stomped upstairs, resisting the temptation to grab a bottle of Jack on the way up; four in the morning was probably too early to start drinking.

Xavier was at the stove scrambling some eggs. "Got shot down, huh?"

"No, I didn't get shot down, dipshit," I snarled. "She just...had to go."

Xavier nodded, pushing the eggs around the pan. "Sucks."

"Yeah, well, what are you gonna do?" I sniffed.

"Got any for me?"

Xavier ignored my question, but ended up answering it by divvying up the eggs onto two plates, with toast and bacon on the side. I poured us coffee and we sat down to eat.

After a few minutes of silence, Xavier glanced at me. "She was hot."

I nodded. "Insanely hot."

"Sounded like the sex was good, too."

I frowned at him. "You're a virgin, Xavier—how would you know?"

He smirked at me. "Well, correct me if I'm wrong, but three hours of screaming seems to indicate quality sexual relations."

I snorted at him. "'Quality sexual relations' he says. Fuckin' dork." I chomped on a piece of bacon, and then sighed as I chewed. "But yes, it was the best sex I've ever had."

"And you let her go?" he asked, his voice disapproving. "Have you learned nothing from our dear eldest brother?"

"It's not that simple," I said. "I wish it were."

"So…you got shot down."

I threw my fork at him, nailing him the chest, spattering eggs all over him. "Yes, goddammit," I snapped. "I got shot down."

Not much fazed Xavier except being touched, so

he just picked up my fork from where it had fallen on his lap, and handed it back to me, brushing the egg off his chest. "You seem vexed."

I gaped at him. "You're a regular Sherlock, ain't ya, kid? What gave it away?"

"Throwing the fork was a pretty obvious signifier," he started, and then stopped, eying me warily. "Oh. You were being sarcastic."

"Yes, I was being sarcastic." I resumed eating, but angrily this time.

"I don't understand," Xavier said, after a while. "You've had a lot of sex, with a lot of different women, and rarely the same one twice. What makes her so different? And why are you so upset?"

"That's part of what has me wigging out," I answered. "I don't know. I mean, yeah, Mara was fuckin' gorgeous, man. Those tits? That *ass*? The way she moved, the sounds she made? She was tight, but she knew what she was doing, and knew what she liked...and then there was just...fuck, I don't know. Something about the way we were together that was just...different. Something about...her, I guess."

"So why don't you try to convince her to go out with you, then? Like, try to...I don't know what you'd call it. Get to know her, or something."

"You make it sound so simple, but that's not how...it's not—I don't..." I trailed off, hunting for an explanation. "That's called starting a relationship, and I just don't know how that shit works. Besides, I don't do relationships."

"You have relationships with all of us," Xavier responded, head tilted to one side.

I laughed. "That's you guys. You're my brothers."

"Is it really so different?"

I laughed all the harder. "Spoken like someone with less of a clue about women than me. Yes, Xavier, it is exactly that different. You guys are my brothers, my family. I've known you my whole life. Plus, you're dudes. Women are…different. They're tricky. Complicated."

Xavier chewed on that for a while as he finished eating. When he was done, he cleared our plates and poured us more coffee, then sat down again, having come to some kind of conclusion.

He eyed me over the rim of his mug. "You're chicken."

I choked on my coffee. "Excuse me?"

"I said…you're *chicken*."

I stood up slowly. "You do realize I can, and will, break every bone in your body, right?"

"You might punch me a few times, but you wouldn't break my bones," he answered smoothly, ever the logical one.

I sat back down. "Yeah, well, you ever been punched?"

He traced a fingertip around the rim. "Yes. Quite frequently, once upon a time."

I frowned. "You have? When?"

"High school. I got picked on a lot. I was beat up like once a week, minimum."

I set my mug down. "You're shitting me."

He stared at me, genuinely baffled. "Why would I jest with you about this?"

"I never knew."

He snorted. "Well, duh, of course you didn't. You were gone."

"Yeah, but the others—"

He kept going as if I hadn't spoken. "By the time I got to high school, you, Bax, and Brock were all gone, the twins had graduated already and were play- ing gigs, which only left Lucian, and he dropped out to get his GED and work on the boat. And Sebastian? He had his hands full keeping the bar afloat. Dad's death came as a shock to all of you because you were gone, but I'd seen it coming. He was…sick. He'd been sick for a long time, he just…finally couldn't take it any longer. He'd been pretty much absent for like… two or three years by the time he died. Like, he was *around*, physically, but he wasn't…*there*. So Bast had to step up, work the bar, make sure I got to school,

all that. Who was going to do anything about the bullies at school?" Xavier shrugged like it was irrelevant.
"The school wasn't going to stop it. I've never really had any friends, and all my brothers were gone or
busy, and my father was a mental case."

"Shit, Xavier, you make it sound like you were
completely alone."

He blinked at me for a long time. "I was."

"Goddamn, kid. I had no idea." I let out a breath.
"And you were bullied at school?"

He nodded. "Badly, yes. They'd punch me in the
hallways, fill my locker with dog shit, steal my books,
and beat me up on the way home. It was rough. But…I
graduated, and got the scholarship to Stanford. None
of those assholes even went to college. They're all still
here working on fishing boats and fixing cars. It's all
they've ever done and all they will ever do."

"Why do you think they bullied you?"

It was his turn to laugh at me. "Spoken like someone with no clue what it's like to be bullied." He took
a hit of his coffee. "They bullied me because I was
younger than all of my classmates by two years, at
least. I was so much more intelligent than all of them
that I might as well have been an alien."

"And people fear and hate what they don't
understand."

"Exactly."

"Shit, kid, I'm sorry that happened to you. I'm sorry none of us were here to protect you."

"You couldn't have even if you'd been here," he said. "But I made it through. I survived, and that's what matters. I'm stronger for it now."

"Back to your original statement, though. You mentioned something about a chicken?"

He nodded. "Yeah, you."

"You better explain."

"You're attracted to this girl at the very least, yes?"

"Yeah," I said, hesitant.

"And she seems to share that base level attraction, yes?"

I nodded. "Right."

"But having examined the subtext of what you've said versus what you've implied, combined with your conflicted body language, I would hazard a guess that you feel a lot more than just a base level physical attraction for this woman. You are unfamiliar with what it feels like to deal with an emotional connection, however, because—and I'm only guessing here, but I would lay a wager that I'm correct—you have learned to shut down your...emotional synapses, so to speak. Your capacity to deal with emotions has atrophied. You deal in the physical. You are strong, fast, powerful, athletic, vigorous, and virile. The physical world is easy for you, it's where you dominate—not to suggest a lack of intelligence, mind you, but your primary prowess is as a warrior. And combat, from what I've read, forces one to inure him or herself to the rigors and traumas of war. Emotions are an unwelcome liability." He paused to think. "But yet, in the real world—or rather, in the larger context of society outside the theater of war, I should say, emotions are the currency of culture."

I blinked at him, trying to absorb and process what he'd said. "You said a mouthful, kid."

"I just mean—"

"Like you said at the wedding, I'm not stupid, Xavier. I know what you meant; I just have to process it. My brain works all right, just not as fast as yours."

"Very few do, in my experience." He said this as a matter of fact, rather than as a boast.

"You're saying I—that I'm in love with her?

Xavier made a face. "In *love*? You just met—all you did was have sex. You know literally nothing about this woman, Zane. There are emotions other than love and lust that you can feel toward females, you know."

"Oh really? Like what?" I prompted, curious and amused.

"Friendship?" he suggested, characteristically oblivious to the subtle note of sarcasm in my voice.

"Respect. Compassion. Curiosity. Need. Desire, but for the company of the person rather than the physical desire connoted for our purposes by the term lust. And really, the range of human of emotion is such a broad and complicated spectrum that I fear we do not have adequate terminology for all of the nuances and varieties that are possible."

I shook my head. "Where the hell do you get this shit, Xavier?"

"I read constantly and very quickly, and I possess an innate curiosity that drives me to explore a broad range of subjects." He pivoted to stare out the window at the pink of dawn on the horizon. "Math, science, electronics and robotics, physics, these are subjects I innately comprehend. I possess a highly logical mind, thus those subjects are easy for me. Humans are not...logical, nor predictable, except that in some ways we *are* logical and predictable...humanity is a difficult, complex topic. Psychology, emotions...these are things I don't grasp as easily as I would differential calculus or quantum physics." He sighed deeply, and I sat in silence, listening, since Xavier rarely spoke of himself. "Like most geniuses, I struggle with expressing myself, and struggle even more with understanding people. I mean, I understand people on an anthropological level, but when it comes to actually dealing with people? I'm much less sure of myself in actual social situations."

"This is probably the deepest conversation I've ever had at…" I consulted the clock on the stove, "five o'clock in the morning."

"Really?" He smiled, gazing off into space. "I often sit with Hajji after our shift, and we talk of many deep and complex issues well into the smallest hours of the morning."

"Who's Hajji?" I asked.

"His name is actually something like Mohammad ibn Ibrahim. Hajji is a title he earned by making the pilgrimage to Mecca, called a hajj."

I nodded. "Ah, yeah. I've heard about that."

"He works at the diner with me, back at school. He's very intelligent, very erudite and well spoken. We are a bit of an odd couple, so to speak, as he's well past fifty and I'm barely eighteen and we're from totally different cultures and backgrounds, but we share a roaming sense of curiosity, and neither of us really feel as if we fit in anywhere."

I chuckle. "You're a fascinating person, Xavier."

He eyed me in utter befuddlement. "Fascinating? What does that mean? How am I fascinating?"

"The things you say, the way you say them? You talk like someone out of…I don't know, Jane Austen or Charles Dickens, rather than an eighteen-year-old punk-ass hipster." I got up and put my mug in the sink, clapping him on the back. "I'm glad we've got this year together, baby brother."

He watched me as I headed to my room. "Me too." When I got to my door, he spoke again. "So... what are you going to do about that girl?"

I shrugged. "Track her down, see if I can figure out some way of getting her to give me the time of day."

"Do you think the aphorism that nothing worth having comes easy applies to women, Zane?"

I stopped and glanced back at him. "I think I'm about to find out, bro."

THREE

Mara

"You did not." This was Claire, sitting across from me in the booth of a dive bar far across town from Badd's Bar and Grill; it was somewhere past midnight the day after I'd walked away from Zane, and I was being interrogated by my best friend.

"I totally did."

Claire was the same height as me and we both had natural blonde hair, but the similarities ended there; she was more waifish, slender, with what she called mosquito bite titties and a boy butt, with her hair cut in a pixie bob—which she'd dyed pink since

the last time I'd seen her. Whereas I'm…curvy, so to speak. I kept fit, but the gym and clean eating can only do so much. It can't, for example, reduce the visual affect of a big D-cup on a five-five frame, nor can it lessen the pop of my booty, which has always been…generous, shall we say.

Beauty is about a hell of a lot more than cup size and jean size, and even though Claire doesn't have a lot of extra padding, she is, hands down, the most beautiful girl I know, and I love her hard.

What I don't like, sometimes, is her unyielding insistence on calling me on my shit. I mean, yeah, it's part of why I love the bitch as much as I do, but *god* it's annoying when I just want to be left alone to get away with my shit.

Like now, for instance.

"Tell me again what he looked like," she demanded. "Details, please."

I sipped my cabernet sauvignon, and then sighed, "I already told you what he looks like, Claire."

"I know, but I feel like it bears repeating, if you're to be believed."

I bobbed my head side to side. "You have a point." Another long sip. "Fine. He's an even six feet tall, and he has to weigh at least two hundred pounds. And honey, that shit is solid muscle. If he's got more than eight percent body fat, then I'm my own great-aunt

Lucille. His body is just…*chiseled*. You know that look we both like so much, right? Where he's not, like, one of those bodybuilders who looks as if he's trying to become one big tanned muscle. He's got all the right muscles in all the right places. That's Zane."

"Arm porn?" Claire suggested.

I pretended to look aghast. "*Arm* porn? Bitch, he's *everything* porn. He's chest porn and abs porn and thighs porn and—"

"Cock porn?"

I shuddered, and this time it wasn't pretend. "Claire…you have *no* idea."

"I wish I did have an idea."

"You do, you really, really do. I mean, if you actually went and slept with him I'd be forced to challenge you to a duel for breaking the girl code, but seriously, the man's dick is…it needs its own area code. He could be a professional dick model."

"You mean porn star?"

I shook my head. "It's not a thing, but if penis models *were* a thing, he'd be a penis model. Because it's just…it's *pretty*, Claire. Like…I just want to touch it and hold it and look at it and—"

"And name him George?"

I coughed in laughter, nearly spitting out my wine. "Yes! I will love him and hug him and squeeze him and I will name him George."

"'I shall call him squishy and he shall be mine, he shall be my squishy. Come here squishy!'"

"Okay, Dory." I wiped my chin with the cocktail napkin. "Seriously, though. It's really that amazing."

She snickered. "We're being serious now, are we?"

I waved a hand. "Don't be ridiculous, we're never serious."

Claire flagged down a waitress and ordered us both more red wine. "Maybe that's the problem. Maybe we should be more serious sometimes. Like, about guys, I mean. Or, about *a* guy. Each of us, I mean. Not both of us about the same guy, that'd be a love triangle and those never go well."

I rolled my eyes as Claire rambled, which, honestly, she was somewhat prone to. Another trait I loved about her, because her ramblings were just so damn cute.

"Claire."

"But what if we decided to be polygamists, like that one show on TLC? Where he has four wives? We could share him, this guy of yours. Especially if he has, what is according to you, the most beautiful penis in all the land, I mean, we could share him. You don't need him all to yourself every single night, do you? You don't need to be selfish. You could totally share him." She glanced down at her lap. "Although,

I'm not sure if I could handle a dick that big, to be totally honest. I'm what you might call petite, and yeah, I'm petite down there too. Not a lot going on between the legs, you might say. Pretty, um, small. That's me. Little Claire, with the teeny tiny titties and the itty bitty booty and, oh yes, that's right, the world's smallest vagina." She patted herself between the legs. "I mean, I love my hoo-ha, but it's *tiny*. The last guy I slept with, he was rocking, like four inches max and was *maybe* as thick as a Ballpark Frank. Had the same curve as one of those curvy-deal hotdogs too. And I was like *ow ow ow ow* the whole time, because I'm *just—that—small*."

I stared at her. "Claire."

She blinked. "What?"

"You're rambling again."

She sighed. "Oh. Oops. Where were we?"

"You were talking about Mr. Curved-like-a-hotdog penis."

"No, before I started rambling."

"Oh. We were talking about Zane's cock."

Claire had gone still, and was staring over my shoulder with a deer-in-the-headlights expression on her face. "This Zane of yours, with the perfect penis…does he have short brown hair and super intense brown eyes, and a jawline like the Cliffs of Dover?"

I frowned at her. "Yeahhhhhhh," I drawled,

starting to cotton on to what she was implying.

"And, um, does he also happen to have a really badass Navy SEAL tattoo on his left arm?"

"He's behind me, isn't he?"

His voice buzzed in my ear. "Perfect penis, huh?"

"Hi Zane," I breathed, flushing in embarrassment.

"You know, my ears have been burning for awhile now. You wouldn't be talking about me, would you?"

I refused to turn around. "Nope. Not a word."

His fingertip brushed my cheek. "Hmm. Not sure I believe you, but I'll let it slide." He slid into the booth beside me. "Mind if I join you?"

I shot him a healthy dose of side eye. "He says, already sitting down."

He just grinned at me, flagging the passing waitress. "Bulleit. Neat, please. Make it a double." To me, then, "What, like you were going to say no?"

I took a sip of my wine and considered the options. I mean, was I going to tell him he couldn't join us? I was already dizzy from his scent, a mix of some kind of spicy cologne, smoke from a grill, and a hint of leather from the battered motorcycle jacket he was wearing. He hadn't even touched me, and I was clamping my thighs together and sitting on my hand just to keep it from sneaking away from me and going to somewhere on Zane's person, somewhere highly inappropriate for me to touch in public. Or at all, considering I'd ordered myself not to sleep with him again.

So yeah, I should tell him to get lost.

For my own good.

But I didn't *want* to. I liked how he blocked out the whole rest of the bar when he sat next to me, how I felt small and safe and secure in his presence. And he really did smell amazing.

But then again…I wondered what he'd do if I did tell him to leave.

"I mean, I haven't seen Claire in six months, and we're kind of having a girl's night. She's only here for—what, Claire, two days?" I said, testing the refusal on both myself and Zane.

The waitress came by with Zane's bourbon; he passed her a twenty and waved off the change.

His eyes flicked from me to Claire and back to me, searching. A smile spread across his lips. "A girl's night, huh?"

"And no, before you ask," I said, "we're not both going home with you."

"We're not?" Claire asked, and I was like ninety-nine percent sure she was just playing along, but with Claire, you never knew—the girl had a secret freaky side.

"We're not," I insisted.

Zane tossed back a slug of his whiskey, and then

stood up. "Meh, I haven't done that shit since SEAL graduation. Two girls at once sounds like a lot more fun than it really ends up being." He bent over and brushed a kiss to the corner of my mouth, then put his lips to my ear, whispering. "Besides, all I really want is another shot at putting my perfect penis inside your perfect vagina."

Gah. Now he smelled like whiskey, and if I kissed him, he'd taste like whiskey, and there are few things more intoxicating for me than the taste of whiskey on a man's breath.

Wait. Perfect vagina? He thought my vagina was perfect?

He was already swaggering away, though, his tight ass molded to artistic perfection in a pair of dark jeans. Those long, strong legs, though. Damn. And that ass? Did I mention his ass? How it was roughly the same size, shape, and hardness as a pair of bowling balls cupped in a pair of jeans?

He sidled up to the bar, finishing his whiskey on the way. The bartender was a woman, tall and lanky and beautiful, tight black tank top showing off a vibrant display of tats. She took one look at Zane and pretty much ran over to serve him, bending over the bar at the waist to give him a nice open look down her blouse at her tits, which were big and fake and amazing. She giggled at him, leaning close as he said something to her. He shot her a bright, flirty grin, nudging his glass at her. She responded with another smarmy giggle, took his glass, and filled it with an absolutely absurd amount of Bulleit. And then, instead of just telling him how much he owed, she went through the trouble of printing out the ticket…so she could very obviously write her number on it.

The bastard wasn't even trying and she was falling all over herself to pick him up.

Zane paid the bill, once again not bothering with change. He took the ticket she'd written her number on, kept it hidden in his hand as he eased away from the bar and ambled to a corner where he could still see me but wasn't obviously watching. I could see him over Claire's shoulder. God, that bastard. Just standing there looking sexy, sipping his whiskey and toying with the receipt from the hot bartender.

I asked a question to get Claire talking, and she was off like a runaway train, chattering happily about her new job, how laid back and fun it was, how they had what she called the rescue cat library, where you could check out a cat to hang out with at your desk all day, and how each cat came with its own box for if-it-fits-I-sits. Which sounded awesome, but I wasn't really listening; Claire and I had an understanding, where she would just let her mouth sort of run away, and I would half-listen while people watching. She didn't really need me to answer, she just needed someone who would let her talk, and I needed someone who understood that I liked to be around a person I trusted without having to talk all the damn time. Thus, our arrangement worked for both of us.

And in this particular instance, our arrangement let me nod at the right time and give Claire half an ear while I focused the rest of my attention on Zane. On the way his arms filled the sleeves of his leather jacket, and on the way his plain white T-shirt clung to his waist and hinted at the superhero abs I knew he had underneath. And on the way all he had to do was stand there and women flocked to him in droves, one after another, and sometimes in pairs—and once even an entire bachelorette party clustered around him, touching his chest and tittering at him and giving him their phone numbers on torn slips of paper. He never touched any of them back, I noticed, and he never gave any of them the slow, sultry, heavy-lidded grin he gave me the first time we met. These girls got a version of Zane I didn't really like, honestly. He gave them a grin that was all white teeth and no warmth in his eyes, and he leaned there in his corner sipping his whiskey as if he had all night and no plans, and he'd listen and nod and was obviously not paying any attention to them whatsoever.

Because his attention was on me.

He'd glance at me with a hint of secret amusement every time he got another phone number, and he'd tuck that paper in the back pocket of his jeans, and eventually the girl or girls would wander off with a ridiculous amount of longing backward glances.

And I couldn't help thinking that if those girls only knew exactly how amazing he was in bed and how big his cock really was and how delectable his abs actually were, they'd be trying a lot harder to get that smile I'd gotten, the one that promised a long night of hard and dirty fucking.

A promise he'd certainly followed through on.

And there went my imagination, running amok with fantasies of what we'd do together if I were stupid enough to let him bring me back with him.

Eventually, Claire ran out of steam, and let the flow of chatter trickle to a stop. Which I didn't notice right away, as Zane was sipping his Bulleit and staring at me over the rim with sex in his eyes.

"Girlfriend, you've got it bad," Claire said.

That got my attention. "What do you mean?"

She waved at me in disgust. "You. I haven't missed the way you and Zane have been eye-fucking this whole time."

"We're not eye-fucking," I protested.

Claire snorted. "Bitch, please. If you could get pregnant from eye-fucking, you'd be nine kinds of knocked up."

I finished my second glass of wine. "Okay, fine, we're eye-fucking. So what?"

"So, why don't you take him back to your hotel and fuck him for real?"

"I already did, well, at his place, but you know what I mean."

"So?"

I gave her a look that said the answer should have been blindingly obvious. "So...one ride per customer, remember? That's how we do things. To protect our hearts?"

Claire was uncharacteristically silent for a moment. "I've been getting sort of tired of that lately. I'm just...not as interested in the endless parade of guys as I used to be. I don't know if it's the move to Seattle or getting older, or what, but...I'm starting to think about getting a boyfriend."

I blinked at her. "Get a boyfriend? Like, long-term, live-in, grunts and farts and forgets to put the seat down *boyfriend*?"

She shrugged. "Yeah. Why not? I get lonely in my apartment at night. It'd be nice to have someone in bed with me, you know? I mean, really, how hard can it be to break in a boyfriend?"

I laughed. "Claire. What are you gonna do, go to the boyfriend store and pick out a boyfriend? Get some boyfriend chow and boyfriend potty training pads? Maybe a nice floral print boyfriend collar and leash?"

She pulled a *well...actually* face. "Yeah, pretty much. Except if anyone was gonna wear a collar and leash, it'd be me."

I sputtered disbelieving laughter. "*Claire!*"

"What? I like being dominated now and then— so what? It's fun to pretend to be all submissive."

"I know you liked being spanked, but goddamn, Claire. I had no idea."

She shrugged, blushing faintly. "I'd only do that when you weren't around."

"Why?"

She shrugged. "I was embarrassed. I thought you'd think I was a freak or something."

I took her hands. "Since when am I that judgmental?"

Claire shrugged again. "It's not that I thought you were judgmental, it's just that you like things... vanilla."

I couldn't answer right away. "Vanilla?"

She nodded. "Yeah. You don't go in for any kink at all. Like, have you ever let a guy tie you up? Or spank you? Or blindfold you? That's still pretty vanilla compared to some of the things a few guys have asked me to do, but for you? You like your guys blah.

Cute, sexy, funny, and blah."

I felt a twinge of hurt and couldn't help myself from firing back at her. "And since we're on the subject, do you *really* like rough sex, or do you just like it rough because it keeps guys from getting attached to the real you?"

She let out a breath from between pursed lips and frowned at me. "Damn, girl, going right in for the kill, huh?" She glanced away from me. "I like it rough because that's something I like, okay? It *is* the real me, it's just…not *all* of the real me."

I blew a raspberry. "Bullshit yourself if you want, but you can't bullshit me." I slammed back the rest of my wine. "And you're wrong about me liking my guys blah, by the way."

"Yeah, Mara, you *totally* like your guys blah. The most blah. Not there's anything wrong with them, they're just…meh. Nothing to write home about."

"Wow. I had no idea you felt that way."

She reached up and tugged hard on a lock of my hair. "You know I love you, right?"

"Yeah." I swatted at her hand. "And I love you back."

"But I think you pick them blah on purpose."

"Why would I do that?"

Claire ordered us each more wine as the waitress came by, and then turned back to me. "I don't know.

We don't really talk about what we did in the Army, and we certainly don't talk about our lives before the Army. So, I don't know. But you like your guys blah, and you don't ever let a guy actually get to know you, especially not if he's an interesting guy…" she jerked her thumb over her shoulder. "Like Zane Badd, he of the epic penis."

"I feel sort of betrayed, Claire," I said. "First you move away, breaking up the Gruesome Twosome. Then you dye your hair pink. And *then* you talk about getting a boyfriend…and now you tell me I like boring guys and insinuate that I'm afraid of intimacy."

"I just—"

I wasn't done though, and kept talking over her. "And when was the last time *you* let a guy get close to the real you?"

"Remember Brian March?"

I nodded. "Tall, super skinny, long goatee, weird taste in movies?"

"Yeah, him."

I shrugged. "I know you slept with him a couple times."

"Try twice a month for a year and a half. He was how I got into light bondage."

"So, you and he…"

"I'd meet him at his apartment after work every other Wednesday and we'd have sex. He'd tie me up, spank me, blindfold me and tease me with ice cubes and feathers and dildos, and I'd suck him off, and then we'd fuck. It was hot."

"You had a bunch of other guys over every weekend."

She sipped her wine as it arrived. "Yeah, well, we had an agreement. We weren't exclusive, we just used each other to express a side of our sexuality we couldn't necessarily show the other people we dated or whatever."

I shook my head. "I feel like there's this whole other Claire I never even knew about."

"It's not like I'm a super spy living a double life. I just did some things I didn't share with you."

"Because you thought I'd judge you for it."

She hesitated, and then glanced down at the table. "Yeah, kind of."

"Why?"

"I guess...it just felt like you wouldn't understand."

I tried to picture how I would have reacted if she'd told me this when we were roommates. And I didn't like the answer at all. "I'm not a good person, am I? Like, I'm a shitty friend."

Claire laughed, shaking her head at me. "You're the *best* friend, stupid. And you're an amazing person. You just..." she paused, frowning in thought. "You need to open your mind more. You need to figure out why you won't let guys even be your friend, why you won't have sex with the same guy twice, much less actually date someone."

"Have you dated anyone?"

She nodded. "Yeah. There's a programmer where I work. We've gone out a few times. Nothing, like, serious. Just...you know, getting my feet wet a little bit, in terms of trying out this whole dating thing."

"What's it like?"

"What? Dating?" I nodded, and she leaned back in her chair, swirling her wine in the glass. "It's fun, to be honest. There's something to be said for letting a guy pick you up, take you to dinner, and just...talking. Walking around, doing stuff. Gabe and I went to Pike Place the other day and just walked around talking. It was so fun. I mean, there are no expectations for either of us. I told him when he first asked me out that I wasn't the dating type, and that I wasn't looking for anything. He said that's fine, neither was he; he just wanted to spend time with me, because he thought I was cool. That's...it's a nice feeling, Mara. Someone who likes me for my personality? Like, actually for real, he just likes who I am? It's better than sex, in a weird kind of way. I mean, I haven't even had sex with this guy, and I'm not sure I'm going to."

I boggled. "Wait, you're dating this guy you work

with, which is weird by itself, by the way—and you don't plan on sleeping with him?"

She nodded. "For one, we don't work together, just for the same company. He's in a whole different department, on a different floor. We met on the elevator, as a matter of fact. And yeah, I'm approaching this whole dating thing as an experiment, right? Like, what will happen if I go into it not expecting anything? If I let things play out on their own, not necessarily expecting sex or a second date or anything, just…take it one step at a time? And I like it. It's new."

"Nah, dating is old, we're just weird."

She pointed at me. "Actually, I think it's the other way around. I mean, maybe twenty years ago you and I, the way we approach sex and relationships, ten or twenty years ago we'd have been weird, we'd be sluts—and to some people we probably still are. But I think the way we do things is becoming more common than you'd think, among both men and women. And I think old school dating like I'm trying it, I think it's actually becoming more and more uncommon."

"And what is all this supposed to mean for me?" I asked, swirling my wine and finally taking a sip of it.

I didn't want to be drunk, or even very tipsy, because if I let too much alcohol enter the equation, I wouldn't be making intelligent, informed decisions when it came to Zane. And if I was going to change the way I lived my life for a guy, I didn't want it be because drunk Mara was in charge.

"I'm not gonna tell you what to do with your life. You're my best friend and you always will be, so I feel an obligation to bust out some truth bombs when I feel like you need 'em." She leaned forward again, giving me the Serious Claire look. "What I will say, though, just as an FYI, is that I've never seen you look at a guy like you've been staring at Zane. You were gushing about him, Mara. That's not usual for you. Remember when you finally got that sexy hipster barista from the coffee shop near the apartment to sleep with you? You said it was the hottest sex you'd ever had and, even then, you had no issue ditching him like last year's purse. You told me all about it, like every detail, but you weren't *gushing*. You were just sharing a nice experience. This guy? Zane? You were gushing about him, and yet you've told me almost nothing about him except that he's gorgeous and has a big dick, and honey, just from the one quick look I got at him, I could have told you that. The bulge in his jeans is so goddamn big it's silly. But then, a big dick by itself isn't that exceptional, right? Remember that plumber you slept with last winter?"

I nodded, making an *oh shit* face. "That was honestly the biggest penis I've ever seen in my life. I seriously don't know how he fit the whole thing in his pants. It was almost too much cock, actually. Like, it took an hour to go from the top of it to the bottom. It was like having the Eiffel Tower in my no-no bits."

"That's my point exactly. If it were just about dick size, you'd have brought Long John Plumber back for a second ride on his Washington Monument. But you didn't. And he was good looking, too, wasn't he? Like, in the face?"

I shrugged. "He was hot, yeah. His name was Eric, and he was actually a really cool guy."

"But you never saw him again, never spoke to him again, and certainly never slept with him again." She tapped the table. "So if it's not just about hot sex, and not just about a big dick, then there's something else about Zane you're attracted to."

I stole a glance at Zane, who had his phone out and was scrolling through a feed of some kind. "I hate you," I said to Claire.

She threw up fake gang signs, lips pursed, head nodding. "That's right! What now, bitch? Li'l Claire for the win, dropping the truthbombs like a boss."

I facepalmed my forehead, groaning. "You are such a dork, Claire. I swear to god."

"Um, hello, computer nerd? It'd be a betrayal to my kind if I wasn't an embarrassing dork."

"Well if that's the case, then you're making a huge contribution to the reputation of your people."

She leaned over the table to hug me. "For real, Mara. I love you, and I really hope you'll do yourself a favor: give this guy a chance. You might surprise yourself." She stood up, finishing her wine. "Now, if you'll excuse me, I see a hottie making it for the bathrooms, and I'm feeling just tipsy enough that a bathroom quickie sounds like fun."

"Um, what?" I asked, but Claire was already gone.

I watched her beeline for the bathrooms, where a good-looking redheaded guy was about to enter the men's room. Claire made it to him before he went in, lifted up to mutter something in his ear. His eyes widened, and he said something that looked a lot like *for real?*—Claire nodded, her hand cupping between his legs and rubbing. The guy glanced around, and then pulled Claire into the men's room behind him.

Gah. The girl was a serious live wire. Even I didn't hook up with guys in the bathroom of a bar. But then, Claire always did things her own weird way.

I sighed, shaking my head at my friend's antics, and got up. Zane was still holding court in the corner, still sipping what looked like the same glass of whiskey. He straightened as I approached.

"Is your friend actually going to fuck that guy in the bathroom?" he asked when I was close enough.

I nodded. "Looks like it." I eyed him. "No. Don't

even think about it."

Zane laughed. "Honey, a public bathroom wouldn't survive the things I want to do to you."

My face heated and I felt my knees go a little weak. "Oh really?"

He leaned closer to me, putting a hand on my hip. "We were both a little drunk last night," he whispered in my ear. "It was sloppy. I was overeager and off my game."

I swallowed some wine along with a gulp of anticipation. "That was you *off* your game?"

"I can do better, I swear. You won't regret it." He said this somewhat tongue in cheek, knowing as well as I did that the sex last night had been off the charts hot.

I pivoted away, hardening my gaze and my voice. "What about that hot bartender? She looked like she was ready to blow you right there on the bar."

"Meh. She's alright...she's got a lot of silicone, though. Not that there's anything wrong with that, but I'm partial to a more natural look." He brushed a thumb almost accidentally across the front of one of my breasts. "Like these, for instance."

I glanced down at his thumb, and my own tits. "Yeah, no silicone there."

"I'm well aware. I became...very well acquainted with these lovelies last night." There was that smile again, the slow, lazy, horny, hungry one. "I gave them my tried and true jiggle test."

"You did, huh?" I breathed, remembering exactly what he was talking about. "What test would that be?"

He saw my ruse for what it was, and played along. "Don't you remember?" He leaned close so he could whisper in my ear again. "I put your legs on my shoulder and fucked you so hard your tits bounced all over the place. Silicone doesn't bounce the way your tits did. That was one hundred percent all natural jiggle."

"Oh," I said, and gulped more wine. "*That* test."

He bit my earlobe, his hand on my waist tugging me close enough that I could feel his hard-on bulging in his jeans. "You know what I'd really like to do, though?"

I held up my glass. "Get me more wine?"

"Nope, no more wine," he said, taking my glass from me and setting it on the counter by his elbow. "What I'd really love is to see you on your knees in front of me, letting me fuck these tits." He cupped one breast over my shirt as he ground against me.

"Is that so?" I was out of quippy comebacks, and had to resort to breathy slut-whispered come-on questions.

"The only way your tits could get any sexier is with my come all over them. And your mouth. And your chin." He bit my lower lip, then, staring down at me. "And your stomach. And that juicy ass of yours, too."

Holy shit. My core was throbbing, and my hands were shaking. "You want to paint me white with your sperm, is what you're telling me."

"Pretty much." His hand, formerly on my hip, was angling toward my ass. "And then clean you off in the shower so I can get you dirty all over again."

I struggled through the haze of lust he'd created inside me, looking for that resolve I'd had for about thirty seconds—the amount of time it had taken to walk from the booth to this corner. In those thirty seconds, I'd had an idea. A stupid, crazy, bound-to-fail idea. Yet...it had sounded just crazy enough even to myself that I'd been prepared to ask Zane what he thought about it. And then he'd started talking dirty to me, and I'd lost my train of thought.

I rested my forehead against his chest and focused on breathing through the raging wildfire that was my out-of-control libido. His hand was exploring my ass over my jeans, which was making it hard to think clearly, because I really, *really* liked the way he touched my butt.

I reached back, grabbed his hand, and moved it to my hip. "Down boy, I'm thinking."

He titled his head to one side quizzically. "About

what?"

I settled my hormones, and gazed up at him. "About something I'd like to talk to you about. But I think we need to go somewhere quieter." I held up my hand to forestall the dirty comment I knew was coming. "No, not my hotel or your apartment. Somewhere public, but quiet."

He scratched the side of his jaw with his fingertips, making a skritching sound on his stubble. "Huh. Sounds intriguing. I might know a place."

FOUR

Zane

I'D BORROWED XAVIER'S BIKE SINCE HE WAS, IRONICALLY, the only one of us with his own wheels—it turned out Bax had only rented that Harley for the wedding, and I'd had to return it for him today. I'd paid the bill, too, since I felt guilty for the nasty slice on his thigh. Thirty-one stitches and strict orders to take it easy for a while. Yeah, the bastard was going to milk that doctor's order for all it was worth. He'd be wheedling his way out of work at the bar left and right, claiming he had to stay off his leg. And I'd let him, because the guilt was a bitch. An inch or two higher and it would have severed his femoral artery and he'd have died. And there was still no guarantee his football career wouldn't be affected by it. They said he'd heal up fine, but still. I felt guilty.

I led Mara out of the noisy bar, and swung a leg over the seat of the bike. "Hop on," I said.

She eyed the motorcycle warily. "You have a bike?"

"Nah, it's Xavier's, I'm just borrowing it."

"Do you know how to ride one?"

I snorted in derision. Kicking up the kickstand, I angled away from the curb, checked for traffic, and then twisted the throttle hard, and kept the front brake squeezed, sending the back tire spinning to push the back around in a tire squealing arc. When I was facing the opposite direction, I released the brake so the bike bolted forward like a shot. As soon as I hit optimum speed, I slowed down a little, leaned forward, barked the throttle and yanked back on the handlebars. The front wheel left the ground and I kept steady on the throttle, popping a wheelie for a good fifty yards before setting it down and braking in a skidding arc to face back toward where Mara was standing.

I pulled forward next to her, grinning. "That answer your question?"

"Show off," she muttered. "So you can ride a motorcycle. Just don't pull any of that shit when I'm on it with you."

"No ma'am," I said. "We'll just cruise nice and easy."

I gave Mara the one helmet and, to her credit, she slid it on without complaining about her hair—the last time I'd tried to get a chick on a bike, she'd bitched about the helmet ruining her hair, so we'd ended up Ubering it back to her place. Mara, however, just jammed that sucker onto her head without hesitation, swung on behind me, and snugged her thighs around mine, her arms clasping around my middle.

"You've done this before," I remarked.

"Yeah," she answered. "My dad has a Harley...I used to ride with him all the time."

There was something dark and heavy in that, which I left well enough alone. As promised, I went easy, cruising nice and slow south toward 3rd Avenue and the Rainbird Trail parking area. It was after midnight and pitch black, but I knew this area as well as I knew my own reflection in the mirror—I used to bring girls here all the time, actually, because it's a damn amazing spot. I parked, swung off, and held Mara's hand as she climbed off, plucking the helmet from her head and shaking her hair out.

"A parking lot?" she asked, looking around.

Dark as it was, and being a tourist, she wouldn't be able to see much apart from the dark bulk of a hillside to our right, and the sky to our left, and maybe a hint of starlight on the water. Not too impressive... yet.

I just grinned at her as I dug through the saddlebags Xavier had added to his Triumph; my youngest brother was a practical and always-prepared sort, and I figured he'd have...aha, bingo—a compact, ultra-bright LED flashlight. I clicked it on and flashed it around, satisfied that it would do the job.

"Up for a short hike?" I asked her.

"In the dark?" She asked, looking up from her phone; she was texting someone it looked like, probably checking in with her friend so someone knew where she was. Smart girl.

"Sure," I said. "I grew up here, and I've been up this trail a zillion times. Just...trust me, yeah?"

She blinked for a moment, and then shrugged, extending her hand to me. "If you turn out to be a serial killer, I'll be really pissed."

I just laughed. "The only thing that's gonna get murdered is your pussy, Mara."

She slapped my shoulder. "Yeah, I'd try and keep that in check if I were you, Rambo."

"You mean that line doesn't make you horny?" I asked, leading her toward the stairs.

"Shockingly, no."

"Huh. And here I thought it'd have you throwing

your panties at me." I grabbed her hand in mine and led her up the stairs, shining the light on the treads ahead of us.

She stopped and hooked a thumb in the waist of her jeans—another pair so skintight they may as well have been leggings—tugging so she could pretend to peer down into her pants. "Um…nope. Still there."

"Damn, it worked for Bax. I'll have to ask him what I did wrong."

"You take pick up advice from your brothers?"

I laughed. "From Bax?" I snickered. "He's the one you pulled the glass out of at the wedding."

She shoved me back into a walk and we headed up the stairs. "The one who drained an entire bottle of Jameson to impress the girls?"

"That's the one."

"Hmmm, maybe don't take pick-up advice from him, if that's his tactic."

There were quite a few stairs so I went slow, unsure how fast she'd be able to take them. I waited until we were at the top to answer.

"Bax is a great guy. He's a bit rough around the edges, I'll admit, but he's got a great heart. And you'd be surprised how charming the guy is, when he wants to be."

"Sounds like you're pretty close," she said.

The forest was close and damp, my flashlight

a white spear illuminating a tiny swath of the path ahead of us. Mara, like I'd hoped she would, pressed close against my side, staring around us at the forest as if worried a bear might amble out of the woods at any moment. On other hiking trails further away from downtown Ketchikan, that'd be a legitimate concern, but here? Highly unlikely. No point worrying her with that, though. I just enjoyed the feel of her soft curves pressed up against my side as we picked our way along the narrow trail.

"Eh, we're getting there," I said. "I joined the Navy right out of high school and made the SEAL team not long after. Didn't get a lot of leave time, so I haven't seen my brothers a whole lot, until recently."

"Did you, like, quit the SEALs, or what?"

I could tell she wasn't sure how to ask what she really meant. "I had to retire, for family reasons."

"Somebody got sick?"

"Sort of," I said. "My dad died. Mom's been gone for a good ten years, but Dad's death was a surprise. He…ah, he left a bit of an odd will. He left us all a bit of money, but the only way we can get it is if all eight of us brothers came home. Bast—Sebastian, the guy that got married, the oldest—he was already here. He never left, but the rest of us were sort of scattered to the four corners of the earth. And Dad wanted us back together, I guess. So the stipulation in his will was that we'd get the money if we moved back to Ketchikan and help Bast run the bar. We have to stay here for a minimum of a year and put in full-time working hours at the bar."

"I'm sorry to hear about your parents."

I shrugged, unsure how to respond. I was still dealing with Dad's death in some ways, and wasn't sure how I felt most of the time. "Yeah, thanks."

"So, tell me about the rest of your brothers."

I glanced at her as we continued walking. She'd bolted the second she woken up this morning, and hadn't seemed interested in sticking around for so much as a how do you do. Now she wanted to know about me and my brothers? My spidey-senses were tingling.

"Well, Sebastian is the oldest. He's the original player of us all. He's been working that bar since he was a teenager. I mean, we all worked the bar as kids, because it was a family business, but Sebastian just took to it naturally. When Mom died, it put a lot of the work on Bast's shoulders. Dad…didn't deal well with Mom's passing. He sort of died inside, I think, and never really recovered. Bast took over pretty much everything after that." I laughed, thinking of Bast's many, many conquests in that bar. "The guy is the smoothest motherfucker on the planet. Tourist chicks just threw themselves at him by the boatload—literally, because of the cruise ships."

She chuckled. "Having watched you get, like, twenty numbers just standing there in the bar tonight, I guess I can see how that might be."

"Bast and I used to have a competition to see which one of us could collect the most digits in a night."

"Who won?"

"Oh shit, Bast always won by a landslide." She seemed skeptical, which made me laugh. "You haven't really met Bast. You'll understand when you meet him."

"So Bast is a player, Bax is a hard-drinking brawler..."

"He's not really a brawler, he just...he's a football player. He's rough by nature." We were getting close the overlook, now, I realized. "Then there's Brock. He's a stunt pilot. Him and Baxter are what you call Irish twins, born within a twelve months of each other. Brock is...he's...I dunno how to explain him. Probably the prettiest of us all and the most conservative. Brock was the straight-A student, the class president, the one who saved his money to pay for his own flight lessons."

"I thought the other two were the twins, the ones playing on the stage?"

"Yeah, they're the identical twins. Canaan and

Corin." I glanced at Mara. "You ever hear of a band called Bishop's Pawn?"

She nodded. "Sure. I actually saw them play in LA once." I saw the dime drop. "Wait, that's them? Your brothers are Bishop's Pawn?"

"That's them." I felt oddly proud that she'd heard of them. I mean, I knew the twins were talented, and that they'd made it pretty big, but when some girl you just met has heard of them, has seen them play? Kind of makes you realize exactly how famous they are.

"That's pretty cool. They're crazy good. They put on an amazing show. Claire and I went together; we took a long weekend in LA." She pushed ahead of me as we reached the overlook. "Wow…now *this* is amazing."

"Quite a view, huh?"

Ketchikan was spread out beneath us to our right, Gavina Island was directly across from us, and the massive bulk of the mountains sheltered us in the dark shadows of the night. There was a fence following the edge of the bluff, so we leaned against it and stared out at the cluster of lights below and the starlight on the rippling water.

"So." She tugged the hood of her sweatshirt over her head against the cool breeze riffling through her hair. "Sebastian, you, Baxter, Brock, Canaan and Corin…"

"Actually, Brock is older by a year," I corrected. "Lucian is next after Bax, and he's a lot different than the rest of us. He dropped out of high school when he was, like, a sophomore I think. He wanted to work the fishing boats. Dad made Lucian a deal that as long as he had his GED by the time he was eighteen, he could work the nets instead of going to school. Luce had that GED in the bag by the time he was seventeen, and the second he had it, he was gone. He got a berth on a tanker and ended up who knows where. He's just an odd cat. He's quiet, intense, and—how would you put it? Wise beyond his years, I guess. Just...he can be hard to get to know."

"And then Xavier is the youngest?"

"Yep. Xavier is...he's a genius, in the literal sense. He builds robots and studies quantum physics for fun, reads hundreds of pages in a matter of an hour...he graduated high school at sixteen, got a full ride to Stanford on academics and soccer. He's gonna be the next Einstein or Hawking, I'm pretty sure."

Mara twisted to lean sideways against the railing so she could look at me. "And then there's you."

I shrugged, unsure where she was going with this. "Then there's me."

She hesitated, thinking, and I stayed quiet, letting her have the time to process her thoughts. "I know I bolted last night, or this morning, or whatever."

I nodded. "You did kind of pull a runner."

She glanced down, picking at the wood of the railing. "Yeah, well, that's kind of my M-O. And I—"

"What *is* your M-O? Just so I'm clear."

"Sleep with someone after the bar, and leave early in the morning before they're awake. No strings, no weirdness."

I nodded. "Same here, for the most part. Although I'm not impartial to breakfast if she seems down with it."

"Yeah, I don't stay for breakfast. I rarely even stay for round two. I just—it's not me."

"Why not?"

She sighed. "Can we maybe hold off on the psychoanalysis for the moment?"

I rolled a shoulder. "Sure. Go ahead, I'll shut up and listen."

"Good plan." She paused to think again, and then continued. "I'm in Ketchikan for a week. I haven't taken vacation days in a long time, and Claire is only here through tomorrow afternoon, so…I'll have some free time, I guess. And—and…I thought we could…hang out, or something."

I eyed her curiously. "I'm not sure what you're suggesting."

"Neither am I!" she said, in a sudden outburst. "I'm, like, *crazy* attracted to you—I'm just not sure what to do with it. I don't do relationships, and I'm only here for a week, so it's not like it's going to be…a *thing*, or whatever. But I would like to spend some more time with you."

I let out a breath, turning to look out at the hometown I'd never expected to be living in again. "Huh. So, when you talk about spending time together, do you mean just sex? Or are you suggesting stuff like spending time together with our clothes on?"

She lifted both hands palms up. "I don't know, Zane. I have absolutely no clue what I'm doing right now. But I was talking to Claire earlier, while you were collecting all those phone numbers, and she said I needed to open my mind a little bit."

"Open your mind?"

She nodded, shoulders hunched as she leaned forward, bracing her forearms on the railing. "Like, start trying things beyond the way I normally do them. But I—I don't know how. Trust is…hard, and I'm just cynical, I guess. None of the guys I've ever met have seemed like anyone I'd be interested in seeing more than once."

"And I'm safe, because you're going back home in a week, so if I turn out to be a raging douchebag, you can just catch a flight home and forget about me."

"Exactly." Her eyes cut to mine. "But please, feel free to *not* turn into a raging douchebag."

"I'll do my best." I pivoted to put my butt against the railing, looking down at her. "So, yeah. I'm game. It could be fun. I mean, I'm not the relationship type any more than you are. Most of my interactions with women happen either naked, or in the pursuit of getting naked. This would be something new for me too."

She smirked up at me. "Hey, you can probably count on getting me naked, because let's face it, you're just too damn good at seduction."

"Good to know," I said.

She straightened, then, standing beside me, still facing the view, arms crossed under her breasts. "But I would also like to try this whole…being together without the sex thing."

I considered what she was proposing. "So basically, we're sort of…practice dating."

She nodded. "Exactly. Practice dating."

"So, is there a ratio or something for how much time we spend dating and how much time we spend naked?"

"Um, good question. I don't know. Maybe we just see how things go?" She eyed me with a teasing grin. "But you can't spend every single waking moment trying to get into my pants, or this won't work."

"No?" I edged closer to her. "Why not?"

Her fingers fluttered like restless birds, and

eventually settled on my chest, playing with the folds in the fabric. "Because you're too good at it, and I'm not very good at resisting. We're supposed to be trying something new, after all."

"Well, I could argue that since neither of us typically sleep with the same person more than once, if we spend this week fucking like newlyweds we *would* be trying something new."

She glared at me. "Goddammit, Zane."

"What?" I laughed.

"That's exactly the type of logic we're supposed to be avoiding, mister."

"It is? Why?"

"Because the whole point of this experiment is to see what it's like having a relationship with someone outside of sex."

"Oh."

She nodded. "Yeah. Oh."

I consulted my watch. "Well, it *has* been at least twelve hours since we last had sex, so…maybe we could start the whole clothes-on part of this practice dating tomorrow morning?"

Mara laughed, her head tipping back, her laughter ringing out through the forest. "You're something else, Zane."

I slipped sideways, wedging myself between the fence and her body.

"You can't even make it through one conversation without trying to slip me your dick," she said.

"I'm not trying to slip you anything," I said, "I'm trying to get you to take your shirt off and give me a blow job."

She blinked up at me. "You want me to take my shirt off and suck your dick?"

"Yeah, why not?"

"For real?"

I shrugged. "Ever since the first time I saw you smile I've been fantasizing about the way your mouth would look wrapped around my cock. So yeah, for real."

She stared at me for a moment, just breathing and looking at me. "Okay."

"Wait, what?"

She slid my jacket off my shoulders and placed it on the ground, leather to the dirt, inside facing up. "I said, okay."

"Really?"

She nodded, and peeled her hoodie off, and then her T-shirt, and then unhooked her bra, setting the clothing in a pile to one side. And holy motherfuck, my cock went ramrod stiff in my jeans. There are few things more inherently erotic than a woman topless, outside, wearing nothing but a pair of jeans and a sultry grin. Something about it is just...fucking hot as hell. I'd suggested it as a joke—mostly—not really expecting her to agree, but there she was, bare from the waist up, nipples hardening in the chill of the September night air.

She knelt on my jacket in front of me and reached for my belt. Unbuckled it, then unbuttoned my jeans and slowly tugged the zipper down. My cock was straining, about to pop out the top of my boxer briefs. She slid my jeans down around my ankles, and then reached up to snag the waistband of my underwear.

She paused, glancing up at me. "If I have to be topless, I think it's only fair that you do too."

I peeled my shirt off and tossed it with hers, then let my hands fall to my sides, waiting for her to make the next move. She grazed her palms over my abs, tracing the ridges between the blocks of muscle. I was glad, then, for the nice little weight room Bast had put together in the storeroom beneath the bar; I'd put in a lot of time down there, benching, squatting, and doing weighted crunches, and it looked like my hard work was paying off, judging by the way her hands ran appreciatively over my body. She hooked her fingers into my underwear again, and this time she didn't pause. She tugged them away from my body to let my erection spring free, and then she dragged them down. I was naked, right out in the open on the Rainbird Trail overlook, Ketchikan below us, stars above us, with the most gorgeous woman I'd ever laid eyes on kneeling in front of me.

Mara wrapped one hand around my shaft and slid it up, then down. Again, slowly. I groaned, aching at the feel of her hand on me.

"Groaning already, Zane?" she teased. "I'm just getting started."

I opened my mouth to answer, but then she bent and put her mouth on me, and I could only groan again; any wisecracks I might have had were blasted out of my head by the pure bliss of Mara's mouth. She caressed me at the root and slid her lips around me, gliding lower and lower, swallowing as I pushed into her throat, and then she backed away, her fist fluttering at my base.

"Jesus, Mara."

"Mmmm-hmmm?" Holy hell, that moan, that hum, the way she sounded like she knew exactly how incredible she was making me feel.

"Your mouth feels like…" I searched for a way to express it, but she felt so warm and wet and soft and her hand was stroking and pumping slowly and it was too hard to think, too erotic to form coherent thoughts.

"Hmmm?" That hum again, encouraging me to keep talking.

"Feels like I never want you to stop. I don't even

want to come, I just want to feel this."

"Mmmm-hmmm?" She hummed, and cupped her other hand under my balls, squeezing gently as her fist slid along my shaft.

"God, yeah." I forced my eyes open and looked down to watch her.

She tilted away from my body and sank to sit on her feet, the angle now allowing her to look up at me through her eyelashes as she drove her mouth on me, pushing closer to my torso, taking more and more of me. Fuck, like this I could watch her mouth take me, watch my cock slide between her lips. My cock was thick enough that her mouth was forced open into a wide **O**, her jaw extended, and I felt her tongue fluttering along my shaft.

She let go of my cock then, her palms brushing over my belly, grazing around my hips to clutch my ass.

God, oh god, oh god. Just her mouth, then her hair in loose golden waves around her shoulders to tickle my thighs, her hands cupping my ass, fingernails digging in fiercely as she moved her mouth back and forth along my cock. She'd swallow as she took me in and swirl her tongue around the head as she backed away, then she'd pause with just the head of my cock in her mouth and give me a series of short suckling little bobs, and then she'd plunge her mouth back down.

She was playing with me, I realized, feeling me tense as the orgasm rose up inside me, and that was when she'd pause and slow down, letting me back away from the edge. And then she'd start over.

She played me to the edge again and again, always pausing and shifting or slowing so I'd lose the edge of the orgasm, and then start over. Again and again, until my balls were throbbing and I was growling in need. How long had she been doing this? Four minutes? Five? I'd never had a blow job last this long. If I'm having sex, I can pull back a lot, keep going for fucking ever. But if a girl was going down on me, the point was to come hard and fast, right? So I'd let it happen as it happened, let her decide when I came. But this? Jesus, this? It was unlike anything I'd ever felt. The pleasure of her mouth for so damn long, fuck, it was enough to make me wonder if I'd died and gone to heaven.

And then, just when I thought she was about to stop playing and bring me to climax, she backed away and let me pop free of her mouth with a loud smack. Before I could ask what she was doing, though, she had both hands around my cock and was…massaging it, I guess you could call it. Way more than just merely stroking it. This was…god, I don't know. My shaft was slick with her spit, so her fists slipped up and down with slick ease, and she was squeezing and twisting on each upstroke, each downstroke, plunging both hands in unison and then separately. When she felt my skin starting to dry out, she formed a cup around the head with her hand and bent over, and I felt warm and wet saliva drip onto me. She spread it around, and now her strokes were speeding up, the tight squeezing massaging touch going faster and faster, until my hips began to move and my cock started to throb and my balls were aching.

"Fuck...fuck, Mara!"

"You're close?" she murmured, staring up at me with that sultry, erotic thrill in her eyes, a lazy, hungry look that said she knew exactly what she was doing to me and that I'd repay her in kind.

"Mara, honey, when I finally come, it's going to be—oh *shit*."

She'd forced me off my train of thought by taking me into her mouth unexpectedly, both hands plunging up and down my shaft, her lips suctioning around the tip of my cock.

For the most part, my hands had stayed by my sides, letting her do this her way. But now...I had to touch her. I rested my hands on her shoulders, caressing everywhere I could touch.

I was edging closer to orgasm now, abs tightening, thighs shaking, hips flexing, and she wasn't stopping this time, bobbing shallowly on my cock while sucking hard, fists gliding at the same slow pace. There wasn't any stopping it this time. I started to groan uncontrollably, uttering curses under my breath, whispering her name. She reached up and moved my hands from her shoulders to her head, encouraging me to bury my fingers in her hair, which I did, eagerly. The sounds I was making at this point were...well, I sounded like a damn caveman, if you want the truth—*unh, unh, oh god, ohhhhh, ohfuckohfuckohfuck*...like that. Nonstop. Loudly.

Everything inside me, everything I was, everything I contained was centered on Mara's mouth, on her hands, on my throbbing cock and aching balls and the crushing need to come. If the entire world exploded right the fuck now I wouldn't care, as long as this moment with Mara didn't end.

I felt it boiling up inside me, then, that hot white pushing pressure that told me I was done.

I tightened my grip on Mara's hair, grunting unintelligibly. I was crazed, honestly. My brain was mush, my heart was hammering like I'd just held my breath until I saw black, and I was helplessly pumping my hips. There are two unspoken rules when it comes to receiving a blow job: one—unless you know for a fact she's down for it, you don't try to act like it's a scene in a porno, meaning don't go all Ramjet the Rookie with the thrusting, and two—when you're about to come, you warn her either verbally or with two tugs of her hair, so she can decide whether to spit, swallow, or let you blow your load elsewhere. In that moment, however, Mara had completely obliterated all of my higher functions. I don't think I'd have known my own name, much less been able to respond.

I couldn't stop it, couldn't even warn the poor girl, I just came with a roar, hips thrust forward hard. And Mara? God, the girl was a fucking goddess. She didn't miss a beat. One hand remained on my ass, pulling me toward her, actively encouraging me to keep moving, and her other hand drifted around between us and her fingers teased over my balls moments before I felt the first wave blast through me, and then right as I started coming she pressed her two middle fingers to my taint, just behind my sac, massaging. Her mouth was suctioning on me like a vacuum, bobbing, sliding. I heard her gulp, and then she was moaning as I lost the last vestige of control, growling like a damn animal. That moan? Dear sweet Jesus. I think I saw stars I came so hard, and it was made all the more powerful by the way she was moaning as she swallowed my come. Faked or not, I didn't care in that moment, it was just so fucking hot, so intense.

It may have only lasted for thirty seconds at the most, but I swear that was the longest, hottest, hardest orgasm of my life, and it felt like it lasted an hour.

Even after I'd stopped actively coming, Mara kept going, backing away, tongue swirling, and then I was out of her mouth and the air was cool on my wet shaft, and her tongue was flicking over my sensitive skin, licking at the tip as droplets seeped out of me. Her hand left my ass and clutched my still hard but slackening cock, stroking, caressing, her tongue flicking, her lips kissing.

And then, finally, she let me go and leaned back.

I sagged against the railing, gasping. "Holy motherfucking goddamn shit."

I had to cling to the thick wooden railing with both arms to keep from collapsing to the ground. And even then, my arms were as limp as spaghetti, like I'd just done fifty weighted pull-ups. I felt myself collapsing, and was powerless to stop it, felt the railing scrape my back, felt the ground rush up to meet me, even as I fought to stay upright.

I hit the ground hard, and Mara burst out laughing. "Ohmygod, are you okay?" she asked, crawling over to me.

The grass was damp and cold, the wood chips rough under my butt, my jeans and underwear tangled around my ankles.

"I think I died and went to heaven and just fell back to earth," I said.

She tugged at my underwear, trying to help me get them back on. "Come on, big guy, lift up for me."

"I can't...I can't move yet." I remained as I was, simply because I was completely unable to move anything but my lips; every other part of me was limp and tingling.

"It was that good, huh?" Her smile was sweet and pleased.

"That good? I...Sweetheart, that was...that was fellatio as art."

She was blushing. "I tried to make it good for you."

"You ruined me, is what you did. You just set the gold standard for all blow jobs. Nothing will ever be able to compare to that for as long as I live."

"Until the next time I do that, you mean, right?"

I blinked at her. "You'd do that again?"

She shrugged. "Sure. I mean, I'll expect something in return, but sure. I like doing that to you, actually. It's hot." Her grin was that sexy, adorable, lopsided one, the grin that first hooked me. "And besides, I already know you can give some wicked good cunnilingus."

I was still bare-assed in the grass, my cock a limp comma against my thigh. "I think you sucked me so good I'm temporarily paralyzed," I said. "But I swear, as soon as I can move, I'll eat you out so good they'll hear you screaming in goddamn Fairbanks."

I noticed she had a small dollop of come at the corner of her mouth; I reached up with my thumb and wiped it away. It was a strange, fiercely intense moment, then, her bright green summer-grass eyes locked on mine, her breasts still bare and draped against my chest, her hands in the damp grass by my hips, her knees between mine. The silence crackled, the tension blazed.

And then Mara parted her lips, her eyes still fixed on mine, and she closed her mouth around my thumb, her tongue sliding soft over the pad, licking away the come, her teeth scraping gently over my knuckle.

Holy shit, holy shit, holy shit—I shouldn't have been able to feel anything down below for at least ten or fifteen minutes, but I swear to god, when she did that, I felt some stirrings happening.

I couldn't help it. I had to kiss her. Had to. I wasn't sure about the rules and parameters of this thing, or where kissing fell in the scheme of things, but I had absolutely no choice but to claim her mouth with mine. This wasn't pre-sex kissing, this was...fuck, I don't know what it was.

Holy shit, who are you and what are you doing to me, woman? That was part of it.

I don't know. I just knew I had to kiss her, and I did.

She fell against me, her fingers stealing up to rest against the back of my neck, her breasts flattened against me, her weight pressing delightfully, warmly, wonderfully, intoxicatingly into me. Her mouth felt as divine and thrilling and maddeningly soft and wet and warm on my mouth as it had my cock, and even better in some ways. Her tongue slid against mine, tangling, pushing, retreating, advancing, dancing. The longer we kissed, the more of her weight she gave me, until somehow I was drifting sideways and pivoting and she was laying on her back in the grass and I was above her, kissing the hell out of her, my palms scouring her ribs and cupping her breasts. Her legs scissored, her back arched, pressing into my touch, a whimper escaping the kiss. I flipped open the button of her jeans, slid my fingers under the elastic of her underwear and found her slit wet and begging.

I lost track of everything and focused on the kiss, on the feel of my fingers sliding through her pussy, stuttering over her clit.

She was writhing, gasping into my mouth, hips lifting as I fingered her into whining, whimpering gyrations.

Her hands slipped and skittered along my back, drifted to my head, palms running over my short hair, then her fingertips were tracing my jawline and her thumb was brushing my cheekbone. I let my hands do the talking, then pulled her jeans down.

She grabbed my wrists to stop me, and then cupped my jaw in both hands again, her forehead bumping to rest against mine. "Wait, wait. I'm getting carried away. I promised myself I wasn't going to let this happen, but you're distracting me with your wizard kisses."

"Wizard kisses?" I said, laughing, pulling back. "And why shouldn't we get carried away?"

She sat up and backed away, re-buttoning her jeans and reaching for the pile of our clothing. "Yeah," she said, handing me my shirt as I tugged up my underwear and jeans. "Wizard kisses. Magical, sorcerous. Your mouth makes me do crazy things."

"If anyone has a magical mouth, it's you," I said. "I'm still tingly all over."

We were both dressed then, she tugging on her hoodie and me my leather.

"Why'd you stop us?" I prompted.

She shrugged uncomfortably. "Because I don't want you to just eat me out, I want to have sex, but I'm not—I'm not quite ready to go that far outside, even here. I just..."

I pulled her close. "Say no more. I get it."

"You do?"

I nodded. "Sure, of course."

She gave me that sweet, adorable lopsided grin.

"We're definitely going to get carried away later, though. When we're, you know, inside."

I grinned back. "You have yourself a deal, Amarantha Quinn."

FIVE

Mara

WELL…HOLY SHIT. WHO KNEW I'D FIND IT SO FUN to suck a dick? I mean, it's not something I usually *loved* doing, but neither did I dislike it. Some guys expected BJs as part of sex, and other guys seemed content to let me decide if I wanted to do it; either was fine by me. So, yeah, I guess you could probably say I've given my fair share of BJs.

But that? What I did to Zane? That was…something else. I've never in my life done anything quite like that, never gone that all out. There just hadn't been a point to it, really. I mean, I was a generous sexual partner, I liked to think. Willing, fun, eager to please. So if the guy I was with was polite and respectful about asking for a BJ, I'd likely give him one. Usually this meant going down on him a bit and then getting to the fucking, but occasionally if he was super hot and super cool, I'd let him come, but that was a rarity, mainly because I didn't care for guys sticking around long enough to get hard again for actual sex.

Yes, I know, I'm complicated—sorry, not sorry.

But that BJ I'd just given Zane was on a whole different plane of existence. I'd wanted on some deep, visceral level to make him feel better than he'd ever felt in his life, to give him something from me that he'd never forget. I'd wanted it to be fucking hot, to be erotic as all hell. I wanted him to let go. I wanted to blow him so good I blew his mind.

Seeing as he literally collapsed to the ground afterward and was still walking funny, I'd say I had succeeded. And I felt pretty damn pleased with myself. The thing that was rolling around in the back of my mind, though, was the question of why I wanted to please him so badly. As I said, I always cared about my partner feeling good; sex was supposed to be a mutual exchange of pleasure, right? But what I'd wanted to prove to Zane was something deeper than that. Not just physical pleasure, but...what? I wasn't sure. And that was what bugged me—that the question existed at all, number one, and that I couldn't figure out the answer, number two.

I followed Zane back along the forest path, keeping hard on his heels, because, jeez, this forest was pitch black and I had no idea where I was going or where to even step without his presence and the flashlight in his hand. Something told me he probably didn't even need the flashlight. Being a SEAL, he could probably see in the dark like some sort of cat. In some places, the path was just a normal trail through the forest, wood chips marking the path. But in other places the path was comprised of giant stepping-stones, primarily where the trail descended the hillside. The stones were damp and slick, but if I went slow and chose my steps, I was fine.

We reached the parking lot after a few minutes of hiking back through the forest; clouds had rolled in while we were hiking, obscuring the moon and stars, making the night darker than ever, a light rain drizzling down. I climbed onto the bike behind Zane, tugged the helmet on and wrapped my arms around him.

This was equal parts comforting and difficult, being on the back of a motorcycle again. Zane hadn't pressed the issue when I mentioned how I used to ride with Dad, although I suspected he'd heard the tension in my voice when I told him. And I wasn't sure if I was relieved that he'd not asked any questions or upset that he didn't seem to care—I decided on relieved, after some reflection, because I just didn't think I was ready to talk about Dad yet. I'd barely broached the subject with Claire, and she was my BFF.

Zane drove slowly through Ketchikan, cautious because of the drizzle. His jacket gradually became wetter and wetter, until the scent of damp leather filled my nostrils. I clung to Zane's midsection and focused on reminding myself that this was him, this was Zane, this wasn't Dad. Yet memories of long road trips with Dad were strong and, despite my best efforts, I felt the old familiar bitterness and sadness trying to take hold.

No, no, no. Don't get sucked in, Mara—it's a black hole, thinking about Dad.

I fought it as Zane guided the motorcycle to the B&B where'd I'd booked a room for the week. Tells you how distracted I was, that I didn't stop to wonder how he knew where I was staying until after he'd shut off the bike.

I stayed seated on the bike behind Zane as I tugged the helmet off. "I have two questions for you, Zane."

He took the helmet from me and hung it on the handlebar, then swung his leg over the seat, pivoted, and swung back on facing backward. "What's up?"

I indicated the B&B with a jerk of my head. "How'd you know where I was staying? And how'd you find which bar I was at?"

"I'll answer the second question first, because that's an easier answer: there aren't all that many bars in this town, so I just went from bar to bar until I found you."

"Alright," I said, conceding the logic of that. "And how'd you know I was staying here?"

He sighed. "I told you Xavier is a whiz at any-thing scientific or electronic, right? Well, he's also pretty quick with the computers. He looked your name up in the incoming flights registers, and then sort of tracked you to where you were staying. Not sure how he did it, just that he did."

"And why did you feel it necessary to know where I was staying?" I eyed him with skepticism. "It feels a little...stalkerish."

He ran his hands along my thighs. "I wasn't ready to let you go last night. I wanted to find you. See if we could hang out some more."

"You mean hook up again."

He grinned. "That too, yeah, no point denying it." Zane's hands traveled to the crease where my leg met my hip. "I wasn't stalking you. I just wanted to be able to find you before you left, see if you'd...give me another shot, I guess."

"What else did you look up about me?" I asked.

"Nothing, I swear." Rain was trickling down his jaw, his forehead, his neck, beading in his hair, but he didn't seem to notice or care. "Just your flight in, and where you were staying."

"So, if you hadn't found me at the bar, you would have shown up here looking for me?"

A shrug. "Probably."

"What if I'd found someone else to take me back to my room?"

His eyes darkened a little, as if he wasn't entirely happy with that suggestion. "I thought about that. If I'd seen you with someone else, I'd—well, I'd like to say I'd have left you alone, but that's probably not true."

I tilted my head at him. "No?"

He wiped at his face, brushing rain out of his eyes. "I'd have still tried to talk to you. Get you to ditch whatever loser you'd picked up."

"What if he weren't a loser?" I was pushing him now, teasing a little, but also sort of…probing his reactions, assessing his jealousy barometer.

"If he ain't me, he's a loser," he insisted, a cocky grin on his lips.

"Oh really?" I tapped his nose. "You, sir, have a high opinion of yourself."

He captured my finger and bit down on it gently.

"We've covered this already. Yeah, I do, but it's not all that misplaced, is it?" He flattened his palm against mine, our hands vertical between us, as if comparing hand sizes: his hands were so big he could curl his fingers down over the tops of mine. "You got something to hide, Mara Quinn?" His voice was playful, teasing.

I should have played it cool, should have responded with some quip to distract his attention. Instead, I was an idiot.

"None of your damn business," I snapped, climbing abruptly off the bike to stalk toward the door of the B&B.

"Well that was supposed to be a joke," Zane said, calm as ever, remaining on the Triumph. "But obviously I touched a nerve."

I halted and spun on my heel. "No shit."

He just eyed me from the seat of the bike, unperturbed. "Notice how I'm not pushing it? Notice as well that I didn't push on that comment about your dad?" His hand scraped over his scalp, flinging water droplets behind him. "You don't have to tell me shit. I'm not asking, and I'm not gonna ask. You feel like talking, babe, I'm all ears. You don't feel like talking? Well, then, that's fine too, no skin off my back. We all got shit we don't like sharing, honey, me included. If you're expecting me to...I dunno...be judge-y or demand you bare your deepest secrets right off the bat, you're talking to the wrong guy."

I walked back to the bike. "I'm sorry, Zane, it's just—"

He put a thumb over my lips, silencing me, and then kissed the corner of my mouth. "You feel like talking about it?"

I shook my head. "No."

"Then leave it. It's fine." He grinned. "Besides, I can think of a better use for your mouth than talking."

I couldn't help a stupid grin from forming, and then I bit his thumb like he had my finger. "I already did that."

"I meant kiss me." He palmed the back of my head, his lips whispering against mine. "Get your mind out of the gutter, woman."

I laughed, and then felt his lips close on mine, his warmth seeping into me, the wet leather of his jacket strong in my nostrils. He kissed me like it was the last kiss we'd ever have, with heat and hunger, eagerness and hints of desperation, his hands wrapped around my waist to pull me closer, then sliding down to grasp my hips.

And just like that, I was all melty and whimpering again, leaning into him, lifting my face to deepen the kiss, my hands gliding up the back of his jacket to curl around the nape of his neck, clutching him to me.

By the time the kiss broke, I was breathless and my thighs were quivery and I was seconds from climbing back on the bike and telling him to take me somewhere private.

Instead, I backed away, somewhat reluctantly. "I should go. I'm meeting Claire in the morning."

He released me, seeming as reluctant as I was. "Will I see you tomorrow?"

I just winked at him. "Call me in the afternoon."

"I don't have your number."

I shot him a glare. "Yeah, it's probably the only number in the city you *don't* have," I said. "I'm sure your brother can get it for you."

Zane lifted up and reached into his back pocket, pulling out a crumpled stack of scrap papers, each scribbled with phone numbers in feminine handwriting. "What...these numbers?" He asked, holding them up. "I don't want 'em. Never did."

The rain had finally quit, leaving everything wet and glistening in the darkness. Zane dug in an inside pocket of his coat, producing a silver Zippo lighter embossed with the SEAL logo. He flicked open the lid and snapped the spark wheel across his thigh in a single fast move, a flame bursting into life. He held the stack of paper upside down and let the flame lick at the edges. I watched in amusement and secret satisfaction as the fire consumed the scraps of paper.

When the fire had caught fully, Zane tossed the entire pile to the ground and we watched it burn until there was nothing left but flakes of ash skirling in the gentle breeze.

He put the Zippo back in his jacket pocket and turned his gaze to mine. "Only number I want is yours, sweetheart, and it only counts if you give it to me." He chuckled. "Fact is, though, if he really wanted to look hard enough, Xavier could probably get hold of your university transcripts, your medical record, your driving record, your credit score—shit, if your info is held in an electronic system pretty much anywhere, he could access it. He wouldn't, though. Just saying…he *could*."

"Is it really that easy?" I asked.

Zane shrugged. "Sure, if you know how and where to look. *I* couldn't do it, but for Xavier? Easier than programming a new remote control."

I patted his hip pockets, his back pockets, and then inside his jacket, hunting for his phone. I found it in the jacket, pulled it out, and handed it to him to unlock. He held his thumb on the home button and gave it back to me. His home screen was a photo of him in full commando gear, an assault rifle held in one hand resting on his shoulder, a helmet on, wrap-around sunglasses on his face. He was in the back of a cargo jet, it looked like, the cargo door open behind him showing the ground blue-green in the distance, with four similarly-geared other men in the photo with him, posing for the selfie with goofy grins.

I stared at the photo for a moment, and then turned the screen to him. "Who are these guys?" I asked.

He named them, starting on the left and tapping each one in turn. "Marco Campo, Oscar Moyer, Luis Valtierra, me, and Cody Kellogg." He paused a moment, obviously remembering, a complicated expression on his face, equal parts nostalgic happiness, and sadness. "They were part of my SEAL team."

"Did you guys have nicknames for each other?"

He chuckled, nodding. "Of course. Marco was Campy, Oscar was either Wiener or the Grouch, Luis was Pinche, which is only funny if you know anything about Spanish insults. Cody was Frosted Flakes, or Frosty, because somebody got ahold of his senior pictures and he had these really wicked cool frosted tips, and his name is Kellogg."

"What was your nickname?"

He glanced at his boots, grinning. "Baddass." He laughed as if embarrassed, and then continued. "You know, because of my last name, obviously. And then there was that time in San Diego, right after BUD/S. I got into a bar fight with a bunch of jarheads from Twentynine Palms. Well, there were, like, eight of them and one of me, so my boys showed up thinking they were gonna have to save my ass. I told 'em I didn't need any fuckin' help, because I didn't."

I eyed him skeptically. "Eight of them? At once?"

He shrugged. "Sure. I mean, I got messed up, but I sure as fuck didn't lose." He lifted his upper lip out of the way with a thumb, pointing at a couple teeth that were a little whiter and straighter than the others. "Lost a few teeth, broken nose, bruised ribs, fucked up my knuckles pretty good, and got my ass chewed off by the X-O, but hell, it earned me a pretty killer nickname."

I shook my head. "You boys and your fighting." I found his contact list and added a new one: *For a good time, Call*—and I added my cell number, then called myself from his phone so I'd have his number, too. I locked the phone and handed it back to him. "There. You have my number and I have yours. See you tomorrow?"

He stuffed the phone back into his jacket and hauled me up against him. "Unless I can convince you to invite me in."

I rolled my eyes and huffed at him, pushing away. "Is that all you ever think about?"

He grinned. "When I'm around you? Yeah, pretty much."

"You're terrible," I said, trying to wriggle out of

his clutches, but he wasn't letting go.

"No, the name's Badd, sweetheart. Two D's." He had me pressed up against him, his hands wandering, and really, I wasn't trying *that* hard to get away.

I groaned. "Jesus. You make puns on your own name." I shook my head, slapping his chest. "Now let me go, for real. I barely slept last night, and tomorrow is my last day with Claire."

He released me, climbing off the bike and pivoting to sit on it properly. "Fine, go get your beauty sleep. Not that you need it."

I backed away from him before my body betrayed my better sense by propelling me back into his hands. "Flattery will get you—well, pretty far, actually."

He grinned, one eyebrow lifted. "In that case, I should mention that I'll probably be awake most of the night, thinking about how beautiful you looked in the moonlight, topless and doing amazing things to me with your mouth."

"Awake doing what, exactly?" I asked, even though I already knew, obviously.

"What do you think? Wishing my hand was your mouth."

I forced myself to continue moving away. "Really? You can't wait until tomorrow?"

"With the mental images you gave me? Hell no."

I had no response for that except a stupid, happy

grin. I waved at him and finally turned away. "Bye, Zane."

"Sweet dreams, Mara."

I didn't look back until I had the door closed behind me, and then I peeked out the window at him as he rumbled away. I went to my room, undressed and pulled on the oversized T-shirt I'd brought as pajamas, and then brushed my teeth, as much to get rid of the come-breath as for the sake of dental hygiene. In the moment, Zane's come had tasted amazing, more because of how much I'd enjoyed his reactions than anything, but now that the flavor had...steeped, so to speak, I was more than ready to brush and gargle it away.

Of course, thinking about Zane's come, and Zane's reactions led to me thinking about Zane, and Zane's cock, and how it had felt in my hands and how it had tasted in my mouth.

And of course, Zane had gotten me pretty worked up before I'd stopped him, so now I was feeling all...tense and horny and needy. I didn't regret stopping him, though, because I knew myself well enough to know that if I'd let him go down on me right then, the next thing I knew he'd have been inside me. I wasn't opposed to sex outside, especially because that spot had been pretty damn secluded and private, so it wasn't that I'd been worried about being discovered, it was more that some instinct was telling me to limit true intimacy with Zane. Keep some level of space between us; keep it impersonal to a degree. That was the instinct, at least, and that was what had me pushing Zane off me.

I'd have relished the magnificent orgasm he'd have given me, but I was also not entirely sure he had a condom, and I knew I didn't, and while obviously I was on the shot, I still wasn't about to run the risk of being part of the one percent if my birth control failed. Plus, Zane bare? Dangerous, that. Very, very dangerous.

I was lying in the bed, trying to fall asleep and failing. Trying to pretend I wasn't horny, and failing. Trying to pretend I didn't have a vivid mental image of Zane naked in the bathroom, one hand braced on the wall, the other sliding hard and fast on his erect cock. He'd be groaning my name, of course, eyes closed, abs tensed as he jerked himself to a cursing, weak-in-the-knees orgasm. I could picture that O, too, the way he'd dip at the knees and groan long and low, the way his cock would spurt a thick white stream of come into the toilet…

The hem of my T-shirt had ridden up, and I had my nice fantasy going. And hey, wouldn't you know I'd brought my LELO? Why pretend, at this point? I fished the vibrator out of my toiletries bag and got back in bed. And then, for some reason, said fuck it and ripped off my T-shirt. I wasn't sure what was coming over me, but as I pictured Zane's fist sliding on his cock, my LELO buzzing around my clit, my eyes kept drifting to my cell phone, laying on the nightstand.

No, Mara.

Nope.

Don't do it, ho.

Do *NOT* sext Zane.

Of course, I didn't listen to myself. I mean, where's the fun in that?

I kept the vibrator on low for the moment, content to draw this out a little. I kept fighting the urge to grab my phone for another…um, thirty seconds, max, and then set the vibrator aside, because I was *so* about to sext Zane Badd. I grabbed the phone, and opened the front-facing camera. I made sure the ambient light was low enough to be sexy but not so dark that I'd need a flash, and then took a couple test selfies. God, my hair was a mess—I finger-combed it to look sexy and sultry, like I'd just been lying in bed looking this good. Part of me demanded that I go put on at least a coat of lip-gloss and maybe some eye shadow, but I resisted it; this whole thing with Zane was turning into an experiment in pushing myself outside my comfort zone. Spending time with Zane outside of bed was a big start, and now I was going to not just text him, not just send him a selfie, but I was going to sext him? Like, send nudes? Way outside my comfort zone. And without any makeup on? Lunacy. Utter madness.

But there I was, lying on my back in bed, hair on point, phone held above me. I played with a few poses until I found one that looked fairly natural, laying so my hips were flat on the bed but my torso was twisted to one side, my arm draped in such a way that my breast was visible but not my nipple. Eyes looking sleepy, a little horny—*click-click-click*.

I snapped a few and swiped through them, satisfied with at least one.

I pulled up Zane's number, saved it in my phone, and started a text message thread.

Me: **You up?**

"Delivered" popped up immediately, and then after maybe twenty seconds switched to "read"; another few seconds, and the gray bubble with the three dots appeared.

Him: *Yeah. I like how you saved your number in my phone. ;-)*

Oooh, I got a winky emoticon? I probably shouldn't read too much into it, but Zane just didn't seem like the type to throw smiley and winky emoticons into every text—just a hunch.

Me: **Thought you'd appreciate that. LOL.**

Me: **WYD?**

Him: *Trying to sleep and failing. You?*

I hesitated a moment, and then attached the best photo from the three I'd taken, and hit 'send' before I could second-guess myself.

Him: *Goddamn, Mara. Can you be any sexier?*

Him: *Wait, I can answer that myself. Yes, you can. Just point the camera down a little further...*

I rolled to my back and held the camera over my head to snap a photo looking down at myself. I didn't like that one, though, because gravity had my tits sagging to either side, which just wasn't flattering. I squeezed my arms against my sides and held the phone with both hands so my arms propped my breasts up and pushed them together; much better.

I sent the photo, and then attached a message:

Me: **Like that?**

Him: *I was trying to wait till I saw you to...you know. But after that photo? Not sure I'm gonna be able to hold out.*

Me: **If you do, send a pic of you doing it.**

Him: *I've never taken a naked selfie before, so I can't promise it'll be any good, but...*

And then a pic appeared in the thread, Zane naked. He'd taken it lying down in his bed, with the camera at an almost upside down oblique angle so it was looking down the length of his body from the top of his head. The angle showed every glorious inch of him, his intense brown eyes turned up to stare into the camera, muscles popping, his cock erect and laying flat against his belly.

Jesus. The man was so gorgeous it was just absolutely unreal. Like, *I* got to touch him? Kiss him? Fuck him? Soon I'd get to have that cock all up inside me, pleasuring me with all those long, thick, hard inches? How lucky was that? I'd be a fool to pass up any opportunity to have him for myself.

I grabbed my LELO and held it up by my face, snapping a photo of me staring at the vibrator in fake shock, sending it with a caption:

Me: **Ooops...where'd this come from?**

Him: *Fuck me, Mara, you're killing me. How about a little video of you using that thing?*

Me: **I'll show you mine if you show me yours...**

Me: **And when you say things like fuck me, I have a tendency to take them as an invitation.**

Him: *I can be at your door six minutes flat, and inside you in seven.*

Me: **I have a better idea. Hold on a minute.**

I fired up the vibrator and pressed it to my clit, gasping as sensation immediately ripped through me. I held the camera up and hit the red 'record' circle, and then panned down, starting at my face. I was already moaning, so I just let myself go, keeping the camera pointed down to capture the shaft of the LELO sliding into my channel, keeping it focused there as I began moving it in and out of myself, gasping and whimpering every time the smaller clitoral stimulator pressed against me. I panned back up to my face, pleased to see myself looking flushed and sexy.

"Oh god," I whimpered, "Oh my god."

Then back down, as the vibrator slid in and out rhythmically, my gasps and breathless little shrieks coming faster and faster as I neared orgasm.

"Zane, holy shit, Zane. I wish it was you...god, *god—*"

And then I came, my hips flying off the bed, biting down on my lip to keep from screaming out loud, recording the entirety of the orgasm.

When I finally finished coming, I was breathless and sweaty, but I turned the camera back to my face. "Now it's your turn," I said, giving the camera my best sexy, sultry, just-fucked look, and then ended the recording. I sent it immediately, and then waited eagerly for his reply.

The wait was agony. It seemed like it was an eternity before my phone blooped to alert me that he'd sent a reply.

The still showed his face and part of his chest, and then when I touched the video to play it, the view panned down to show his big, hard cock with his fist around it, sliding slowly; he was still in his bedroom, laying on his bed. I heard a click off-camera, and then a small bottle of lube appeared and I watched him squirt a small amount onto his cock. His fist slid faster now, squelching wetly. Faster, faster, and I heard him gasping and groaning, and every now and again he'd pan up to look into the camera as I'd done before returning the camera to the action.

I'd just come, but watching his fist slide on his cock was turning me on more than ever. I put the vibrator inside myself again and started moving it in and out to the rhythm of Zane's fist jacking himself.

Even watching him, I could tell when he was close. His abs flexed and his hips lifted, and his groans went guttural.

"Fuck, fuck. Mara, god," he groaned, his voice low and rough. "Even now, all I can think about is— oh fucking hell, I'm so close—is the way your mouth felt on my cock. I wish it were you right now. Shit, oh shit, I'm—"

Thank god he kept the camera focused on his cock, because that moment when he came, was one of the hottest things I'd ever seen, hot enough to push me over the edge for the second time, searing pleasure shooting through me at the sight of Zane orgasming. His jerking strokes blurred and his hips flexed off the bed, and then he growled low in his throat as he came. Come spurted out of him in a white stream, splashing across his stomach and up onto chest. He kept jerking himself as another spurt left him to pool on his stomach, again and again.

I thought of what he'd said, how he wanted to come all over me, and in that moment, watching him jerk off onto himself, I could very easily imagine how it would feel to have his come on my flesh. I'd done a lot of things, but never that. I'd never let a guy demonstrate any kind of dominance over me, never done anything that smacked of me demeaning myself. But somehow, it felt like if I let Zane come on me, it wouldn't be demeaning...it'd be hot. It'd be erotic as hell, and thrilling. Sexy. I'd lick it away and smear it all over myself and tease him with it, make him taste himself on my mouth.

Me: **And I just came again watching you**

Him: *I watched your video like three times. You are so hot it's ridiculous.*

Me: **You know what I think is hot?**

Him: *What?*

Me: **The thought of you doing that again, but on me.**

Him: *Onto you where?*

Me: **Anywhere? Everywhere?**

Him: *Paint you white with my sperm is what you're saying?*

Me: **LOL exactly.**

Him: *I literally JUST came, and now I'm getting hard again thinking about you with my cum all over your tits.*

Me: **Hold that thought until tomorrow.**

Him: *Like I said, I can be there in six minutes.*

Me: **I really do need to sleep now. Plus I just came twice in ten minutes, so I'm all tuckered out now anyway.**

I took a photo of myself pretending to sleep, twisted slightly to the side so my boobs looked good, the vibrator visible in the lower corner.

Him: *Okay, okay. Till tomorrow then. Good night.*

Him: *By the way, I'm gonna save the video and photos, but I hope it goes without saying that I'm the only one who'll ever see them.*

Me: **LOL here I was thinking I'd show Claire the dick pic, just so she'd believe me about how big your cock really is.**

Me: **Only kidding. Mostly.**

Him: *Do what you want with it, but just know I'm sure as hell not going to be sharing you with ANYONE.*

Me: *Claire and I actually do tend to overshare details with each other, but in this case I'm feeling a little possessive of my new toy. ;-)*

Him: *There was a guy in my unit that had this really hot GF who would send him nudes pretty regularly, and he'd pass them around. She knew, and was fine with it, but I always thought it was kinda weird. Like, if I were to ever have a hot GF sending me nudes, I sure AF wouldn't be sharing them with my buddies.*

Me: **Yeah, see with Claire and I, we just share everything. I'd never show any of my other friends, but Claire is kind of like my sister, or an extension of myself. I wouldn't pass it around for everyone to see. Claire is just...Claire, I guess. IDK.**

Him: *I know what you mean. That's how I was with Campy. Super close. He showed me pix of his wife right after she gave birth to his son, and Campy was ridiculously private. Not many of the guys even knew Marco was married or that his wife was pregnant.*

Me: **Are you still close with him?**

Him: **He was killed a few days after my dad passed.**

Me: **God Zane I'm so sorry.**

There was a long pause, then.

Him: *Yeah, me too. Lost my dad and my best friend within days of each other. It sucked. Still sucks.*

Him: *We all knew the risks when we signed up. It just especially sucks because he had a wife and a brand new baby boy. Reasons to live, I guess. The rest of us were just single jackasses and horny douchebags, but Campy was the real deal, man. Honorable, truly coura-geous, and the best damn friend anyone could ask for.*

He was the real badass, not me.

Him: *Some days I think it should have been me, not him. Then his kid would have a dad. Nobody should have to grow up without their dad.*

Me: **I don't know how to express this without sounding...cold or selfish or whatever, but I'm glad it wasn't you. I'm sorry about your friend and for his wife and kid, but I just can't be glad it wasn't you. Does that make me a horrible person?**

Him: *Shit I'm such an asshole. Ruining the whole thing we just had with my dark bullshit. I'm sorry for making it heavy. I don't know what came over me. I never talk about this shit, even with my bro's.*

Me: **You don't need to apologize, Zane. We're trying out this practice relationship with each other, right? Well, you're practicing opening up. You can talk to me...friends talk.**

Him: *Friends. I like that.*

Him: *I thought you had to sleep?*

Me: **I do. But I don't mind this. Although, if I stop answering, it's because I fell asleep.**

Him: *Sleep. Have fun with Claire tomorrow.*

Me: **Okay. Call me at like 4?**

Him: *I will. Talk to you at 4, then. Good night Mara.*

Me: **Night Zane.**

I put my phone to sleep and plugged it in, and

then switched off the lamp. As I drifted to sleep, I found myself thinking about Zane. Surprising, I know. But for the first time since I'd met him, I wasn't thinking about his body or even his eyes or smile. I was thinking about *him*. The man. The bits of himself he'd shown me, his deep respect for his friend, the hint of the pain he obviously still felt but kept buried deep down. He'd shown me that, and it seemed to have surprised him as much as it did me.

I also couldn't help but notice that I hadn't reciprocated the sharing. Kind of felt like a bitch for it, since he'd shared something that was clearly deeply personal. But…how did I share about Dad? I just didn't even know where to start.

I fell asleep thinking about Zane, and how this "practice relationship" had suddenly started feeling a lot more like real.

SIX

Zane

I WOKE UP WITH A RAGING HARD-ON LEAKING PRE-COME. I'd been dreaming of Mara and the way she'd looked in the moonlight up on the Rainbird. Huge, firm, perfectly-shaped tits pressed against my thighs as her mouth slid up and down my cock...fuck, fuck, fuck. And then, later? That fucking video? Jesus.

I couldn't help myself. I cued up the video and started it, watching her slide that pink vibrator into her pussy, listening to the way she moaned and watching how her breasts bounced as she started to come, her hips pumping.

I shot jizz all over myself yet again, groaning her name through gritted teeth. Which then meant a shower, because I'd only cleaned myself up with some toilet paper last night, so I was a little…crusty.

Once I was clean, I contemplated calling her early, but held off, so she could get in some quality time with her friend. I wasn't due downstairs for work until ten thirty, and it was just past five in the morning—sleeping in for me, since I usually woke up at four with or without an alarm. I was feeling cast adrift, more unsure of myself than I'd ever been in my life. I didn't know what to do with myself.

For reasons I was unsure of, I found myself with my cell phone in hand, staring at a particular contact entry, one I'd not called in a long time. Too long. Way, way too long.

I touched the "call" symbol on the screen, letting out a breath. Held the phone to my ear. Waited as it rang several times. I was about to hang up when the ringing stopped and I heard the muffled sound of a phone being fumbled.

"'Lo? Zane? What—um…is everything okay?" Annalisa Campo, Marco's wife. She sounded sleepy, groggy.

"Hi, Anna. It's…it's Zane."

"Yeah, I know. Are you okay?" A pause. "Not to be rude, but why are you calling at eight o'clock in the morning?"

I swallowed hard. "Shit, I'm sorry. I wasn't think-ing. I just...I figured you'd be up by now." I cleared my throat. "I'm calling to check in. See how you're doing. Make sure there's...see if there's anything I can do."

I dug the heel of my palm into my eye socket, as if to rub the raw emotional pain out of myself through direct force.

Annalisa was silent for a long time. "It's been sev-eral months, Zane. Why now?"

I hesitated. "I don't know. I don't know. I just...I don't know."

She blew out a breath. "Let me make some coffee. I'm just gonna put you on mute for minute, okay?"

"Yeah, fine."

There was a good minute or two of dead silence, and then I heard Annalisa click back onto the line. "Hey, I'm back." I heard her take a sip of coffee, and then she spoke in a low tone, meaning her son was sleeping somewhere. "So you're checking in, huh? I don't know what you want me to say, Zane. Things are hard."

"Tell me the truth, I guess, whatever it is."

"I miss Marco, that's the truth. I don't know how to cope without him. I mean, he wasn't around much, but we got to FaceTime, and I got letters from him pretty regularly, plus he'd get leave once in awhile, so I'd actually get to see him." She sniffled. "He never met Tony. Tony never...he's never known his father. All he's ever known is me and my parents. So...I miss him. I just miss him. He's gone. He's dead, he's never coming back and I'm alone and I don't know how to do this."

I felt my eyes burn and my throat close up. "Shit. I know. I keep going to call him, or text him, and then I remember."

She sniffled again. "We get some money from the government, but it's not much. It doesn't cover... everything. My parents aren't young anymore and they're retired, so they can't help much, and...I'm working midnights at a nursing home, which is why I was still asleep. I just got home from work an hour or so ago. I'm struggling, Zane. That's how I'm doing."

"Fuck. Why didn't you call me? Or Luis or—or any of us? You know we'll do anything for you."

"And say what? 'Hey guys, I'm a poor war widow, please send money?'" She snorted. "Yeah, right. I've got *some* pride."

"Fuck pride, Anna. We *owe* you. You're Campy's wife. He was our brother and that makes you our sister, and his kid is...goddammit." I cleared my throat. "Text me your address. I'm calling the guys. You're getting help, Anna. You shouldn't have to work mid-nights to make ends meet, not when you've got all of us."

"I'm not accepting your charity or your pity, Zane. He died doing what he loved. You didn't get him killed any more than Luis or Oscar or any of the other guys did. There's no guilt for any of you. You don't owe me anything." Her voice softened. "Thanks for calling, Zane. It's good to hear from you."

"Anna, goddammit, it's not charity or pity. Just give me your address." I barked the last as an order, gruff, harsh.

She just laughed, a soft, sad huff. "Fine. I know better than to argue with you. You'll just have your baby brother stalk me online or something."

"I would never," I protested.

She laughed again. "Would, and have. Remember when you had Xavier hack into Marco's email account? You sent everyone in the unit creepy clown porn from Marco's email address."

I laughed. "God, that was hysterical. He was *pissed.*"

"That one you sent? Where the clown has to take off the fake nose to go down on the girl? Marco almost passed out from laughing so hard."

"You watched that shit?"

"Of course we did. We watched the clown porn

and then we got it on like Donkey Kong. He kept honking my boobs like they were a clown's nose." She laughed, but it turned into sniffles. "He was only pretending to be pissed at you. He thought it was funny."

"I know. He was shitty at being mad at people. He couldn't hold a grudge if his life depended on it."

"I broke up with him three times while he was in BUD/S. He'd be pissed for a day or two, but then he'd call me and convince me I hadn't really broken up with him. He refused to let me."

"You're what got him through BUD/S," I told her.

She couldn't quite answer clearly. "I—I know."

"And he got me through it," I said. "So yeah, I do fucking owe you."

She sighed. "Are you coping, Zane?"

"I don't know. I'm trying."

"It's not your fault," Annalisa said, her voice soft.

"Just text me your address, Anna."

"Okay."

"I'll let you go now. Sorry for waking you up."

"It's okay." A brief hesitation from Annalisa. "It's good to hear from you, Zane."

"You too, Anna. Bye."

"See ya."

I tossed the phone aside, rubbing the bridge of my nose. She was working midnights? Jesus. I'd dropped the ball.

I grabbed my phone again and sent a group text to Luis, Oscar, and Cody, detailing my plan to take care of Annalisa. We'd each send her four hundred dollars a month, which between the four of us would equal to sixteen hundred a month, not a huge number, but hopefully enough to offset things for her. I got replies immediately from all three of them, agreeing to my plan. They were all still active duty with the SEALs, so they were making good money anyway, which made me suspect they'd probably kick in more without asking, just because that's the type of guys they were. I just felt like shit for having let it go this long before checking in on her.

I got another text, this one from Annalisa, containing her PayPal account details, and a note saying that if we really wanted to help out, it would be easier to send money digitally than writing out a check and sending it in the mail, which was what I'd planned.

I forwarded this update to the guys, and then created a PayPal account for myself and linked my Navy Federal account to it, and then immediately sent Annalisa a thousand dollars.

I'd been in the Navy for ten years, most of that as a SEAL; I'd never spent much on myself over the years, never bought a car or any expensive shit, so I had quite a lot of money banked. The bar was slammed all the time now, which meant all of us were making insane bank each night we worked, which I stashed in my account and rarely touched, only adding to my nest egg. Meaning, I could afford to shoot some cash to Annalisa. I was tempted to send more, but I knew the other guys would be doing the same thing, feeling similar guilt and obligation, and I also knew if we went too far overboard Annalisa would refuse to accept it.

I was at odd ends again, now. Trying not to think about Marco, trying not to think about Annalisa, trying not to think about Mara…what was left to think about? Not a lot.

So I went down into the storeroom under the bar, slid a pair of forty-five plates on each side of the bar and started benching until I was shaky.

When in doubt, work it out. It doesn't solve any problems, but it's a better way of pushing aside your problems than drinking.

Especially at six in the morning.

Fuck me; it was going to be a long day.

SEVEN

Mara

Imet Claire at a nearby diner at nine the following morning, feeling refreshed even though I'd not fallen asleep till well after two and was up again by seven thirty. I normally need a lot more than five hours of sleep, but something about the way I'd fallen asleep had made me sleep more deeply than normal. I wasn't about to examine that too closely, though, because I suspected it had everything to do with Zane and the multiple orgasms.

I arrived at the diner first, so I got a booth and settled in to wait for Claire; punctuality wasn't really in her repertoire of personality traits, you could say. If we were supposed to meet at nine, she might show up at eight and sit drinking coffee and working on her laptop for the next hour, or she might not show up until fifteen or twenty minutes past the meeting time. She just…didn't have a solid grasp on time, and it was something I'd just gotten used to over the years of knowing her.

Today, thankfully, she showed up only ten minutes late, a spring in her step and a mischievous smile playing on her lips.

She sat down and immediately stole my coffee. "Ohmygodcoffee. I got up like ten minutes ago and ran straight here."

"Up late partying, huh?" I asked, knowing what the bounce in her step and the shit-eating grin meant.

A passing waitress brought a mug over for Claire and poured her a fresh cup, and Claire started slugging it back steaming hot and black. "I dunno if I would call it partying, exactly," she said, waggling her eyebrows at me suggestively.

"Partying…on your back?"

She giggled. "Um, more like partying doggy style, and then standing up partying, and then shower partying, and then reverse cowgirl partying. *Aaand* there might have been some absurdly high quality muff diving, and then some really quality fellatio. And then something brand new even for me: post-party snuggle time. Which I highly, *highly* recommend, by the way."

"Well damn, girl, that's a lot of partying."

She gave a sassy flip of her hair. "What can I say? I'm a party girl."

I laughed. "I think I'm reaching semantic satiation with the word 'party', my friend." We paused to order, and then when the waitress left I turned back to Claire. "So, who was the lucky guy? The guy from the bar bathroom?"

"Oh, no, someone else—this local guy I met."

"So wait, that was all with the same guy, in one night?"

She shrugged, pretending to be demure. "He had a *LOT* of stamina."

"Well, obviously, if he can go that many times in a single night. Jesus. Can you walk okay?"

"Well..." she said, wincing, "I *am* feeling a bit bowlegged, since he was...um...*insanely* well-endowed. But, all in all, I discovered that my vagina can stretch more than I'd ever thought possible, given proper lubrication and lots of, what I've decided to call, pre-game orgasms."

I guffawed at that, almost snorting piping hot coffee out my nose. "Pre-game orgasms. Are you going to see him again?"

She lifted a delicate shoulder. "Eh? Maybe." She wasn't looking at me when she said this, looking rather preoccupied with stirring her coffee…which was odd since she hadn't put cream or sugar in her coffee.

"Claire…"

"Amarantha?"

I knew she was serious when she used my full name. "You're going to see him again, aren't you?"

"Yesnowshutup," she mumbled under breath. "How about Zane, that smug, sexy motherfucker from the bar? You gonna see him again?"

"I saw him last night," I said.

"Well, no shit Sherlock, we both saw him last night."

"No, I mean I saw him again later. When you took that rando into the bathroom, I left with Zane."

The waitress arrived with our food then, and we paused the conversation to dig in. After a few bites, Claire stabbed the air in my direction with her fork. "Good girl, I was hoping you would." She took another bite. "So? Spill."

"Wait, I just thought of something. The guy from the bar bathroom and the local guy, they're different?"

"Yeah, that guy from the bathroom got all excited super quick and I could tell he wasn't gonna go the distance, so I gave him a handy and then bounced. I met the other local guy at a different bar later on, not long after you texted me."

"But you're going to see the local guy again?"

"YES, I'M GOING TO SEE THE LOCAL GUY AGAIN," Claire bellowed. "Now, will you let it go? You're gonna jinx it."

"Jinx what?" I was honestly confused, seeing Claire get this worked up.

"Me...this guy...the *thing*. There's a thing going on with us, and I don't want to jinx it, so can we please not talk about him anymore?"

"You have a *thing* with this guy?" I asked. "I'm sorry, I'm just confused."

She sighed, spearing a breakfast potato with her fork and waving it around, gesticulating. "I don't know, Mare. I really don't. It's a thing. What is the thing? Fuck if I know, and neither does he. But it's a thing, and we're gonna go very slowly and cautiously and try out this...*thing*."

"Like a rela—"

"SHUSH!" She snapped. "Do NOT say that word. No more talking about it. One more word and I'll shove these potatoes down your throat."

An effective threat, since I hated potatoes. "Fine, but when you can speak coherently about it, I expect details."

"Agreed." She crossed her wrists and stuck out her pinky fingers; I crossed my wrists and hooked my pinkies into hers, and we shook. Stupid and childish, but a promise-making tradition we'd had since boot camp. "Now. Zane, he of the epic penis. I need all the gory details."

I sighed. "He took me to a scenic overlook and I gave him the most epic blow job of the century…" dramatic pause, "…and maybe possibly kind of decided to practice date while I'm in Ketchikan for the week."

Claire clapped her hands over her heart, tilted her head to one side, and made an *awwww* face. "My little girl is all grown up, now."

"Oh, shut up." I threw a sugar packet at her. "I wouldn't go that far. But I'm giving it a try."

"For realsies, I'm happy for you, pumpkin."

I blinked at her. "Pumpkin?"

Claire laughed. "I'm experimenting with cute terms of endearment. I want to find one to use semi-ironically with this guy I'm maybe sort of not really but kind of almost seeing."

"Yeah, don't call me pumpkin. That's weird."

"Honeybuckets?"

"Uh, no."

She tapped her chin. "Diddly-dinkums?"

I threw another sugar packet at her. "You need to be stopped." I dipped my fingers in the glass of melting ice water and flicked it at her, repeatedly chanting,

"The power of Christ compels you."

She put her hands in front of her face, shrieking. "Okay, okay, I'll stop!" When I stopped, she threw the sugar packets back at me. "And besides, you don't say 'the power of Christ compels you' for an exorcism."

"How would you know?"

She frowned at me. "Um, because I grew up Catholic? As in, I went to a private Catholic academy from pre-K through high school, attended mass every week, and was in the church choir?"

I sat in stunned silence. "Shut the hell up." I pointed at her. "Yet another thing I didn't know about you. What other secrets are you keeping from me?"

"It wasn't a secret, it just never came up. Once I graduated high school, I stopped going."

"Wow. So...what else hasn't come up that I should know about my best friend?"

She paused, obviously thinking about how to reply to my question. "Um...I got my wisdom teeth out? I had an appendectomy my junior year because my appendix exploded and I almost died?" She looked at me in the eyes and then threw out one more, casually. "I had a D-and-C when I was twenty."

I gasped in shock at the last one "A D-and-C? Like the thing they do after a miscarriage?"

She nodded. "Yep. I got pregnant and had a miscarriage. On my twentieth birthday, actually."

"Damn, Claire. You've never talked about this before." I sat in stunned silence for a long time. "Like, how did I not even know you grew up Catholic, much less that you had a fucking D-and-C?"

She shrugged. "I just don't talk about myself, that's all."

"Understandable," I said, although I was surprised she had not shared this, given our close friendship. "I just...I feel like I don't even know you, in a way."

"You're still my best friend, Mara, that'll never change. She sighed. "But yeah, the miscarriage itself was brutal. I hadn't even really had time to process that I was pregnant, and then it was over. It was messy, too. Like in the movies where it looks like a Quentin Tarantino movie happened between the girl's legs? That's not an exaggeration." She stirred her coffee again. "I, um, don't talk about it because of the other effects the whole thing had on my life...and not just because of the emotional trauma of the miscarriage itself."

"What do you mean? What happened?"

"My dad disowned me. My mom is super traditional and she refuses to openly disobey Dad, so the only way I can see Mom or my sisters is if they sneak out while Dad is working."

"Damn, honey."

She nodded. "Yeah, it sucks. Six years have passed, and I still have to be all sneaky and secretive if I want to see them."

"He hasn't relented?"

She shook her head. "Nope, and he never will. He forced the rest of them to have new family photos taken so I wouldn't be in them."

"Because you had a miscarriage?"

"Because I got pregnant out of wedlock."

"That's archaic."

"That's Dad." She paused, and then stuck a finger in the air. "Also, Dad is a church deacon."

"I don't know what that means."

"Sort of like a priest, but they can be married if they were married before becoming ordained." A shrug. "It just means he's, like, a super church man and very strict when it comes to religious dogma. He works for the church in a permanent, paid capacity."

"Oh. Does that mean he won't ever forgive you?"

Another sigh. "That's so unlikely as to be impossible." She waved a hand, dismissing it. "Or, if he did, it'd be conditional. I'd have to confess my sins and be absolved and say, like, forty million Hail Mary's and do a bunch of penance and other stupid bullshit. He's a stubborn asshole, and I'm just as stubborn as he is, only I'm going to be more stubborn than he is about this because I'll be damned if I'm going to apologize, and certainly not for *him* disowning *me*."

"God, I'm so sorry, Claire. I had no idea."

"It is what it is. I'm used to it, now." She shrugged, then poked the back of my hand with her fork. "That was a very nicely done deflection, by the way."

"It wasn't a deflection, it was an honest question…a rabbit trail in the conversation, but I'm glad you told me about it."

"Well, thanks, but let's get back to the topic at hand, namely, you and Zane."

"Me and Zane? There's not much to say. We're going to keep having excessive amounts of super crazy hot sex, and also, we're going to hang out and do stuff that isn't sex. Just to see how we both like it."

"And you're calling this a practice relationship."

"Correct. Because he lives here and I live in San Francisco, and neither of us are ready for a real relationship, but we feel pretty compatible, so we're gonna see how it feels to pretend we're in one, in case we decide we want to try it for real later on."

"So, like me and Brian at work, only with sex?"

"Exactly. If we hadn't already had sex, I might actually try and see how a no-sex dating thing would go, but since we've already done it, there's no point in stopping now."

"I guess that makes sense," Claire said, pushing her now-empty plate away. "Now, can you go back to the most epic blow job of the century? I wanna hear more about that."

I shrugged. "I mean, I wasn't planning on doing it. I had been planning on talking to him about my idea regarding the whole practice dating thing, and then the conversation just sort of got dirty—"

"Understandable when you're talking to a hot guy with a massive dong," Claire put in.

"Right," I agreed. "And then he was like, so how about a blow job, and I was, like…sure."

"And?"

"And I sucked him off so good he actually collapsed to the ground afterward and couldn't walk for several minutes."

Claire blinked at me. "Well good goddamn, girl. You must have some sort of secrets you haven't shared."

"Yeah, maybe." I grinned. "I mean, it was helpful that I just…I dunno…I really, really wanted to give the best blow job he'd ever had. I mean, if we only have a week together, I want it to be the best damn week of our entire lives, right? And obviously I've given plenty of BJs before, but this was different somehow."

The waitress came over right then, and had to hold back a snort of laughter as she refilled our coffee.

"Different how?" Claire asked.

I sighed. "I don't know. I wish I did. I've been

trying to figure that out myself. It's not just that he's gorgeous, which he is, and it's not just that he has a massive, gorgeous dong, which he does, and it's also not just that he's an incredible sexual partner, which he is, nor is it just that he's a god among men when it comes to cunnilingus…it's all of those things at once, and…something more. I don't know. It's frustrating."

"It's chemistry, babe," Claire said. "It's ineffable."

"Ineffable?"

She nodded. "Something so incredible, so amazing, so perfect that you just can't put it into words."

I threw another sugar packet at her head. "I know what ineffable means, whore-face."

She threw the same packet back at me. "Well, then don't say it like you've never heard the word before."

"I just…I'm trying to apply it to Zane, and the whole thing between us." I lapsed into silence for a moment, thinking. "It's just…if you'd asked me last week if I thought the word 'ineffable' could be applied to a man in any capacity, much less this weird quasi-relationship we've got, I would have laughed in your face. But…it's not so stupid now, somehow."

She nodded seriously. "Believe me, poopsie, I understand more than you know."

"Poopsie? Really? That sounds like something a minivan-driving soccer mom who shops exclusively at

Whole Foods might call her potty training kid's turd."

Claire snorted in laughter, trying to keep in a mouthful of coffee. "Goddammit, I just scalded my sinuses," she said, wiping coffee from her nose and chin. "Then what do you think I should call this guy in the heat of the moment?"

"What's wrong with the classics like honey, baby, sweetie—things like that?"

She waved a hand in dismissal. "He deserves something original. He's like no one I've ever met."

"Now *that* I understand," I said.

"I just thought of something weird," Claire said. "What are the chances of us both meeting hot, incredible guys who challenge the status quo of the way we live our lives and view relationships...in the same week, in the same city, both local guys, but at different times and in different places, without actually being together when we met them?"

I stared at her. "Now that you put it that way, it is kind of..."

"Statistically so improbable as to be laughable?"

I nodded. "Exactly. But then, we are the Gruesome Twosome." My phone chimed in my purse, and I lifted it out to check it.

My boss had sent me an urgent email; I was on vacation, but my boss knew I checked my email religiously, so he was prone to sending me emails even when he knew I was home or gone, because he knew I'd check it and likely reply. Which I did, even though I hated that my boss used my cell phone addiction against me. When I finished the email, I looked up to see Claire typing on her own phone, but judging by the soft, amused, yet slightly horny expression on her face, she was texting her guy and not her boss.

I set my phone on the table and slid out of the booth. "I have to pee. Don't pay the check without me."

Claire snorted. "As if," she muttered, not looking up.

I used the bathroom and returned to the booth... and found Claire with my phone in one hand, her other hand clapped to her mouth in shock, her eyes wide. Claire knew my passcode and I knew hers, and we'd always been open enough that we felt comfortable going through each other's phones; this was the first time I felt weird about it in the years I'd known her.

"Holy mother of fucks, you weren't kidding about an epic penis, Mara. Jesus. That thing is a monster." She swiped a finger, touched the screen, and I heard a familiar sound, a low male groan of pleasure—"*I wish it was you right now*—"

"Oh...my...*god*." She touched the screen and moved the slider back to start the video over, checking around her and then hunching over the screen, fending off my attempts to get my phone back. "That has got to be the hottest minute and a half of video in existence. Can you forward that to me?"

"No I can't forward it to you!" I snatched the phone back, more angry with my best friend than I'd ever been. "God, Claire, I know we've always shared pretty much everything, but this is..." I wasn't even sure what to say.

I was bubbling with anger I didn't understand, and that itself was freaking me out. I'd shown her my dick pics before, and she'd shown me hers. Any other time in our friendship, if Claire had snooped through my phone and found a dick pic or whatever, I'd have laughed with her. I wouldn't have gotten angry. It would have been totally fine. But this time....

Claire was eyeing me intently. "But this is different, isn't it?" I nodded and she grabbed my hand, meeting my eyes. "I'm sorry, Mare. I really am. I wasn't snooping for anything like that—I was just... messing with your phone. I was gonna change your lock screen or something, just to be funny, and I happened to see the dick pic he sent you, and I couldn't stop looking. That thing *is* gorgeous. Not just because of the size, though, like you said. It's just...pretty."

"Claire—"

She held up a hand. "I didn't mean to see it, for real. But now that I have, we might as well talk about it, right?"

I sighed. "I guess. I'm sorry I overreacted; I'm just being weird about this. What's funny is that I sent him a few photos and a video, too, and he was like 'Obviously I'm not going to share this with anyone, just so you know,' and I jokingly said I'd only ever show you, because that's how we've always been, but then I thought about it later, and realized I wasn't sure I wanted to share him with you in that sense. I mean, I've shown you photos before, but—"

"But that's more because ninety-nine percent of the time when a guy sends a dick pic, it's comical rather than hot."

"But *that's* a hot dick pick, though."

"I'll say," Claire sighed. "Seriously hot. I think I'll send my guy a few nudes and see what he does."

"Tell him if he jerks off to the photos he should video it and send it to you."

"I think I'll do just that." She grinned at me. "And I'll send it to you when he does, because Mara, babe, my guy's dick? Equally as epic, I must say."

"Maybe we should agree to keep all dick pics and jerking-off videos to ourselves for the time being?"

She nodded. "I'll agree to that. I can see how I might be a bit possessive if I had that video on my phone."

"If I get any other unsolicited dick picks, though,

I'll totally send them to you so we can laugh together."

"You better. Laughing at unsolicited dick pics is one of life's greatest pleasures."

"I know, right? Like, what are they thinking when they send those? Do they honestly think we sit around looking longingly at pictures of average-guy penis?"

"I never can quite fathom their thought process-es. Like, objectively speaking, penises are kind of... weird, and not something I like to just sit around star-ing at. Like, show me a sexy set of abs or a nice chest, and I'll be impressed. Your dick? Not as much. Even if it's above average, if I'm not interested in you, I'm not gonna want a photograph of your penis. I'm just not. Hell, until I saw *that*, I honestly never thought there'd ever be a situation in which I'd willingly *want* a dick pic. But that shit right there, that convinced me."

"Exactly how I've always felt. I mean, it's not like we'd ever go, 'Hmmm, I wonder how I can get this random guy on Tinder to like me? Ooh, I know, I'll take a close up of my va-jay-jay. That'll turn him on!'"

Claire bobbed her head to one side. "I dunno, I think most guys would actually respond to that pret-ty well. Vaginas are more inherently and objectively sexy than penises are."

"True. But guys aren't hard to turn on. Show 'em some titties, and...*boing*, they've got a chubby."

Claire reached across the table to poke one of my

boobs. "Especially those puppies. Show a guy those, and he's yours, right, Boobs McGee?"

"Shut up. Future lower back problems is a real thing. And do you have any idea how many times I've been asked if they're real?"

Now Claire threw a sugar packet at me. "Oh, cry me a river. You know how many guys ask me if I've ever thought about getting implants? That's got to be just as insulting, if not more so. Like, no, jackass, not all of us are interested in having giant water balloons attached to our chests for you ogle. Some of us are content to helm the good ship Itty Bitty Titty. I own one bra, and I only wear it when I don't want my nip-pies showing. I don't have to wear a bra when I work-out, because I've got nothing to bounce around, and I've never had to deal with the horror of an underwire poking me in the tits."

"True, but you also don't know the sheer, unadul-terated pleasure of taking off your bra at the end of a long day, or how nice it is just sit watching TV with your hands under your boobs. Or how convenient it is to put something in your bra when you don't have pockets."

"Plus, you could have a face like a bag of moldy potatoes and the personality of Cruella De Vil and you could still get any guy on the planet to sleep with you at least once just based on the perfection of your boobs." She cupped her breasts over her shirt and jiggled them. "These pathetic little A-cups? Good luck finding a guy who's a hot, sexy alpha male who doesn't mind a complete lack of breasticles."

"You *have* them, they're just small."

"Even with the most bombshell push up bra Victoria's Secret has ever made, I still only look like a small B."

"So?"

"So…I've mostly come to terms with it, I guess. I'd never get surgery because overall I love myself and I love my body, but there are still times, even now, at twenty-six, that I sometimes wish I was more well-endowed."

"What about this guy?" I asked. "What's he think about them?"

She sighed, staring out the window. "He worships them like they're the most amazing things he's ever laid eyes or lips on. That's part of why I'm so enamored with him, because he doesn't give off a vibe like he's being disingenuous about it. It seems like he honestly feels that way. He says they may be small, but they're a perfect handful each, and perfectly shaped. I'm still not entirely sure I believe him, but it's nice to hear, and it's a good part of the reason he got so much sex out of me last night. I just can't resist well-crafted flattery, and goddamn, the guy is seriously silver-tongued."

"And you won't even tell me his name?"

She shook her head. "Nope."

"Not fair." I held up my phone. "*You* saw Zane's dick *and* watched him jerk off, but I don't even get your guy's *name*?"

She leaned forward. "I'll tell you all about him. I'll even let you meet him, I promise. Just...give me some time to keep this to myself, first, okay? It's new, and it's weird, and it's scary."

"You *really* like him, don't you?"

"I really do."

"And this is from spending one night with him?"

"Sometimes you don't need a lot of time with a person to know there's a connection." She lifted a black restaurant check folder. "Also, I totally paid the bill while you were going pee. Now let's get out of here. You should show me the overlook where you gave Zane the world's best blow job."

"Only if you promise to let me pay the next time," I said, trying to ignore the deeper elements of what she'd said.

"Nope." She stood up and sauntered out, forcing me to follow her. "By the way, did I mention that the company I work for is looking for an H-R manager? I already put in a word for you. You can move to Seattle and we'll be the Gruesome Twosome again."

"Really?"

She nodded, taking out her phone, pulling up an email thread, and showing it to me; it was a conversation between her and the HR department head, wherein Claire talked me up and the department head sounded interested. It seemed I had a job waiting for me as long as I didn't totally fuck up the interview. It would be a promotion of several degrees, meant more money, and a chance to be near Claire again.

I teared up. "Bitch, you made me cry."

"I ended up at a department head lunch one day recently, totally by accident, and got talking to Thomas, and I guess I mentioned you at some point, and then two days later he emailed me asking if you'd be interested in the position. They haven't really even started looking yet, so if I were you I'd send Thomas your résumé, like, today. You could have a job by the time your vacation is over." She glanced at me sideways as we wandered on foot in the general direction of the Rainbird Trail; I sort of remembered where we'd gone last night, and if not, Google Maps would show me. "There is one other little tidbit of information, which may or may not interest you."

"What's that?"

"It's only an hour and forty-five minutes by air from Seattle to Ketchikan, and my guy happens to be a pilot."

My heart skipped a beat or ten. "Um. That's neat, but just, you know, out of curiosity…why would that be a factor?"

Claire continued the nonchalant charade. "Oh, no reason. Except that you could then continue to see Zane, he of the epic penis and godlike cunnilingus skills. You could catch a ride up here with me on the weekends. We could double date, do that whole four people sharing a milkshake thing."

"That would make the practice relationship real, though."

She nodded. "There would be that. But face it, snickerdoodles, you're already fighting the urge to think in those terms. I know this because I'm going through the same thing. This way, we could go through it together. We could stop each other from intentionally sabotaging our own relationships."

"Why would we do that?" I asked. "And don't call me snickerdoodles, either."

"Because we're a pair of big old scaredy-cats who are terrified of real intimacy due to the fact that we both have serious daddy issues."

"Oh, that."

"Yeah, that."

She wasn't wrong. About any of it.

"Do you have any idea how annoying it is that you're right all the damn time?" I asked.

Claire nodded without a hint of irony. "I do. I annoy myself, sometimes. Being right all the time can be a serious burden." She quirked an eyebrow at me. "We've all got our burdens to bear, after all. You've got those giant tits you have to lug around everywhere, and I'm almost never wrong."

I snorted at her, but there was, of course, a kernel of truth to her words.

EIGHT

Zane

I WAS SCHEDULED TO OPEN THE BAR, SO I WAS DOWNSTAIRS by ten thirty setting things up, getting the kitchen opened and taking the stools off the bar and tables, cutting garnish fruit, stocking the alcohol, and counting the register drawers. The place was busy the second I opened the doors, since it was a weekend during tourist season. It was a blessing, though, because it meant I had zero time to let my head run away from me…either the big head or the little one. I was slammed from the time I opened the doors until Brock floated in at three-thirty, a stupid grin on his face as he stared down at his phone.

He tucked a bar towel in the back pocket of his jeans and joined me behind the bar, checking the coolers and shelves to see what he had to restock before he took over for me. He'd put his phone away, but he still had the stupid grin on his face.

"What's up your ass, sunshine?" I asked, setting a pair of beers on the service bar for Lucian to take to his table; Luce, it turned out, had offset his savings by waiting tables and tending bar during his travels, so he was an experienced and skilled addition to the bar.

Brock just winked at me. "Nothing. Nothing at all."

I grabbed a ticket as it printed from the service bar printer. "Bullshit. Only one things puts a grin like that on a man's face, and that's prime pussy."

Brock left and returned with two cases of beer held on one shoulder and three bottles of liquor clenched in his other hand. "Yeah, well…a gentleman never kisses and tells." He said this with a sly grin.

"That prime, huh?"

"Let's just say it's a good thing I'm tending bar instead of flying today, because I'm running on, like, maybe three hours of sleep."

I snorted. "Pussy. Try staying awake for seventy-two hours, boots on the ground in enemy territory, completing a mission, and then having to swim six miles in full gear to reach the E-Z."

"And *you* try performing death-defying aerial stunts in six cities in five days while flying yourself from venue to venue."

Lucian collected his drinks from me. "How about you two quit measuring dicks and get to work?" He took his drinks and moved back into the bar to deliver them without a backward glance.

Brock and I glanced at each other and chuckled.

"And Lucian schools us both," Brock said.

I started stacking pint glasses, rocks glasses, and shot glasses into the washer. "For real, though," I said. "You're floating around with a goofy-ass grin on your face. Must've been pretty damn good."

Brock shrugged while shaking up cosmopolitans for a gaggle of giggling blonde tourists. "Zane, brother, there are no words. I died and went to heaven...six times in one night."

I stared at my younger brother with renewed respect. "Well, damn, son. That's the way it's done, I'd say."

The group of thirty-something blondes he was mixing drinks for had overheard us and were whispering loudly to each other while staring between Brock and I.

Brock nudged me and leaned close. "I'm seeing her again next weekend."

"Really?"

"*Really*." He shot me a look. "And you know, you've been rocking a pretty dumbass grin yourself most of the day. Don't think I haven't noticed."

"I have not," I groused.

Lucian set four glasses on the bar and filled them with ice and Coke. "Have too." He dug his cell phone out of his pocket and pulled up a grainy, blurry photo of me he'd obviously taken on the sly and, yes, I was sporting a grin exactly as described: big and goofy. "Exhibit A." And then he was gone, having done his damage; typical Luce, dropping a bomb and sauntering off.

"The asshole took a *picture?*" I snapped, staring after my second-youngest brother.

Brock just snickered. "You mentioned something about a relationship between goofy grins and prime pussy?"

"Yeah, well...she's way more than just prime pussy, so show some respect, you little bastard." I grumbled.

"Hey, you don't have to explain that to me. Those were your words, not mine."

"Shut up," I growled, and pulled a handful of limes out of a refrigerator and set about slicing them...a little too vigorously, possibly.

"Awww, did poor widdle Zaney-wainey get his

feewings hurted?" Brock mocked from across the bar. "Methinks the lad doth protest too much."

I stopped slicing and turned to fix an evil-eye glare at Brock. "Hold your hand up against the wall," I told him.

"What? Why? What are you gonna do?"

"Just do it, asshole."

Brock held his hand against the wall at the end of the bar, fingers spread wide, back of his knuckles against the wood. I flipped the knife in the air and caught it by the back of the blade, hesitated in the name of dramatic pause, and then whipped the knife at my brother's hand. The blade flipped end over end and buried itself point-first in the wood between his middle and ring fingers, handle quivering.

"Remember that I can do that the next time you feel like mocking me, dickhead," I snarled.

Brock slid his hand away from the knife and yanked it out of the wall, staring at it like he'd never seen a knife thrown before. "You could have hit my hand, jackass."

I took it from him, washed it, and went back to slicing limes, ignoring the smattering of applause, stares, whistles, and whispers my little display had gotten. "Oh, please. I could do that from twice the distance in the dark with a hatchet."

"Bullshit."

I frowned at Brock. "What do you mean, bull-shit? My unit and three others held knife-throwing competitions every year, and I won every time. Got to the point that they'd only let me compete with a handicap, meaning kitchen knives and hand axes and shit instead of actual properly-weighted throwing knives like everyone else got."

Brock shrugged. "Huh. Never knew you could do that." He scooped the lime slices from the cutting board onto the tray.

"There's a lot of shit I can do that you don't know about."

"Like getting offended too easily?" He suggested, pouring a pint of beer for a customer.

"Like beat your scrawny, pretty-boy ass if you don't shut the hell up," I snarled.

Brock just laughed. "Case in point." He shook his head as he handed off the beer and made change for a $10. "You're crankier and tetchier than usual, even for you."

"Jesus, you dork, who even uses words like 'tetchy'?

"I do, Crankshaft."

"Crankshaft?" I asked, staring at him.

"You know, the comic strip about—"

"I fucking know what *Crankshaft* is, cock-waffle."

"Yeah, well, you're acting more curmudgeonly

than Crankshaft. Which is at serious odds with the id-iot grin you were floating around with all morning."

I glanced at the time on the register screen; 3:55 p.m. "I gotta go. Got shit to do."

"Classic avoidance technique, brother."

"I'm not avoiding anything, I just—I'm supposed to call Mara at four. And if you say a damn word, I'll castrate you in your sleep."

"The nurse from the wedding? You're...*calling* her...on the phone?"

"No, you dick-turd, I'm gonna stand on the roof and shout."

"Dick-turd?" He paused in the act of pulling a pour-spout from an empty bottle of Jameson and stuffing it into a fresh one.

"Yes. Dick-turd." I washed my hands and then collected the tips from the tip jar by the register. "Ass-muffin. Douche-canoe. Shit-goblin. Scab-eating shit-sucker. Walking moose knuckle. Sheep-fucker. I got more—should I keep going?"

"Please, no. You're offending my delicate sensi-bilities with your crude, barbarian epithets. I might faint." He delivered this dripping with monotone sar-casm. "Where do you even come up with this stuff, anyway?"

"Long flights to insertion with not much to do except find new and ever more creative ways of insulting each other," I said.

"Well I'll give you an A for creativity, that's for sure."

I laughed, counting the bills and sorting them. "Seriously, we'd do that for hours. Those are tame compared to some of the shit we'd come up with. Your ears would shrivel off your proper little head if you heard what we'd come up with after six or eight hours in the back of a C-130. The goal was always to be as vile and offensive as possible."

"Go. Call your woman. We got this."

"She's not my woman. We're just...practice dating."

Brock stared at me for a long moment. "There's so much to unpack from that statement I don't even know where to start."

"So don't start. Just let it go."

He shrugged, hands raised in surrender. "Okay, okay. But you realize I'm gonna psychoanalyze you later, right?"

I waved and stuffed the cash into my pocket. "Yeah, yeah, egghead. I'll see you later."

I jogged upstairs and changed into clean jeans, a plain black polo, my combat boots, and my leather jacket. I hesitated for a moment, and then stuffed a few condoms in my back pocket, just because it never hurts to be prepared, especially considering the intense physical chemistry between Mara and I.

Xavier was gone on his bike so I was left on foot, a situation I'd have to rectify posthaste if I was gonna live here another eight months, minimum. To be honest, I could see myself being here in Ketchikan for a little longer. I was enjoying being around my brothers, being back at home, living a little boring civilian life for once. I'd been in the Navy for ten years, the bulk of that as a SEAL and my life had been anything but normal, so this was new and kind of weird and I was enjoying it.

I slipped downstairs and outside, then started walking toward the dock where I knew Mara's friend Claire's cruise ship was docked. I dialed Mara.

She answered on the third ring. "Hey you."

"Hey. Have fun with Claire?" I heard noise and voices in the background, which definitely put her at the cruise ship docks.

"Yeah, it was a fun day. We hiked more of the Rainbird, took a Duck tour, had some lunch."

"Funny, I grew up here and I've never done one of the Duck tours."

"Yeah, well, I've lived in San Francisco for half my life and I've never been to Alcatraz or the Muir Woods. When you live somewhere, you don't tend to do the touristy stuff."

"True," I said. "So are you at the docks? Want to

meet somewhere?"

"Yeah, I am. I just dropped Claire off, actually. Do you have your brother's bike?"

"Nope, he's got it, so I'm on foot. I was just thinking I should buy a truck or something. This walking everywhere is bullshit."

"Aren't you a soldier? I thought you'd be used to marching."

I laughed. "I was in the Navy, not the Army. And as a SEAL, we don't do a lot of unnecessary walking. It's not an efficient way to infiltrate, for the most part."

"Infiltrate what?"

"Eh, whatever the mission target was. Way behind enemy lines, onto a boat in the middle of the ocean, behind compound walls. It varied."

"So how do you infiltrate, then?" She asked.

"Well, again, it depends on the mission. If we were hitting a drug lord's shipment way out in the middle of the ocean, we'd jump out of a helicopter and swim to it, or if the boat was big enough we'd even do a HALO insertion."

"What's a HALO insertion?" she asked, and then spoke before I could answer. "And where are you, anyway?"

"I'm close to you. Just stay where you are, I'll find you."

"Okay. So HALO insertion. Go."

I was close to the docks by then, so I started scanning the crowd, wishing I had Bast's extra four inches of height to see over the crowd. Finally I spotted her on the boardwalk near one of the gargantuan cruise ships. She was facing away from me, so I crept up behind her.

"Well," I started, "HALO stands for High Altitude Low Opening. It's just a really complicated way to skydive, basically. It means we jump at thirty thousand feet and dive to anywhere from four thousand to two thousand feet A-G-L."

"And A-G-L is what?"

"Above ground level." I was close now, I kept my voice down so she wouldn't hear me, though the crowd was thick enough there was little chance of that anyway. "So we'd free-fall for several minutes and reach something like a hundred miles per hour, easily."

"And why do these HALO jumps?"

"Because at thirty thousand AGL, the aircraft isn't visible from the ground with the naked eye, so the target won't be able to see us coming. In a regular fun jump, you go at fourteen thousand AGL, and you open pretty high up, so you have a lot of time floating down. That's fine when it's for fun, but when you're inserting for a military operation, you don't want the bad guys to see you coming, right? So you free-fall hard and fast and open at the last possible second, so there's as minimal a chance of being spotted as possible."

"Oh, I guess that makes sense." Her voice lowered. "And what other kind of...insertions did you do?"

"All kinds," I said. "My favorite insertion method was to just sneak in nice and slow..."

I cut the connection, stuffed the phone in my pocket, and closed the last few feet between us. Mara was still facing away, obviously cottoning on to the fact that I'd hung up or that the connection had been lost. She pulled the phone away from her ear and stared at the screen.

"Zane?" Her head pivoted, scanning the crowd around her.

I was within touching distance, now. I sprang, wrapping my arms around her and burying my nose in her neck, then whispered in her ear. "I was always really good at the slow kind of insertions."

"Oh, yeah?" She'd jumped when I first grabbed her, but had immediately relaxed when she realized it was me. "You'll have to show me that slow kind of insertion, then. It sounds...interesting."

I slid my hands across her belly and up beneath her breasts. "The trick is go really slowly, just sort of…*slide* in, you know?"

She tilted her head back to rest it on my shoulder, slipping a hand between us to trace the ridge of my zipper. "I think I might have an idea how it works. Pretty sure I'll need a demonstration, though. Just in case."

"Oh yeah?" I let my hand drift down to cup her core over her jeans.

"Not—not here, though," she murmured, catching my wrist. "I'm not quite ready for exhibitionism yet."

"No, me neither." I bit her earlobe. "So how about you show me your room?"

"Doesn't that usually happen *after* the date?"

"I think that's up to us," I said. "I'd like to think we can decide for ourselves how we want this to work."

"And you think sex first is a viable plan, huh?"

"And after." I tickled her ear with my tongue. "And maybe even during. You never know."

"During?"

I took her hand in mine and led her in the direction of her B&B. "Yeah, during. You wear something more…accessible, and I can do all sorts of interesting things to you."

"Is that so?" she breathed. "And…and what if I didn't bring anything more *accessible*?"

"You didn't?"

"I might have brought one skirt."

"I think you should change into that, then." I put my lips against her ear. "No underwear."

"I never go commando," she answered. "It's weird."

"That's fine," I said, an idea flitting through my head. "Wear underwear with the skirt. I can work with it"

She eyed me. "And what does *that* mean?"

I just grinned. "Oh, you'll see."

We didn't talk much the rest of the way to the B&B, since we were both kind of power-walking. I know for my part, all I could think of was the video she'd sent me, the glorious, erection-inducing visual of beautiful Mara with her thighs spread apart, that pink vibrator sliding into her pussy. I kept seeing that over and over, the way her tits had bounced while she came, and how badly I needed to be the one to make her tits bounce.

Just thinking about it had me going hard in my jeans, which was a problem because we'd reached the B&B and my cock was pointing down, which meant I needed to adjust myself...a difficulty when the living room of the B&B was crowded with guests. Mara said her hellos as she veritably hauled me through the room to the stairs. We reached her room, and she unlocked it in record time and shoved me through, slamming and locking the door behind herself.

"Naked," she murmured. "Get naked."

I peeled my jacket off, tossed it aside, and then yanked my shirt over my head. "Eager, huh, Mara?"

"All damn day I've been thinking about that video you sent me. I can't get it out of my head."

I bent to unlace my boots, kicked them and my socks off, and then shucked my jeans and underwear before reaching for Mara. "I've been having the same issue."

She toed off her shoes and socks while I started tugging down the skintight jeans she favored, leaving her in a red thong and her T-shirt. "You have?"

"Hell yeah. I might have had to relieve myself because of it this morning."

"And you didn't record it?"

"Should I have?"

"Hell yeah." She grasped my cock and stroked it slowly. "Always record it, and always send it to me."

"Ditto, in that case."

I decided to play with her a little bit, so I left her shirt and bra on but slid her thong down. I pushed her back against the door and traced her slit with my middle finger, then again, and penetrated her ever so slightly, teasing her pussy gradually until my finger was inside her and she was writhing against my finger.

A fist rapped tentatively against the door at that moment. "Miss Quinn?" The voice was elderly, thin and sweet.

She blinked, hips flexing as I slid my finger slowly in and out of her channel. "It's Mrs. Kingsley, the hostess," she whispered to me, and then twisted away from me and opened the door a crack. "Hi, Mrs. Kingsley. What's up?"

I palmed her ass as she leaned into the sliver of an opening, just her head and shoulders visible on the other side; Mara batted at my hand, but I ignored her, sliding my hands over her marvelous ass, then cupping her hips, then carving both hands around to palm her pussy. I teased her opening once, twice, a third time, and Mara's hips began flexing as I flitted the tip of my middle finger against her clit.

"Hello, dear. I just wanted to see if you were planning on joining us for dinner this evening. I'm doing a nice beef stew, and Mr. Kingsley has some fresh salmon he's smoking. It'd be nice to know if we can count you in or out so I know how many settings to put out."

"I...um—" Mara stuttered, hips fluttering as I circled her clit; she had a death grip on the side of the door, trying desperately to hold still and not give anything away, but I could tell by the way she was moving her hips that she was nearing the edge of climax. "I don't—I don't think so. Oh—god—goddammit!"

I heard a surprised gasp from the other side of the door. "Is everything all right, dear?"

"I just—I stubbed my toe against the door, is all. I'm fine." She was writhing in earnest now.

"Are you sure? You're acting awfully strange." Suspicion tinged Mrs. Kingsley's voice.

I had Mara on the cusp then. I delved two fingers inside her, gathered her wetness and withdrew my fingers to spread her juices over her clit, then sped the circling of my fingers. I saw Mara's knuckles go white on the edge of the door, watched her shoulders tense, and then she couldn't stop herself from moving with my touch, her hips pushing to grind into the rhythmic pulse of my fingers on her clit.

"I—um, T-M-I, maybe, but I was just about to go the bathroom. So I'm—*ohhhh*...I'm doing the potty dance. So, yeah. I have plans for dinner, but thank you very much, Mrs. Kingsley."

"Well, if you change your mind, just let me know." A pause. "And if you do decide to join us, let me know how many I should expect, all right? You could bring a...*guest*, if you wanted." There was laughter in her voice, as if she were wise to the game.

"Okay, thanks. Maybe I—*mmmm*...maybe I'll see you for dinner after all."

"All right, dear. I'll leave you be."

And then Mara was shutting the door and twisting the lock; the second I heard the lock slide home, I was on my knees in front of her, hands on her hips, turning her to face me. She ran her fingertips over my scalp as I buried my face between her thighs, lapping at her slit, my tongue eager. She gasped as I probed her opening, her hips flexing nonstop now. I slid two fingers inside her and flicked my tongue against her clit, and then she was clutching my head to keep my face buried against her pussy, writhing against me.

"Oh yeah, Zane, right there. Just like that. God, yes." She dipped at the knees, thighs spread apart, grinding down against my mouth. "I'm there, Zane—oh, fuck, yes...make me come."

I thrashed her clit with my tongue and slid my fingers in and out, going hard and fast with both, pushing her to the edge and then over it. I felt her come, felt her pussy clamp around my fingers and her thighs quiver, and she was gasping and writhing and grinding.

"Oh fuck, oh fuck, oh fuck," she moaned through gritted teeth, hips flying wildly.

I kept going, kept licking, kept fingering, and she kept writhing, and then I pulled my face away and stood up, sliding three fingers inside her and pressing the heel of my palm against her clit and fucked her hard and fast with my fingers, palm grinding, and she went crazy, groaning out loud, head pressed against the door, spine arched, hips pressed forward.

"Zane…*Zane*, I'm—oh, oh, *oh*…oh my god! I'm gonna—I'm—*ohmyfuckinggod!*" she wailed, curling forward.

Her forehead pressed against mine, her hands gripping into my shoulders like claws. I used my other hand to yank her bra cup down far enough that I could pinch her nipple, squeezing and twisting it to the rhythm of my touch between her legs, and then, as I felt her start to come, I clamped down hard and held on as I worked her pussy as fast as my hand would go.

Her face slid down to my shoulder and her teeth sank into the muscle along the side of my neck, a guttural groan escaping her as her hips gyrated.

"*Oh—oh—oh—oh…*"   she   chanted, "I'mcomingI'mcomingI'mcoming so hard it hurts, oh god it hurts, ohmyfuckinggod*ZANE!*"

She shattered, then, her whole body spasming, arching backward and then curling spastically forward, my palm grinding in a blur against her clit. She cried out wordlessly and a thin stream squirted out of her in a long arc just as I moved out of the way.

I scooped her into my arms as she collapsed, holding her against my chest. She was shaking all over, shuddering, eyes closed, little whimpers seeping past clenched teeth.

I laid her on the bed, gently stripping her of her shirt and then her bra. She cooperated sluggishly, moving her arms just enough to allow me to get her arms free of the bra straps. When she was fully naked, I took a moment to appreciate her body, her beauty, the flushed glow on her face, the messy tangle of her naturally blonde hair.

"You're beautiful all the time," I said, reclining beside her on the bed, my mouth inches from hers, "but right after you've come? You're absolutely breathtaking."

"You made me squirt," she mumbled.

I laughed and touched my lips to hers. "Yes, I did."

"I can't feel my legs."

"Does this make us even for that blow job?"

She opened her eyes finally, scintillating and brilliant and vividly green. "Based on intensity alone? Yes." She gazed up at me, her eyes soft, lazy, and satisfied. "You should shut up and kiss me."

I complied willingly, giving her my mouth. I was lost in the kiss. Consumed by it.

I could do nothing but kiss her, nothing but put myself into the kiss. My hands buried in her hair, clutched her closer, and she rolled into me, her hands scraping down my back to palm my ass, her hips pressing against mine. Heat seared through me at the ferocity of the kiss, need piling on need. I was a live wire, the detonation of a fragmentation grenade compressed into the touch of lips to lips, belly to belly, thighs to thighs, hands on skin and tongues tangling. I lost my breath and found it in her lungs, lost my ability to think or function or move, and found it in the writhing of her hips and the clutch of her hands all over my body. All of me was focused on her, on this woman, in this moment, mesmerized by her, drawn in by her. I couldn't breathe, but I didn't need to, because she was all the breath I needed, her mouth on mine.

"Zane…" she breathed.

"Mara." I pulled back, my eyes on hers. "What's happening?"

"I don't—I don't know," she whispered, and then pressed a kiss to my jaw, my chin, my cheekbone, kisses peppering across my face with delirious fervor, eliciting gasping groans from me at the wet, warm bliss of her lips, the affection in the kisses. "But I don't want to stop."

"Me neither."

We were on our sides facing each other, tangled together. My cock was aching, throbbing, pulsating with bursting need. I could feel every inch of Mara pressed against me, her breasts flattened against my chest, her arms around me, her hands scouring my arms, my hips, my thigh, my shoulders, palming over my scalp and teasing the shell of my ear and my nape and my back.

She pressed closer to me, snuggling so tight there was not a single atom's worth of space between us. A breath of a moment later, Mara draped her thigh over mine, her hand on my ass pulling at me.

"Zane." She buried her face in my neck, breathing hard. "I need you."

I inhaled the scent of her hair, my hand on her hip. "I need you too."

She flexed against me, then, and I couldn't stop the way my hips ground against hers, and I felt her slit sliding damp against my cock. "God...*Zane*—" There was a hint of a whimper in the way she said my name.

A pivot of my hips, and I felt her open for me, felt her slick warmth welcome me. I groaned into her hair as I pushed in, bare and trembling.

Mara moaned with me, clinging to me with all the strength in her body, shuddering against me as I sank into her until we were hips to hips, flush, her thighs wedged around my waist. I rolled to my back, taking her on top of me, and she drew her body downward, lips stuttering across my chest, her spine arching outward, her hips grinding backward, crushing me deeper and deeper and deeper. I gripped her hips, then forced my hands to release, hands shaking more than they ever did before combat. I traced the knobs of her spine with my fingers, walking my touch up her back until I reached her neck, and then slid my hands into the blond mass of her hair.

Her head lifted, then, and her eyes bored into mine like lasers, daring me to look away, daring me to break this moment, daring me to stop this. I couldn't, I didn't. What I did was bring her face down to mine and kiss her, renewing the breathless delirium of our earlier kiss, except the ferocity and need was redoubled now, because I was buried inside her to the hilt, her pussy clenching around my cock.

When my tongue slid into her mouth, she moaned, and began to move. A slow slide at first, is all it was, but then as one moment bled into the next, she growled into the kiss and moved faster. Her hands clutched my face and her tongue slashed mine and her hips rolled faster and faster.

Something niggled deep down, way in the back of my consciousness, but I couldn't grasp the thought. All I knew was Mara, her mouth on mine and her ass brushing against my thighs as she moved on top of me. I moved with her, palming the heavy, taut globes of her perfect ass, encouraging her motion, pulling her against me, gripping my fingers into the generous swell. I tasted the heat of her mouth and felt her pussy clenching in throbbing rhythm around me.

She controlled this moment. It was her movement, her body writhing on mine. All I could do was move with her, push into her thrusts.

A rasping moan bubbled past her lips and we moved together, thrusts becoming ever more wild, ever more forceful, Mara guiding our pace. Faster, faster…her moans nonstop, her pussy gliding around my cock in a tight, slippery slide. Her forehead pressed into my chest and she pushed, arching her back, hips tight against mine to keep my cock thrust deep inside her. She rolled her hips in wide circles, and her fingers stole between her thighs, and she touched her clit. I kept moving, keep thrusting even though I was pressed as far into her channel as I could go, feeling her hand between us, her knuckles moving as she fondled her clit.

Her moans went ragged, became whimpers, and then breathless shrieks, hips grinding harder, faster. "Zane—god, Zane. I'm—ohhhhhh…"

She couldn't even finish her statement, but I knew. God, I knew. I felt it, felt her body spasm, felt her pussy ripple and tighten around me. In the moment of climax, she yanked her hand away and gave in to riding me through the orgasm.

Her groans, her gasps, the clamping clench of her pussy around me, the hot silk of her flesh against me, under my hands, her body writhing above me, juddering…

It was my undoing.

"Mara, god…I'm—ohhhh god—I'm right there, I'm so close…"

Her eyes flew open as I felt the release building inside me. "Oh, no! Zane—don't! Not inside me!"

At the very last moment, I rolled her off of me and pulled out. Went to my knees above her, snarling and grunting as I felt the orgasm build and build to an imminent, explosive crescendo. Mara reached for me, both hands wrapping around my cock, fists plunging. I let go, then, hips pumping, cock sliding through her hands.

I came with a wordless shout, a geyser of come spurting out of me. Her fists plunged hard and fast, her attention rapt as the first stream shot out of me, splashing onto her pale skin. I growled through it, watching my come lay in a thick white stripe along her belly and up her ribcage. She shimmied down as I came again, and this time it pooled on her breasts, sliding down between the mounds of taut, firm flesh. She didn't relent, but kept stroking me through each successive wave until I was breathless, a viscous string dangling between the tip of my cock and her skin.

She lifted up, licked the string away, and took me into her mouth. She sucked the last of it out of me, fist still sliding, until I was too spent to stay upright any longer.

I fell to the side, gasping, Mara next to me. She was staring down at herself, index finger tracing through the puddles of my come.

As we lay in companionable, easy silence for several minutes, the reality of what we'd just done, what had almost happened, began to rifle through me.

"Mara, I—" I started, but had no idea what I'd been about to say.

She held up her finger, sticky with my come, stuck it into her mouth and pulled it out, and then her eyes met mine. "I'm sorry, Zane."

"You're sorry? For what? It was me, I should've—"

"No, I mean, I'm sorry that I told you to stop. That you didn't get to finish the way we should've finished. I wanted you to…to finish inside me. But—" she fondled my now-slackened cock. "I just—I'm not—I wasn't ready."

"I shouldn't have let that happen."

She inched closer to me, laid her head on my arm and gazed at me. "I don't regret it. I don't, I can't—being with you bare like that? Zane, that was…it was *so* amazing. I want it like that all the time. That's what's dangerous about it."

"We can't, though, can we? I mean, I'm clean, but—"

"I'm clean, too, and I'm on the shot, so we're protected."

"But still."

She nodded. "But still."

Her room in this B&B had a tiny but full en suite bathroom; she rolled away from me and danced gracefully across the to the bathroom, beautiful, naked, and enticing. She didn't bother closing the door; instead, she let me watch from the bed as she cleaned up. It was a strange, intense, and almost shocking intimacy, watching the way she soaked a washcloth in the sink, wrung it out, the way she wiped her skin clean with it, scrubbing her breasts and then her belly and then between her legs, then soaked and wrung out the washcloth again and wiped herself down once more. She dried herself with a bath towel, and then soaked the washcloth and wrung it out several more times before returning to the bed. She leaned over me, standing beside the bed. Gently, almost lovingly, she cleaned my cock, starting at the tip and then the head, then holding it with two fingers and angling it this way and that as she wiped me down with the warm, damp washcloth.

That was a first for me, and it was just as bizarrely, emotionally, and intensely intimate as it had been watching her wash herself. Why? I wasn't quite sure. It just was. Combined with the fierce vulnerability we'd shared as we moved together, the moment was fraught and delicate as porcelain.

My heart hammered, clenched. My breath caught. I couldn't look away—Mara was too beautiful, too mesmerizing. The way her hair cascaded in long sunlit waves over her shoulder, the flick and shift of her grass-green eyes, the high, full roundness of her breasts, the generous swell of her hips, the flawless ivory of her skin…

How could I ever give her up? The thought battered through my head with all the undeniable force of a Stinger missile.

I choked on the thought, froze under it, paralyzed by the ravaging intensity of it.

Holy hell, I wasn't ready for that.

This was supposed to be a week of fun with a gorgeous, charismatic, down-to-fuck girl, with a little extra non-sexual fun on the side.

Not…*this*. Whatever this was.

The problem was, Mara Quinn was quickly metamorphosing from a gorgeous, DTF girl into a breathtaking goddess, into the woman of any red-blooded man's dreams. My blood ran red, ran hot, and this woman was exactly that, the kind of woman I could see being at the center of all my dreams.

And that was scaring the piss out of me.

NINE

Mara

I SAW IT HIT HIM, LIKE IT HAD HIT ME. I'D BEEN CLEANING myself up—the bathroom was so small it was nearly impossible to close the door unless you got in the tub first, so I'd left the door open. I hadn't intended to let him watch, and it had been nerve-wracking in the extreme to stand there washing his come off my skin while he watched. It had taken everything I had to act casual about it, to not hyperventilate. But his gaze while I washed up…it had been so intense. Fierce. And the moments just before I'd stopped him from coming bare inside me, those moments as we moved together had been…searing enough to flay right out of me any notions of this being casual sex anymore.

And I saw it hit him, watched the intensity hit him, watched the moment when he realized that we were creating something between each other that I know neither of us were ready for, that neither of us had expected.

I finished cleaning him, tossed the washcloth into the tub, and re-joined him in the bed. I remembered Claire's insistence that I try post-coital snuggles…but given the intensity we'd just shared, snuggling with Zane seemed a little too much like tempting fate.

So instead of curling up against his side, my head on his chest—like I dearly, desperately wanted to, deep down—I propped myself on an elbow next to him and drank in his masculine, muscular, rugged beauty. He didn't reach for me, either, and I suspected he was going through a similar tangle of thoughts and emotions.

"So." He mirrored my pose, reaching out a hand to trace my figure from shoulder to hip to thigh and back up. "Dinner?"

"With Mrs. Kingsley and the others?"

He shrugged. "Sure. Sounds like fun."

"And then a movie?"

Another nod and shrug. "The theater here only has two screens as I remember, so the selection is limited. But that'd be fun." He let his hand rest on the swell of my hip. "It'll be proper date, then."

"A real date." I wrinkled my nose. "I haven't been on a *date*-date since high school."

He chuckled. "Me either, actually."

My hand had a mind of its own, apparently, because I watched it drift out to fondle his dick. Still slack, but under my touch it began to stir.

"Tell me about your last date," I said.

He let out a breath. "Her name was…uh—Ashley. MacNamara? I think that's it, Ashley MacNamara. My senior year of high school, and she was a freshman at U-A-S."

"An older woman, huh?" I teased, toying with him still.

He flicked a thumb against my nipple. "Nah, only by, like, six months."

"So what'd you guys do?"

"Walked the boardwalk, and then I took her to Bar Harbor, and then to a movie." He rolled my nipple between his thumb and finger, sending little thrills fluttering through me. "Um…*The Holiday*, I think we saw."

"You remember the movie?"

He grinned slyly. "Yeah, well…more because we didn't actually see much of the movie."

"Too busy making out, huh?"

He chuckled. "You could call it making out, I suppose."

I quirked an eyebrow at him. "In the movie theater?"

"Way up in the very back."

I had him at half-mast, by that point, hard enough to really begin stroking him. "You went all the way with her…in the theater?"

"Nah, not all the way. Second base, I guess you'd call it."

"And that was the last real date you went on?"

He nodded. "I graduated not long after, and shipped out for RTC."

"RTC?"

"The Navy's version of boot camp—Recruit Training Command, in Great Lakes, Illinois."

"And you and Ashley MacNamara? What happened there?"

"After that date, she informed me she'd prefer to meet at her apartment. I'd bring carryout after school and we'd watch a movie in her room, and…you know, Netflix and chill, only this was before Netflix. *Real World* and chill, it ended up being, most of the time."

"So that was a long term thing?" I asked, my fist moving slowly up and down his shaft.

He circled my areola with a fingertip, his gaze on my breasts rather than me. "Um, sort of." His voice went tight and clipped, verbal shorthand for *drop it*.

But I wasn't going to.

"Meaning what?"

He sighed and glanced at me. "You really want to hear this?"

"Of course."

"Now?"

I nodded, and he shifted closer to me, allowing me to reach him more easily, and him me.

"Well…" he said, sighing, and starting over. "That was my first and really only taste of heartbreak, if you really must know. I was into her. I'd dated a few girls up to that point, nothing serious, mainly just being a horny teenager, you know? Sleeping around, being a general douchebag. Ashley was cool, though. She was a college chick, which gave me points with the guys, but it wasn't about that. I was genuinely into her. Like I said, though, after that date she made it obvious she wasn't interested in dating me, just sleeping with me. Which was fine—like I was going to argue with not having to set up dates all the time? Should've been wiser, but I was a horny kid and she was hot. I mean it should've been obvious, looking back. I thought we had something, I thought she just liked being around me in private. But then one day I was out with Brock and Bax and couple other guys from school, just a bunch of dudes horsing around, whatever. And we saw Ashley with a bunch of other kids, guys, girls, a big crowd of people. And Ashley was hanging on this guy, this older guy. Like, she was nineteen and he had to have been twenty-four or five, I guess. Just hanging on him, kissing him, holding hands. Being the arrogant punk I was, I went up to her. And she was like, 'Oh, hey, Zane. This is my *boyfriend*.' She emphasized the word boyfriend and gave me this look that said don't say a fuckin' word. That was when I realized I was just a piece of ass for her. A side piece. So I quit going to her place, focused on finishing school, and then left for RTC."

He was fully and magnificently hard by then.

"That sucks," I said. "She sounds like she was a bitch."

He shrugged. "It was a learning lesson."

"What lesson did you learn?"

"That dating sucks, and don't trust anyone."

I turned my attention to my hand gliding along his length. "And now?"

He watched me touch him. "Now? I mean, nothing I've ever seen has convinced me otherwise." He hesitated. "Until Bast met Dru, at least. And now... you."

"And now me, what?"

"I mean, we're not really dating, but you...you're starting to make me think maybe if the right person comes along, dating could be all right, and that it might not be so bad to try and trust someone."

When he said *we're not really dating*, I felt a pang of pain. But he was right. By my own suggestion, this wasn't really dating. What we were doing had a built-in shelf life. I wasn't sure there was a term or a box for what we had—more than a one-night stand, but less than a relationship.

"The right person, huh?" I asked, hoping to disguise the sudden flux of disappointment I was feeling, which was stupid, because he was right and there was no reason I should feel disappointed, but I did, and I couldn't deny it, only ignore it and hope he didn't notice and that it went away.

"The right person," he echoed. "She'd have to be really special, though." His hand drifted down, down, found my legs parted just enough to allow him access.

"Special?"

"Yeah. They'd have to be particularly gorgeous."

"Obviously."

"And I mean, I have to admit I'm partial to blondes." His fingertip found my clit, and I wiggled, stifling a gasp.

"Go on," I said, twisting and squeezing my fist around the broad, springy head of his cock.

"And green eyes. There's something about that combination that just...gets me, you know?" He nudged me and I rolled to my back, spreading my thighs to let him touch me, keeping my stroking, twisting grip on his cock going slow and steady as he levered over me, murmuring down to me. "I mean, her hair has to be a very specific shade of honey and wheat and late afternoon sunlight, and her eyes have to be the green of really lush, healthy grass."

God, my heart. What was my heart doing? His words were like bullets hitting a bull's eye, each one thunking into my heart.

I lifted my unoccupied hand and twisted a lock of my hair, going along with his game, pretending to be unaffected by his touch or his words. "Huh. Would you look at this? *My* hair is kinda that color."

He nodded. "I've noticed. But there are a few other stipulations."

"Like what?" I asked, going breathless now as his touch skillfully brought heat and pressure and plea-sure building up inside me.

"She has to have the body of a goddess. Her tits have to be just the right size, you know, full and round, and just...perfect. That's very hard to find, naturally perfect breasts." He cupped a breast as he said this, then leaned down and flicked his tongue over my nip-ple. "Almost as hard to find as a perfect ass. Heart-shaped, and juicy but firm. The kind of ass that you just can't keep your hands off of."

I rolled toward him, grabbed his wrist, and guided his hand to my butt. "Like this one?"

"Exactly like this one." He paused to breathe and gather his thoughts, groaning low as I continued to stroke and fondle and caress him, and then continued, acting unaffected. "But she's got to have more than just a perfect body, though."

"Do tell."

"She's got to be strong; she's got to have a personality that can match mine. I can be hard to handle, hard to deal with. She'd have to understand what it means to know that I've seen combat." He had me writhing and gasping, and I knew he was feeling the urgency in my touch too, but neither of us was willing to break first. "She's got to be funny, and smart, and easy to be around."

"That's a tall order, Mr. Badd," I said, and then managed a saucy grin, giving his cock a squeeze. "You might be interested to note that I happen to find you rather pleasant to...*handle*."

"That *is* interesting," he mused. "There's one other thing, though, one last requirement." He punctuated this by slipping two fingers into me and unerringly finding my G-spot.

"What's that?" I was going to be the one to break the game, to give away the need.

"She has to be an *animal* in bed. She's got to

challenge me, not just passively go along with whatever I want." Those fingers of his...god, they were
magic.

Sliding in, hooking, finding my G-spot and making me crazy, then slipping out to tease my clit.

"Get a condom," I said, finally.

He rolled off the bed, lithe and quick despite his
muscular size. He dug in the back pocket of his jeans
and produced a string of three condoms, ripped one
free and tossed the rest onto his jeans. Tearing open
the foil, he rolled the condom down his length and
then crawled onto the bed.

He hovered over me, huge and hard and muscular, cock erect and bobbing between us, his eyes fierce.
"You wouldn't know anyone like that, would you?"

I lifted up and bit his lower lip, sucked it into
my mouth. "You know, I just might." I clung to his
shoulders and wrapped my heels around his back.
"Although, this person I know, she might have a few
requirements of her own."

"Oh?"

I reached between us and fit the head of his
cock between my nether lips, then hesitated. "Yeah.
He'd have to have a body so perfect it'd put Channing
Tatum to shame."

"Don't know who that is."

I laughed, despite the situation. "An actor. Big

muscles, lots of abs. Really sexy."

"Betcha I could bench press him," Zane boasted.

I laughed again. "That wouldn't surprise me." I moved slightly, taking an inch or so of Zane's length into me; I was starting to wonder when he would take charge, when he would get tired of letting me be in control. "He'd have to have a huge, and I do mean *huge* cock. But not just big, his cock has to be shaped just right, and would have to fit in my hands just right, and my mouth, and inside me. The fit is imperative."

Zane pressed his forehead to mine and sank into me. "Like this?"

I gasped. "Yes, god yes, just like this."

He stilled when he was rooted fully within me. "What else?"

"He'd have to be a badass. I've known some badasses in my life, and this guy, he'd have to be the most badass of them all." I found myself caressing the back of his head and gazing up at him as I spoke. "But also kind, and funny. A sharp sense of humor is really important."

"I was voted class clown in high school," he said.

I snickered. "You were not."

He shook his head. "No, I wasn't. But I did make the X-O crack up so bad during a briefing once that he had to leave the room."

"X-O?"

"Executive officer."

"Ah."

"Any other requirements?" Zane asked.

"Um…" I pretended to think as Zane began slowly thrusting into me. "Hmmm…there was one other thing, but I'm having a hard time remembering what it was."

He bent and claimed my mouth with his, lips scouring mine, tongue searching, demanding. It was a dominating kiss, one that reminded me who he was, what kind of man he was.

"That jog your memory at all?" he asked.

I was shaking all over from the kiss, and found it genuinely hard to think, to follow the conversation. "Oh, ummm…yeah. The last thing is kind of a two-parter. He has to be the most amazing kisser in the entire world—like he has to be able to kiss me literally stupid and breathless."

Zane obeyed the implied suggestion, doubling down on the hot, dominating kiss, moving into me in rhythm with his probing tongue, making it no longer just a kiss but an extension of the union of our bodies, a continuation of the physical chemistry, the connection, the searing intensity I know we both felt as he thrust into me.

This was more than just the merging of our bodies; I knew it, and he knew it…and the kiss proved it.

"The other part?" Zane prompted, after breaking the kiss.

"He has to just instinctively, innately know my body. He has to be able to make me come in thirty seconds flat. And there has to be...something about the way we have sex that's just..." I trailed off, finding it impossible to summon the right word.

"More than real?" Zane suggested.

"Yes, exactly," I said, moving with him, now. "More than real."

There was just us moving in synch, then, breathing matched, eyes locked, bodies slipping and sliding and sweating together. No hurry, no tricks, no weird positions or thinly veiled suggestions, just us, just our bodies and our hearts and whatever this thing was we shared.

He was moving slowly, still, though. Holding back, maybe.

"Zane?"

"Hmmm?"

"You're holding back."

"A little, yeah."

"There's no point to everything we just said if we're not both all in." I lifted up and kissed him, one hand on his waist, the other wrapped around the back of his head.

His movements faltered, stopped, and he stared

down at me for a moment, and then he grinned at me. "You asked for it."

A beat of silence, in which I was about to ask what he meant, but never got the chance. He pulled out of me and gripped me by the hips, flipping me to my belly.

Oh.

I moved to my hands and knees, ready and willing to take him like this. He slid his hands over my ass, and then shifted closer to me, upright on his knees behind me. I watched over my shoulder as he gripped his shaft and guided himself into me.

"Oh god," I murmured.

"Ready?"

"Give it to me, Zane."

He pushed into me, once, gently. "Like that?"

"More."

He moved faster, thrusting harder. "Like that?"

"Yeah," I breathed.

His hands gripped my hipbones and pulled me back into his thrusts, which were getting harder and harder with each successive slap of his hips against my ass.

"More, Zane."

"More?"

"More...everything."

He slowed, then, in seeming contradiction to

what I'd just said. Withdrawing slowly, he hesitated at the apex and then slammed into me, forcing a cry of surprised bliss from my lips as he filled me so suddenly. Like that, then, slowly pulling back and fucking in hard, again and again, until the slow pull-outs grew faster and the thrusts in harder, until he was grunting, yanking me back into his thrusts, fucking me so hard I felt my ass jiggling, felt my tits swaying back and forth, and all I could do was whine and whimper and groan through it and slam back into his beautiful, powerful, uninhibited thrusts.

"Don't stop, Zane," I begged. "Keep going. Come for me. Come inside me."

"Couldn't stop now even if I wanted to, honey," he murmured. "I'm close."

"Yeah?" I breathed. "How close?"

"Fuck, *fuck*, Mara—so close."

"Are you gonna come hard?"

"You have no fuckin' idea."

"Show me, Zane. Come for me," I groaned, slamming back into him.

He groaned long and low in his chest, then, his thrusts faltering as he buried himself deep. "Now, ohhhh god, Mara—*Mara*."

"Yeah, Zane. I like it when you say my name while you come."

"Mara."

"Say my whole name, Zane. Amarantha. Shout it while you come inside me."

"Even your name is the most beautiful thing," he growled. "Amarantha! Now, now, god, *now*, Amarantha!" Zane shouted, fucking me with raw abandon, driving into me with all the power he possessed.

I felt it then, felt him pour into the condom.

And I knew something, right then, as the force of his orgasm released one of my own—

As amazing as it was to feel him come like that, so hard, so powerfully...I needed to feel him come inside me. Bare. Raw. Nothing between us. I *needed* it, no matter what. And I knew the next time we did this, there wouldn't be anything between us.

"Goddamn, Amarantha," he gasped, when we were both spent.

He pulled out of me and collapsed to his back, and this time I didn't deny myself the comfort of nuzzling into the shelter of his arms.

Claire was right: post-coital snuggles were the best.

There was a knock at the door, then, the same light, tentative rap. "Miss Quinn?" Mrs. Kingsely called. "Dinner is in fifteen minutes, if you and, um... your guest...would like to join the others."

"We'll be right out, Mrs. Kingsley."

"Okay, dear."

There wasn't really a chance after that to get into the weird, roundabout conversation Zane and I had had, but it was running on repeat in my head the whole time we were having dinner with the other B&B guests.

Mrs. Kingsley was small, frail, and sweet, but her gaze was sharp and knowing as Zane and I—each of us having showered as quickly as only former military personnel can—emerged, dressed and trying to act like we hadn't just been banging each other's brains out. Mrs. Kingsley knew, though, judging by the twinkle in her eye as we took our places at the table.

She'd set out two places for us, between a young couple from Utah on their honeymoon and an upper-middle aged woman who claimed to be going through a mid-life crisis, which, according to her, involved traveling the world and imbibing copious amounts of red wine.

Mr. Kingsley was tall, slender, silver-haired, and quiet, pouring wine and bringing out bowls of salad. There were four other people at the table, two more couples; a man and woman in their mid-thirties who seemed content to eat in silence and listen to the chatter, and another young couple from Sydney, Australia, who seemed determined to monopolize the conversation in between bouts of hurling playful insults at each other and making sex eyes at each other.

As she and her husband served the entrees, Mrs. Kingsley shot a glance at me. "Miss Quinn, You're from San Francisco, I believe?"

I nodded as I took a bite of salad. "Yep. My friend was on a cruise that stopped here in Ketchikan and I was due to take some of my vacation days, so…" I shrugged, hoping it would stay there.

But, judging by the looks Zane and I were getting, it wouldn't happen like that. The walls were thin, and Zane and I hadn't exactly been…discreet.

Mrs. Kingsley glanced at Zane. "So how are you liking the cruise, then?"

I decided to just bite the bullet and make the conversation interesting. Before Zane could answer, I did. "Oh, no, my friend's boat already left. Just an hour or so ago, actually. She lives in Seattle."

Mrs. Kingsley reddened and busied herself removing empty salad bowls as the diners finished eating. "Oh, um, I see. So you and your boyfriend…"

I winked at Zane, who hid a grin behind a bite of stew. "Zane and I just met, actually. We've known each other—what? Like forty-eight hours?"

Zane shrugged. "Um, yeah, about that. Maybe a little more. The hours have sort of all…blurred together at this point, if you know what I mean."

Mrs. Kingsley coughed in scandalized shock. "Oh. Oh, I see." She glanced at Zane, still trying to salvage the conversation. "And you're from where?"

He took a sip of wine with a delicacy that I wouldn't have thought him capable of. "Oh, I'm from Ketchikan, actually. Born and raised." He left a dramatic pause. "I'm Zane Badd."

Mr. Kingsley's eyes narrowed and his jaw tightened. "I knew your father." He took the stack of bowls from his wife and headed for the kitchen.

Zane nodded. "I expect you did. Just about everyone knew Dad. He was a hard man to miss."

"I was sad to hear of his passing."

Zane nodded. "Yeah, so was I."

"Condolences," Mr. Kingsley said, and then vanished into the kitchen, his contribution to the conversation apparently over.

"I've heard all of you Badd boys have come back to Ketchikan," Mrs. Kingsley said, and then frowned at her own unintentional turn of phrase. "I mean, you and your brothers."

Zane chuckled. "We're the Badd brothers, Mrs. Kingsley. The name fits us, and none of us have ever pretended otherwise."

Mrs. Kingsley shifted uncomfortably from foot to foot, possibly regretting opening the conversation. "Yes, well...your elder brother, Sebastian, he did a remarkable job keeping your father's bar open."

"That he did," Zane said, finishing his food. "And now we're all back in good ol' Ketchikan, all eight of us. All grown up now, too. Last time all eight of us were under one roof, half of my younger brothers were just kids."

"All eight of you," Mrs. Kingsley said, as if the full force of what that meant was sinking in. "Oh my."

"Yeah, exactly." Zane laughed. "I'd advise keeping your granddaughters indoors, next time they come visiting. They were shaping up to be real heartbreakers if I remember correctly, and Canaan and Corin would be right about their age."

"That's about enough of that talk," Mr. Kingsley bit out from the kitchen doorway.

Zane just laughed again. "I was just kidding. Mostly." He stood up and extended a hand to me. "You ready, hot stuff? Movie starts in thirty."

I stood up. "Thank you for dinner, Mr. and Mrs. Kingsley. It was delicious."

"Our pleasure, dear. Have fun." She turned to listen to whatever it was the Aussie couple was bickering about.

We were outside in the golden evening light,

then, the air cool but not cold, warm but not hot. Zane took my hand and we walked unhurriedly toward downtown.

I glanced up at him. "What was all that about? With the Kingsleys?"

"I was messing with them, that's all."

I frowned at him. "What's that mean?"

He shrugged. "Well, our mom died going on eleven years ago. It was sudden, some kind of cancer that struck hard and fast, nothing anyone could do. Which left dad to raise eight boys by himself while running a bar. He'd been a hell-raiser himself, back in the day, until Mom got ahold of him and tamed him a bit, but we've all got a lot of Dad in us, which means they'd have had their hands full even if Mom had lived. But raising us alone? Dad didn't stand a chance, and he was a mess over Mom's death anyway." He paused, and then continued. "We ran wild. No mom, Dad was busy and emotionally unavailable or whatever...so we all fought, drank, and fucked our way through this town. The name Badd is synonymous in with trouble in this town. We're the Badd brothers. We always stuck together, looked out for each other. So, yeah, I knew the Kingsley's would know my name."

"And the thing about their granddaughters?"

Zane laughed. "Oh, that. Well, Rachel Kingsley,

their daughter, she always had…pretensions of grandeur, I guess. Thought she was better than all of us in this stupid little town, that was the air she always put on. Married this hoity-toity investment banker over in New York City. They come visit every now and again, with their twin daughters, Aerie and Tate. Same age as Cane and Cor. And like I said, they're heartbreakers, Aerie and Tate are." He pronounced the first name *AIR-ee*. "Those girls are seriously stunning, and seem to have escaped inheriting their parents' sticks-up-the-ass. The last thing Rachel Kingsley would ever allow, though, is for her daughters to be caught so much as *looking* at any member of the Badd family."

"I see. And you think this is funny?"

He nodded. "Yep. I sure as hell do. We earned our reputation, and we're proud of it. But we're not bad people. We'll help you, if you need help. We didn't go around boinking underage girls or married women—although there was that one time Bax got caught with a guy's wife, but she hadn't told him she was married, so that was on her, not him. Point is, we were rough boys and didn't follow anyone's rules but our own—we're still like that, come to think of it—but we weren't cruel or mean. We weren't bullies. And Bax, he never told anyone, but he volunteered sixth period through all of senior year in the special education room. He was really close with all those kids, good friends to them. Anyone picked on the special ed kids, Bax would pound 'em. But still, a lot of the locals look down on us. Or at best, aren't quite sure what to make of us. They were all thankful when Xavier left, because that meant all the Badd brothers except Bast had left Ketchikan....meaning their daughters were safe, as long as they stayed away from Badd's Bar and Grill. And now? Here we are, all eight of us."

"And the virtue of all the single women is at risk, huh?" I teased.

He shrugged, conceding the point. "Pretty much. Although Bast is married now, so that takes one of the biggest threats to Ketchikan's female virtue out of the equation."

"And you're mine," I heard myself say, and then stumbled to cover the gaffe. "For this week, at least."

He didn't miss anything. "Amarantha." He halted as he said my name, pivoting to face me, hands on my arms.

I stared up at him. "Yeah?"

"We both know something happened back there, so there's no point denying it."

"Okay?"

"So, yeah, I'm yours." He paused, as I had. "For this week, at least."

"And after this week?" I couldn't help asking.

He let silence build between us, not letting go of my arms. "Are we really gonna have this conversation right here, right now?"

I shook my head, realizing how right he was. "No." I pulled out of his grip and re-threaded my fingers through his. "No, we're not."

We walked another half mile or so, reaching downtown and the movie theater. There were only two movies playing, as Zane had said there would be—an action movie, and a rom-com; Zane told me to pick, so I went with the rom-com. He paid for the tickets and led us into the movie theater...all the way up in the very back against the rear wall, in the corner farthest from the door.

As we waited for the movie to start, he glanced at me. "You know, I've told you a bit about myself, and I'm realizing I don't know dick about you." He rubbed a thumb over my knuckles. "You don't have to get into anything gnarly or super deep, but...I'd like to know a little about what makes Amarantha Quinn tick."

I sighed, long and slow. "Okay. Well, what do you want to know?"

He shook his head. "Nope, that's not how this works. You tell me what you want to share, and if I have questions, I'll ask, but you're not obligated to answer if you don't want to."

I tapped a finger against the armrest. "I'm an only child, so there's that. Which means I truly do not understand your family." I hesitated, because that was about as much as I usually shared. "I grew up in a little podunk town in Indiana. My mother is a dental hygienist. I played varsity volleyball in high school. I had a horse, a Rocky Mountain mare named Ethel."

"The horse's name was Ethel?"

I laughed. "Yeah. We bought her from a breeder, and he named her that, not sure why though."

There was silence then, with Zane eyeing me expectantly. When I didn't burst forth with any more intel, he frowned at me. "That's it?"

I shrugged. "What else is there?"

He tugged on a lock of my hair. "Quite a bit. You didn't mention your dad, for one thing."

"That's a touchy subject."

Zane sighed. "Look, I'm really not trying to push. But I just feel like like maybe you don't really trust me. Which I get, I guess. But I thought this was supposed to be us practicing opening up to each other. But so far, I'm the only one doing any trusting. I told you about Marco. Not even my brothers know Campy had a kid."

I groaned. "It's not about trust, Zane. It's just...I don't talk about Dad. You want to know about my boyfriends in high school? I'll tell you. I dated Brad

Riley my freshman year. He was my first boyfriend, my first kiss, and the guy I went to second base with for the first time. He broke up with me after three months to date the captain of the cheerleader squad—who also happened to be the school slut. I guess I wasn't moving fast enough for Brad? I don't know. He just gave me a generic break up excuse and was tongue-fucking Cherry the cheerleader in the hallways the next day." I lowered my voice as the lights dimmed and the previews started, although we were the only ones in the theater, so far. "I dated Dane Howell in tenth grade, to whom I gave my virginity on prom night, in the back of his shitty Ford Taurus. We dated most of tenth grade. Eleventh grade was Tom Wyland, Jeremy Ring, and Morris Morrison."

"Morris Morrison?"

I snickered. "Yeah. He went by Morrie. Hated his name, hated his parents, and drove a brand new Mustang he'd bought himself dealing pot at the elementary school playground after school." A teen-aged couple entered the theater and sat a few rows down from us, giggling together. "Senior year was Joey Fustinelli, but I only dated him a few weeks as a 'fuck you' to my mom. He was a major douche-bag, and I never even slept with him. Kyle Pruitt, who was nice, but a little slow. Greg Michaels, a Harvard-bound soccer star, and a stuck up prick who I only dated because he had a BMW and a credit card and used me as a fuck you to his parents, which worked out for me because I got cool points in school and a couple really nice Coach purses. And last, but not least, Isaac Horowitz. Sweet, poor as dirt and nearly illiterate, but good-looking in an unassuming way, and would legitimately give you the shirt off his back if you asked for it. He was the epitome of wrong side of the tracks. His mom was black, and his dad was a non-practicing Orthodox Jew. Isaac was...amazing, actually. Really, really amazing. Probably the most genuinely kind person I've ever met."

Zane was quiet for a minute, and then he twisted that same lock of hair around his index finger. "Can I ask what happened?"

I had to breathe slowly for a moment or two before answering. "He was bullied his whole life. All through elementary school, junior high, high school. Beat up, made fun of, treated like shit. He never let it get to him, just kept on being himself despite it. We were assigned to be partners for an AP physics project. He was nearly illiterate because he was dyslexic, but he was a wizard with numbers and things, and physics wasn't really my thing, but I was smart enough to make the AP class. I joined late, and Isaac had been left without a partner because nobody wanted to work with him. So I was stuck with him. That's

how I saw it at first, too. Like everyone else, I just
sort of either pitied or looked down on him, because
I didn't understand him. Then we were partners on
the project, and I got to know him. Discovered what
kind of person he really was, you know? Saw past the
crappy, dirty, third-hand clothes and the way he stuttered through English class, and how painfully shy
and withdrawn he was."

"Not liking where this is going."

I shook my head. "Whatever you might be thinking, it's worse." I swallowed hard. "I stuck up for
him. Became his friend, and then eventually we were
spending all our time together. I lost all social standing at school, but Isaac had made me realize how
stupid all that was. I...I don't know. We never talked about being in love or anything, but Isaac was...
special. Super, super important to me. The bullying
got worse. They started targeting me. This is rural
Indiana, remember. Lots of the kids were...um, let's
just say they were closed minded. Learned it from
their parents. Not that everyone was like that; I'm
not saying that. There were some really nice, sweet
people. But there were others who were just...cruel.
They spray-painted swastikas on his locker and then
went to his house and burned crosses in his yard. Evil
shit like that. I'm not talking just pushing him around
and punching him a few times, this was hard core

antagonization." I had to swallow again. "Um. Like I said, when Isaac and I went open with our relationship, it got...ugly. Really, really ugly. The whole town got sort of...dragged into it. His dad got beat up so bad he was hospitalized and lost his job at the factory, his mom was fired by her racist boss, and they started egging my house, slashing my tires, all sorts of nasty stuff."

"Jesus."

I nodded, blinking hard. "One day, um, I was driving Isaac home. He lived a long way outside town, so you had to drive through a whole bunch of nothing, just endless cornfields. No traffic, no neighbors, no gas stations, just the highway and the corn. Well, I got rear-ended. Lost control, ended up in the corn. Hit my head and passed out. When I came to, Isaac... uh—shit. Isaac had been—they'd dragged him out of my car and beat him...beat him so badly he..."

I couldn't keep going, and Zane sat holding my hand, waiting.

I cleared my throat. "A semi saw the headlights in the field and stopped. Radioed for help. But by the time the cops came, Isaac was gone."

"Jesus fuck. What happened to the kids who did it?"

I laughed bitterly. "Not a damn thing. I never saw them...nobody saw anything. I mean, never mind the paint on the back of my car where they'd hit me, or the fact that everyone knew exactly who it was that hated Isaac so much. But yeah, there wasn't even a real investigation. A sort of cursory, 'Oh no, this kid nobody liked died, how sad, guess it was an accident. Someone from out of town, probably.' And that was it. His parents moved, and I wanted to quit school. Mom wouldn't let me, and so—I finished, got my diploma, and joined the Army."

"Goddamn, Mara."

I shrugged. "Yeah. It was...it was bad. What really gets me is that the bullying only got that much worse when we started dating. I know—I know it's not directly my fault, but I'm still partially responsible. I mean, *they* did it, they killed him. But they hated him even worse for daring to date me...I'd been pretty popular, you know? In the inner circle of the cool kids. So when I started dating Isaac, they looked at it as Isaac stealing me from them, tainting me, somehow."

The movie was starting, but neither of us was paying attention, and neither was the teenage couple, so our conversation wasn't disturbing anyone.

I hesitated, and then let out another sigh. "So, that's Isaac. What else is relevant and important? Um...I was date raped while I was in the Army. He drugged me and I woke up naked and sore in an alleyway. That was fun. Of course, in that case the guy that did it failed to realize how close we were in the medical unit. My entire unit found the guy, and… uh, curb-stomped him, I guess you could call it. Shitty part of that was it wasn't the first date I'd gone on with that guy either. I'd been seeing him sort of casually for like a month. We'd even slept together once. And then he put GHB in my drink and raped me. Sort of soured me on guys, you might say. Sort of hard to trust anyone, you know? After Isaac, and then Chad, yeah…dating seemed stupid and dangerous and pointless, so I stopped doing it."

Zane was quiet for a while, staring at the screen but obviously not watching. "I don't know what to say."

I took his hand. "You wanted to know, and I told you. That's all part of what makes me tick." I squeezed his hand. "Nothing you need to say. You're listening, and that's what's important."

"I'm sorry you went through all that, Mara."

"Me too. I mean, I can't change it, and it made me stronger, but it's why I'm having a hard time getting myself to open up to you." I sat in silence half-watching the movie for a few minutes, sitting beside Zane, and yet there was only one thing on my mind. Or… one person. "You want to hear about my dad?"

Zane twisted in his seat to look at me. "Of course,

but only if you want to talk about him."

I lifted a shoulder. "I mean, I've told you about Isaac, and I told you about Chad, so I might as well tell you about Dad." I nodded my head at the red-lit exit sign. "Want to get out of here? I'm not really feeling the movie."

Zane stood up and led me out of the theater without hesitation. We found a nearby bar, slid into a corner booth, and ordered some drinks. When we were settled in, Zane sitting beside me, I began peeling the label off my light beer.

"Uh oh," Zane said. "You're peeling the label. That's not good."

I shook my head. "Nothing like what happened with Isaac or Chad. It's just...complicated." I spent a moment or two thinking. "My dad was a normal guy, a normal dad. He worked a nine-to-five job selling insurance, went to all my piano recitals and theater productions, played with me in the backyard. Drank Budweiser sitting on the front porch after work, watched wrestling and NASCAR, kissed my mother when he left in the morning. He was just...Dad. But then, when I was twelve, he bought a Harley, sold his insurance agency, and left."

"Midlife crisis?"

I shook my head. "No, not really. He was only thirty-five. It wasn't a crisis, and it wasn't as random as it may have seemed. Then, to me, at twelve, it was the most unexpected and shocking thing in the world. I just came home from school one day and Dad's F-150 was gone and there was a motorcycle in the driveway. He had a backpack packed, and he was wearing leather chaps and a leather jacket. Mom was screaming at him, and he was just taking it. Which wasn't Dad, you know? They bickered as much as any married couple, but nothing crazy. Mom never screamed, and Dad never yelled, but he also wasn't passive. I didn't understand. He gave me a kiss on the cheek, told me he'd send me letters, and that he'd see me soon, and then he got on his bike and rode away."

"Just like that?"

I nodded. "Just like that."

"How is that not random?"

"Well, do that math. He was thirty-five when I was twelve: he was twenty-two when Mom had me. Mom was born in town, but not Dad. He was a drifter, I guess. Blew into town one day on a motorcycle, met Mom at a diner...and then ended up falling in love and staying. Mom had me, and he sold his bike, got a job selling insurance, and ended up owning the agency. Mom thought he was content, he had her, he had me, and he had a good job that paid well. We weren't the richest people in town, but we were pretty well off. Then, out of the blue, he decided he'd had enough domesticity, and left."

"You ever hear from him again?" Zane asked.

I nodded. "Yep. But not for a solid year. He didn't send a letter, didn't send a birthday card, nothing. He sent Mom cash in an unmarked envelope every month, but that was it. She wrote him off, and so did I. Then, about a month after my fourteenth birthday, right at the beginning of summer break, I was reading a book on the front porch and I heard motorcycles. I knew it was him. He rolled up on his Harley, wearing a vest with a bunch of patches on it, new tattoos on his arms, a big beard—he was different, but it was Dad. And there were about twenty other bikers with him, all in the same club. I didn't understand it then, of course, I just knew that there was a whole shit load of big scary tough looking guys on motorcycles, with a bunch of hard-looking women behind them, or on their own bikes."

"He took you?"

I bobbed my head side to side. "Yes, and no. He didn't kidnap me. He came up and asked if I wanted to spend the summer with him. I was a fourteen-year-old girl and I was still mad at him for leaving, but I also just missed my Dad. And I was curious. Like, what was it that was so much better out there than here at home with me and Mom? So I was like, sure. He told me to pack everything I could fit into a backpack and leave a note for Mom."

Zane made a face. "You didn't."

I nodded. "I did. Stuffed a bunch of jeans, under-wear, socks, and T-shirts into my backpack, threw on a hoodie, and left. I wrote Mom a note, that I was spending the summer with Dad and that I loved her, all that kind of thing."

"I bet that went over well."

I laughed. "Oh yeah. We made it maybe ten miles outside of town before about six state troopers showed up with lights and sirens going. The whole gang pulled over and the troopers went in guns drawn like I'd been snatched. Not an outlandish assumption to make, especially since that's what Mom had told them."

"What happened? Cops versus bikers never goes well, from what I understand."

"Dad had me talk to them. I told them I was with Dad voluntarily, so there wasn't anything any-one could say. Mom and Dad had never divorced, so it wasn't like he was violating a court visitation order."

"So you spent a summer with your Dad's biker gang."

"Yep. It was amazing, honestly. Total freedom. Ride all day, hang out with the guys at night. Dad let me drink, kept an eye on me, and kept the younger guys from sniffing around after me. If it was a nice night, they'd just stop wherever they wanted, pitch some tents, light a fire, and camp on the side of the highway. Or there'd be a motel, somewhere not too ratty but not flashy."

"That doesn't sound so bad."

I shook my head. "It was incredible. He brought me back a week before school started. Just dropped me off, gave me a kiss, and rode away without looking back. And then I didn't hear from him again until the first week of summer the next year. And guess what?"

"You spent your summers on the back of your Dad's Harley?"

I let out a breath and nodded. "I sure did. Every year until I joined the Army."

"How'd your mom take it?"

I shot him a wry grin. "Not well at all. That first time, I was grounded the whole first month of school, and she refused to talk to me. I mean not a damn word. Stopped getting me up for school, stopped making my breakfast, stopped doing my laundry, stopped packing my lunches, stopped driving me to school, stopped giving me allowances."

"Damn, that's harsh," Zane said, chuckling.

"When you're fourteen, yeah, it's harsh," I shot back.

He raised his hands. "Hey now, I was being

serious. He's your dad, and she was making you choose, essentially. I mean, yeah, he probably should have, like, called you or sent postcards now again, but he showed up. He was involved, just…his way. She shouldn't have guilted you into choosing her over him."

I felt oddly relieved that he understood. "Exactly. My mom is a world champion at holding grudges, I've learned. She doesn't let go of things. You know how guys will joke about their girlfriends, like 'she has flowcharts and graphs and flashcards for every single thing I've ever done or said'? That's Mom. She never forgave Dad, and she never got over him, either. Never divorced him, never dated, never took him to court. I mean, why would she? He was gone nine months of the year and he sent her an envelope full of cash once a month, every month, without fail—and looking back, I think he had to have sent her a couple grand every month, easily. And then, for the three months of summer, she got to be completely alone, do whatever she wanted, no kid, no one to look after or clean up after. She got to spend an entire summer single, basically. I said she never dated, but I suspect she spent those summers I was gone dating while I wasn't around to see. And me, well, she never forgave me, either. She saw it, like you said, as a betrayal. According to her, I should have refused to ever talk to him again, because he'd abandoned us both.

"And yeah, I was always a little angry with him for leaving like he did. I still am, in a way. But he showed up, and he invested in me. The summer trips were a birthday present, too. He'd let me do what ever I wanted, within reason. I learned how to drink around Dad, learned how to throw a mean right hook, how to ride a motorcycle, how to change a tire, how to change oil. I saw the country on the back of a Harley, in the company of my dad and a bunch of other amazing people." I paused to take a drink of my beer, which had started to go warm. "Mom never forgave me. We established a status quo, but I was taking care of myself from then on. She did the grocery shopping and paid the bills, but I was responsible for myself. I got a job when I was fifteen and bought a car with my own money when I turned seventeen."

"How are things now?"

I looked down and picked at the label of my bottle. "Well, Mom still lives in Elvira, Indiana, still works for the same dentist she has since I was in high school, still lives in the same house. I don't see her that much. I refuse to set foot in that town, not after what happened to Isaac, not after the way even the so-called 'good people' turned a blind eye to what Jimmy Price, Kevin Lyle, Patrick McKnight, and Reggie Kowalski did. Those are all the sons of city councilmembers, F-Y-I. They're the ones who killed Isaac and no one says anything. It's just this dirty little town secret, except it's not, like, someone's a secret drug addict or someone got someone else's wife pregnant. It was premeditated murder of an innocent kid. So yeah, I don't go back. I buy Mom a plane ticket every December and she spends a month with me in San Francisco."

"What about your dad?" Zane asked.

I sighed. "Two years ago, he was convicted of grand larceny, money laundering, possession of and intent to distribute schedule one narcotics, and possession of a firearm without a license."

"Oh." Zane blinked, processing. "So…he's behind bars for a while."

I laughed bitterly. "A while, yeah."

"So when you were on those trips with him…?"

Another bitter laugh. "Those were his vacations, too. The rest of the year he and his gang were… well, your average gangsters. Drugs, guns, hookers, the whole nine yards, and my dad was one of the ring-leaders. He kept it from me all through high school and while I was in the Army, and then one day, bam, I got a collect call from him. He was behind bars and wouldn't be getting out for something like twenty years, minimum. Turns out he'd been lying to me the whole time. I mean, I always kind of wondered where he got the money to send Mom, and how he could afford to just scamper off with me for three months and spend money on me like it was no big deal. The last week or so of our summer trips, we'd swing by Indianapolis before he took me home, and we'd go shopping. He'd buy me whatever I wanted and then we'd ship it all to Mom's house. He'd drop several grand at a time without blinking. Should've been a hint, but I was just..."

"A girl being spoiled by her dad."

I nodded. "Exactly. It was easier to not think about it, not ask any questions."

"I notice none of the charges he was slapped with are violent offenses."

I shrugged. "Yeah. I think he had others do that kind of dirty work when it needed doing."

"Do you ever visit him?"

"Nope. I will, eventually, but I haven't forgiven him yet. It's another betrayal, yet another way he abandoned me."

"Understandable." We both finished our drinks at the same time, and Zane pointed at mine. "Another?"

I shrugged. "Nah. You want to just...walk around?"

"Sounds good."

And that's what we did. Hand in hand, just strolling the boardwalk next to the cruise ships and fishing boats and sailboats, telling stories about our child-hoods. Zane did a lot of the talking, which was fine by me; he had an endless stream of hysterical stories about his brothers.

And then things turned to our experiences in the military, and I told him a few of the antics my unit had gotten up, pranking each other mercilessly, and he talked more about his friend. Specifically Marco, the one who'd been killed. I had a feeling he found it cathartic to talk about Campy with me, since I would understand the strangely intense bonds you form with people in your unit, especially if you've seen combat, which I had, since I'd been a "Sixty-Eight Whiskey", a 68W—a line medic, meaning I went with the Joes on hazardous missions to provide trauma care.

We eventually ended up on a bench near the docks, looking out over the water as the sun set behind the mountains, and we were there when the moon rose, still talking.

I don't think I've ever spoken to one person for that long in my life. Even Isaac, we'd only get to see each other for a few hours at a time, and honestly, we didn't exactly spend a lot of time just talking—we were teenagers, after all. But this? With Zane? I just couldn't fathom ending the conversation. The thought never even entered my head. We sat, and we talked, and so many hours passed I lost track. And then, when the sky started to go hazy gray with on-coming dawn, he led us to a place called Pioneer Café that was open twenty-four hours on the weekends, and we ordered an early breakfast and talked until the sun was high.

Eventually, I was yawning and my eyes were burning, and even Zane, conditioned to long hours of being awake, seemed to be dragging.

"I need to sleep," I said, pushing away my now-empty plate.

Zane wiped yolk off his plate with the last of his toast and stuffed it in his mouth, eyeing me. "I have a suggestion," he said between chews. "Feel free to call me crazy."

"All right," I said, sounding as wary as I felt.

"Come back to my place with me."

I made a face at him. "Why would that be crazy?"

He quirked an eyebrow at me. "That wasn't the crazy part."

"So what is?"

"We go back to my place, we get in my bed…" He trailed off dramatically.

"Yeah…" I prompted. "And?"

He leaned forward, whispering conspiratorially. "And we just sleep."

I sank back against the booth, blinking at him. "That *is* crazy." I ripped up the remnants of my napkin. "Just sleep?"

He nodded. "Just sleep." His fingertip traced the bumps of my knuckles. "I don't work until four to-morrow, so we can sleep in. I'll make you breakfast—well, actually, Xavier will make you breakfast and I'll take credit."

I nudged my plate. "Isn't this breakfast?"

"Nope. Breakfast is whatever meal you eat after you wake up, regardless of what time it is."

"Oh."

He tossed a pair of twenties on the table and tilted his head at me. "So, Amarantha. What do you say?"

"I say…I like the way you say my full name, and I also say…let's go non-euphemistically sleep together."

TEN

Zane

WE WALKED BACK TO THE BAR, STILL TALKING, THIS time about our favorite movies and actors.

I've never been much of a talker, never was one to stay up with the guys chewing the fat all night. Brock, Xavier, Bax, Cane and Cor, they can all talk till the cows come home. They'll talk your damn ear off if you let 'em, especially Bax. But me? I like to listen, like to sit back and watch. I'll talk when I've got something to say, but once I'm done, I just don't have any more words. But with Mara, there just always seemed to be something else to talk about. I think I told her more about myself and my life and my time as SEAL than I have anyone…maybe even everyone I've ever known put together. I told her shit I never even talked to Campy about, and that man was my best friend in the world. She just…brought it out of me.

The bar was dark when we got back, all the stools up on the tables. I led her upstairs to the apartment and, unsurprisingly, Xavier was at the kitchen table, some kind of thick textbook on the table, a laptop next to it, with a bunch of electronics bits and pieces and doodads and gizmos and gadgets spread out around him. He was reading the textbook at lightning speed, flipping pages every few seconds, and every once in a while he'd do something with the wires and motors and computer chips, tap at the laptop, fiddle a bit more, and then go back to reading.

Mara stopped at the table, watching. "What are you doing, Xavier?"

He blinked at her for a moment, as if registering that she was there and that he was expected to respond. He kind of goes into a trance when he's working like that, so he was a little slow on the uptake.

"Oh, hello Mara," he said, finally. "I'm, um, studying."

"Studying what?"

He flipped the textbook closed to show the cover. "Advanced Computational Mathematics."

She gestured at the laptop and robotics. "And all this?"

Xavier just blinked at her. When he was in his head like this, it always took him a while to re-gear into a socializing mindset. "Um, it's basic robotics, I just..." he glanced at me uncomfortably.

I laughed. "Boy genius here has focus problems."

"But...he's doing two super advanced things at once," Mara pointed out.

"Yeah, well, Xavier's focus problem is the opposite of everyone else's. He reads so fast and his brain comprehends so quickly that it's like...listening to the radio while driving for the rest of us. He has trouble sitting still and paying attention if he's not mentally occupied. So he has to do something to entertain all of his brain." I picked up a finished robot, a three-legged little thing, and showed it to Mara. "He builds these robots while he studies. They're simple little things that only do one or two things."

"I *can* answer for myself, you know," Xavier said, his voice sharp with sarcasm. He glanced at Mara. "But what he said is correct, even though he spoke for me."

Mara examined the robot; it was just a box with three tiny pegs for legs, one each on opposite sides of the cube, and then a third on the front forming a sort of off-kilter tripod. "So what's this one do?"

Xavier took it from her, set it on the table in front of his textbook, and flipped a switch on the bottom. The little box sat on the two primary legs with one edge touching the table, and then rotated backward flat to the table so it was sitting down, so to speak. When the legs and corresponding cube face were parallel to the table, it suddenly flipped into the air, did three somersaults, and landed again, then used the single "front leg" to push itself back into a sitting position, at which point it reared back and repeated the simple performance.

Mara laughed delightedly. "Oh my god, that is so cute!" She crouched to watch the little robot do its jump and flip, laughing every time it launched itself into the air. "And you do this just for fun?"

He shrugged modestly. "Sure. Just to keep myself busy while I'm studying."

She picked up the robot and turned it off, then examined it again. "You ever think about selling them?"

Xavier did the blank, blinking stare again, the one that made it seem like you'd spoken in Swahili or something. "Sell them? To whom?"

Mara laughed. "Anyone! Online, or downstairs in the bar? You put in one of those USB rechargeable batteries and put a cute little face on this? I bet you could get twenty or thirty bucks out of it."

Xavier stared at the robot like he'd never seen it.

"That's, like, maybe five or ten dollars in parts. The most expensive part is the chip, and I get a wholesale discount from a supplier I know."

"Exactly. Huge profit margin, and you make them in your spare time."

Xavier turned the robot on and watched it flip. "You really think people would buy them?"

"Absolutely." She dug her wallet out of her purse and set three tens on the table, and then took the robot. "There. I'm your first customer."

Xavier poked at the money like he'd never seen a greenback before. "For real?"

Mara laughed again. "Yes, sweetheart, for real. This thing is amazing! I could watch it flip for hours while I'm doing paperwork. I know for a fact if I put it on my desk at work, before lunch at least five people would ask me where I got it."

Xavier pointed at a slot on one side. "It already has the USB battery, because that's just the easiest way of charging and being able to reprogram it."

"See? And everyone has a mini USB cord somewhere around the house, so there's no need to include one. I think you just make it look more like an animal or monster or something, just a little head and eyes or whatever, give it a cute name, and you're in business."

"A cute name?"

Mara nodded, tapping the robot on the head.

"Like, I'll call this one Flipper. Like the old TV show about the Dolphin? Only this actually is just a flipper, so it's…stupid, but—"

"No, that's cute. I see what you mean." He was already on his laptop, tapping away. "I could design a basic starter website in like an hour. I'd just need a PayPal account, and some way of packaging them…" And then Xavier was gone, mentally, mumbling to himself, fingers clacking and flying on the keyboard.

I laughed and led Mara toward my room. "You know he has crates full of those things in his room? If he sits and studies or reads for three or four hours, he'll put together four or five of them. And they're all like that, simple, cute, funny, and endlessly enter-taining. I think you just created the CEO of the next Apple Corporation."

Mara smiled at me. "It'll start there, and then he'll design a more complex one, and next thing you know, he'll be selling his IPO for half a billion."

"Exactly," I said, closing the door behind us.

"Is he always up at this hour?" she asked, glanc-ing at my alarm clock, which read 5:48am.

I nodded. "He sleeps maybe four hours a night max. He'll go to bed at one or two and be up again ready to go at five or six. Usually, though, he goes to bed at three or four and wakes up at seven or eight." I shucked my shoes and jacket, setting them aside.

"He's always going, doing, studying, reading. He's ex-hausting, is what he is."

There was an awkward moment, then. Mara stood just inside my room, the door closed behind her, her zip fleece in one hand, purse in the other, staring around my room, at the bed, at me, looking unsure.

Like, where do you start when it comes to just literally, physically sleeping with someone? How do you approach it? It's weird.

I slid off my socks and tossed them in the ham-per near my closet, then approached Mara slowly. "Hey, look, this doesn't have to be weird or awkward, okay?"

She tilted her head to the side and made a face. "Yeah, well, it already is, isn't it? I mean, what do you wear to bed? Which side are you sleeping on? Do you brush your teeth before bed? How am I going to take off my makeup?"

"I usually wear nothing or just underwear to bed, but I can go with shorts if it'll make you more com-fortable. I usually end up on the left side of the bed, but I'm fine with whatever you're comfortable with. We have a bunch of extra toothbrushes around, and Bast's wife has a bunch of girly makeup shit in the bathroom, so I'm sure if you poked around you'd find what you need." I grinned. "Anything else?"

She frowned. "I can't just *poke around* another woman's makeup, especially one I've never met. That's…it's…anathema."

I shrugged. "She won't mind—she's cool. Plus, she and Bast are in Baja on their honeymoon, so it's not like she'll ever know anyway."

"I'm not rifling through your sister-in-law's makeup collection. I'll just wash my face with soap and water."

"Suit yourself." I went to my bureau and pulled out one of my faded, worn, washed a million times Navy T-shirts, handed it to her. "You get changed while I find a toothbrush for you."

It had been weird at first, getting used to having a woman living with us. Dru had stuffed our once-bare medicine cabinet in the bathroom with all sorts of weird shit, and our bathroom towels were all folded all the time, and she'd bought a fancy toilet paper holder instead of just leaving the roll on the back of the toilet where it had been for as long as I could remember, and I had to remember to knock if the door was closed. And there were bras hanging from Bast's bedroom doorknob, panties on the floor of his room, tampon and pad wrappers in the bathroom garbage—and there *was* a bathroom garbage in the first place. She bought all sorts of food we never stocked, did the dishes for no reason whatsoever, vacuumed, dusted even—don't get me wrong, for an apartment filled with a bunch of bachelors, we were plenty clean. I'm former military, so I've got that stereotypical neat-and-orderly bug, and Bast had been in charge of the rest of us growing up and he hated mess and dirt, so it wasn't like we were a bunch of slobs. But we were dudes, and we lived a dude life in a dude's pad.

Then Dru moved in and all that changed. For the better, mostly, but she did yell at us when we left the toilet seat up in the middle of the night or missed the bowl. It's kind of impressive, honestly, how easily she fit herself into our life, surrounded by a bunch of guys. The other brothers lived over the studio a block or so down, but this was the home base for all of us, so often as not there'd be someone passed out on the couch or playing Xbox or making food, since Dru had taken over grocery shopping and kept this place stocked like a restaurant.

I changed into my shorts and then browsed in the medicine cabinet for a new toothbrush; I found one, and, conveniently, several little white packages that said "makeup remover pads" right beside them. After pissing, brushing my own teeth, and washing my hands, I snagged one and brought it and the toothbrush to Mara.

"Look what I found!" I said, showing her. "She's got like four of these packages in there, so I *really* don't think it's a big deal if you use some."

And then it registered what I was seeing: Amarantha, wearing my favorite Navy shirt, looking sleepy and sexy and gorgeous…and just so perfect and so right, so natural in my environment, lounging on my bed scrolling through her phone. The way she was lounging left it obvious that she wasn't wearing a damn thing under the T-shirt, which didn't help me in my determination that we were just going to go to sleep, and nothing else.

She looked up at me as I came in, and gave me that cute, quirky, lopsided grin. "Thanks. Taking off makeup without remover is tricky." She eyed me, then. "Why are you looking at me like that?"

The emotion I was feeling was hard to pinpoint. Soft…tender, possessive, comforted…all of those at once, and more I didn't have the words for.

I let my gaze linger. "Just…you," I said. "In my bed, in my shirt, looking incredible."

She blushed. "There you go with that flattery again."

"It's also just having you here, like this. It's…." I trailed off, hunting for the right words.

"Comfortingly domestic, in a bizarre and unfamiliar sort of way?"

"Exactly."

She sat up. "I may look like the picture of

confidence and cool, collected, adult rationality, but inside, my heart is going like this..." she patted her chest over her heart in a quick rhythm. "And I'm not at all cool or collected."

I sat on the bed beside her, pressed her hand over my heart; her hand was warm and smooth and soft. "Feel that?" My heart was hammering like drum. "You're not the only one, babe."

She gazed up at me, her hand still on my heart. "Why are we being so weird about this? We're just sleeping."

"I know. I was wondering the same thing. It's stupid for me to be nervous about this, but I am." I laughed. "Put me in the back of an airplane with a backpack and a rifle, about to drop thirty thousand feet and attack a bunch of bad guys who'd love to kill me...and my heart will be steady as a rock. Not so much as a single missed beat. But this? Going to bed with a woman I've already slept with, a woman I like more than anyone I've ever met in my life, and I'm— I'm like a boy about to kiss a girl for the first time."

She laughed and sank against me, putting her arms around my waist and her cheek to my chest. "How do you always know what to say to reassure me?"

I could only shrug, my breath stolen by the soft, sweet tenderness of Mara with her arms around me, nuzzling against me, whispering to me. Feeling like she belonged here.

She just held on for a long moment, and then stood up, taking the makeup remover and tooth-brush. "Be right back."

I snagged my cell out of my jeans pocket and plugged it in, then reclined in the bed, pulling up my text thread with Bast.

Me: **You up?**

Him: *Yeah. What's up?*

Me: **Random question, and you can't get up in my shit about it. How'd you know you wanted to be with Dru? Like, that it was a real thing with her?**

Him: *That hot medic, huh?*

Me: **The boys have been talking? Gonna have to beat some ass.**

Him: *Nah, I saw you take off with her at the wedding.*

Me: **So? How'd you know, with Dru?**

Him: *I fucking hate that I'm saying this, but...you just know, man.*

Me: **That's a shitty answer.**

Him: *I know. I'm sorry. But it's the real answer. If you can't make yourself let her go, then you know. If the idea of her leaving and never coming back makes you crazy, then you know.*

Me: **So let's say, hypothetically, that I'm about**

to sleep, JUST sleep with her, and my heart is pounding and my hands are shaking worse than before my first combat drop?

Him: *Then I'd say you probably know.*

Me: **So what do I do?**

Him: *How the hell should I know? Don't let her go? Figure it out. If you can earn a bronze star, you can figure out what to do about a woman you're hung up on.*

Me: **How'd you hear about that?**

Him: *Why, is it a secret?*

Me: **I just don't talk about it.**

Him: *Marco?*

Me: **Yeah.**

Him. *Sorry.*

Me: **I told Mara about Marco.**

Him. *Damn.*

Me: **I know.**

Him: *You'll figure it out, and if not, we'll be here for you, bro. Now, I'm gonna go back to sleep with my wife.*

Me: **Why didn't you tell me I woke you up?**

Him: *Because you're my brother and you wouldn't text me at 5:45 in the morning if it wasn't important.*

Me: **Well thanks.**

Him: *NP. Later.*

Me: **Later.**

It was weird texting Bast—he'd been kind of a

caveman when it came to technology of all kinds, as in he hadn't had a cell phone, computer, game console, nothing. The first thing Dru had done when she moved in was instruct him in no uncertain terms to "go get a cell phone and learn how to fucking text, you goddamn Luddite." Dru could and did curse like a sailor, and having been a sailor myself, that's saying something impressive.

I set the phone aside as Mara came in, her hair brushed, face clean of makeup, eyes flicking around, fingers plucking at the hem of the T-shirt. I tossed aside the blankets and held out my arm; Mara hesitated at the foot of the bed for a few moments, and then climbed toward me, slid her feet under the blankets, and nestled her head against my chest. My arm curled around her waist and palmed her thigh, her hand fluttered around before coming rest on my chest, under my chin; we were both stiff for several minutes, until I laughed, reached out to shut off the lamp, and tugged her more fully against me, sliding lower in the bed.

Gradually, we both relaxed.

"This is…really nice, actually," I said, feeling sleep finally tug at me.

"Mmm," she answered, her voice muzzy. "The nicest. I'm glad I thought of it." I heard the sleepy grin in her voice.

"Yeah, well, you're pretty damn smart."

"I have all the best ideas."

"Sure do."

Silence, then, for a long time. I was on the verge of sleep when I heard her speak again. "Zane?"

"Hmmm?"

"I get nightmares a lot, still, and disoriented, sometimes. If I wake up and I'm crazy—"

I pressed a kiss to the top of her head; I hadn't thought about it, it had just happened automatically. "I do too. If it happens, we'll deal."

She made a quiet, innocent little humming noise in her throat in response, and then nuzzled closer to me, her whole body curled around and draped over mine, my arms wrapped around her. I could smell her hair, the faint odor of toothpaste, and just…Mara.

I've never fallen asleep so fast in my life.

She never woke up with a nightmare.

I woke up slowly, gradually. Sunlight streamed into the bedroom from my window, seagulls cawed loudly…and a woman snored softly.

I blinked my eyes open and glanced down—Mara was facing away, body curled into a comma, blond hair tangled and messy and draped over her face, obscuring her features. She was pressed back against me, back to my chest, thighs against mine, ass nestled against my hips.

Her mouth was partially open, a soft, feminine snore snuffling out every few breaths—and that was, possibly, the most adorable sound I'd ever heard. My heart clenched, squeezed, skipped half a dozen beats, and then started up again, pounding and hammering.

I didn't deserve this. Not her, not this peace—

Deep, deep, deep down, that was the fear that plagued me.

That was the reason my heart was pounding so hard I felt it slamming against my ribs. That was the reason I'd frozen, my hand on her hip, my nose in her hair—I was scared to death I wasn't good enough, that I didn't know how to be a guy she could stay for. Not saying it was easy for Bast and Dru, but neither of them had watched best friends die bloody, violent, pointless deaths. Neither of them had fought off dozens of insurgents alone, standing over the body of their blood brother. Yeah, I got a fucking stupid bronze star—people expected me to flash it around and swagger like a cocky badass because I got a medal. Sweet, great, I'm proud of it; I am, too, in a way. But I'm also ashamed of it. Marco *died*. He took a bullet, just inches away from me. I see his eyes go glassy in my nightmares, a hole in his forehead. He fucking died, and I went apeshit, and got a stupid piece

of bronze for it. Marco is still dead, and his kid is still
without his daddy, and that bronze star won't bring
him back. Worse yet is that I'm not really supposed
to talk about how I got the star, or that have it at all,
because we were on a covert mission, and the only
reason I got it is because my actions saved the rest of
my team and the extract crew. I didn't do what I did
for honor or glory or for the extract team or even the
rest of the guys...I did it to avenge Marco.

Deep down, I feel gnawing, acidic guilt and
shame: Marco should have lived. He should be on a
ranch in Tennessee, playing with his baby boy and riding horses with his wife. Not in a box six feet under
the Tennessee soil. I shouldn't be here. It should be
me in that box, covered in the Stars and Stripes.

That's the fear. That's the insecurity. I'm a Navy
SEAL. I'm hardcore, I'm tough, I've got a lot of skills,
I know I'm good looking, I'm good in bed, and I'm
loyal as hell to my brothers. But way deep down,
there's that insecurity, the knowledge that it should
have been me that died instead of Marco, but it wasn't
and now I'm here, alive, with an amazing, incredible,
gorgeous, sweet, sexy, smart woman in my bed, snug-
gled in my arms, one who understands the invisible
scars combat leaves, the survivor's guilt. She gets it.
We don't have to talk about it to know we both get it.

I don't fucking deserve her.

The thought finally hits, finally moves through me in so many words. I don't deserve happiness with a woman like Mara Quinn. I let my best friend die. I let his wife and son suffer. I lived, and he died, and that's a fucked up amount of unfairness I can't make right. But how do you make yourself feel worthy? No one would understand if I said anything about this. Not even Mara—she gets combat, she gets the nightmares and flashbacks and all that, but survivor's guilt? I don't think she can understand that. I know the term for what I'm going through, but that doesn't help me fix it, that doesn't make it easier for me to go through it, and doesn't give me the tools to address the problem.

Marco should be alive right now, not me; that's a truth I can't shake. God, how can I ever be good enough for a woman like Mara when I shouldn't even be alive? I should be in a box six feet under. My brothers should be the ones with the folded flag stowed away somewhere, not Annalisa Campo.

I don't know what to do. I'm here, in my bed with Mara in my arms, and I don't feel good enough. I'm not enough—I wasn't enough to save Marco, to keep my best friend alive, and I'm not enough now for Mara. But...I can't let her go.

I don't deserve her, but I don't know how to let go.

She stirred in my arms, stretching and groaning,

spine arching. And then she froze, breath catching, her hand sliding along my forearm, as if she was disoriented and confused as to where she was and who she was in bed with.

"It's me, Mara," I whispered, leaning close, lips to her ear. "You're in bed with me. You're safe."

She stayed tense and frozen for a moment, and then gradually began to relax, muscles softening, breathing resuming. She wiggled back against me, twisted her head sideways. Her hand slid up to cup the back of my head, pulling me toward her.

"I've never enjoyed waking up so much before," she murmured. "Normally, I'd have been disoriented for a lot longer."

"Waking up with you in my bed...I can't think of anything better," I whispered, the guilt and the feelings of inadequacy still powerful inside me, but not enough to erase or minimize the potency of what it feels like to have this woman in my arms.

She pulled me closer, touched her lips to mine, softly, hesitantly, her eyes open and wide and searching mine from centimeters away. "No? You can't think of even *one* thing that might better?"

And then Mara pressed up into the kiss. Claimed my mouth as hers. The kiss was gentility personified, tenderness and silk and heat and drowning sweetness and beauty. I groaned as we kissed, my palm grazing up her thigh and under her shirt to explore the warmth and softness of her flesh. She reached down behind herself and tugged at my shorts, helping me kick them off, leaving me naked under the blankets, her ass grinding against my throbbing, aching, hard-as-iron erection.

"Mara…" I breathed, palming her breast.

She just hummed hungrily in response, claimed another kiss, a hotter one, a harder one, a deeper, fiercer kiss. She used one hand to peel her shirt off, and then slipped her hand between our bodies again. She grasped my cock, angled me between her thighs, shifted her hips, and then I was sliding into her silky wet heat, snug and perfect. Bare and beautiful. She whimpered against my lips and rolled her hips, taking me deeper, and her hand clutched at my ass, pulled at me, silently begging me. Whimpered again as I pushed against her, thrusting deeper, and then she was kissing me, and the kiss was something I've never experienced before; a delirious, drowning hypnotism.

An expanding, all-consuming, white-hot, heart-throbbing glory.

Enveloped by Mara, subsumed within her.

Surrounded by her warmth and softness and heat, our movements in perfect unison, exchanging breath and driving our kiss higher and hotter.

I felt her hand slip between her thighs to circle at

herself wildly, her other hand on my ass, clawing deep into the flesh and muscle, pulling at me, encouraging me to move harder and faster and deeper. Her mouth on mine, her lips moving, her tongue seeking. Her soft breast in my hand, her hair spread out in a tangled golden cascade.

Lost in her.

Buried in her.

Kissing, moving, joining.

I felt her twitch and heard her groan, tasted her whimpers on my lips, felt her clamp down around me as she shattered in my arms, and I let go with her, poured myself into her, kissing her through our mutual concussive luxuriating release. I groaned and writhed and breathed her name and devoured her, sucked her breath into my lungs and reveled in the way she gasped my name a thousand desperate times.

When we finished, we were gasping in synch and sweating together, still joined.

I moved to pull out, and she shook her head, holding me in place. "Just...stay with me. Just like this."

"Okay."

And so I do.

We fall back asleep together, joined like that.

And, like Bast said I would...

I just...*know.*

ELEVEN

Mara

THE WEEK PASSED IN A BLUR. ZANE AND I SPENT EVERY waking moment together whenever Zane wasn't working. Even when he was behind the bar, more often than not, I'd be parked in the booth closest to the service bar, sipping beer and catching up on all the reading I'd been meaning to do. My TBR list had gotten kind of out of control—my Kindle library was filled with books I'd purchased and had meant to read but had never gotten around to. So, for the six or eight hours that Zane worked behind the bar or on the floor, I caught up on reading and let myself get a little tipsy.

Xavier would bring me food, whatever he felt like making, and one of Zane's other brothers would scoot into the booth with me now and then and chat me up. I met all of his brothers except Bast, who was still on his honeymoon.

Brock was sharp-witted and sweet and a great conversationalist, and possibly the most absurdly beautiful human being I'd ever met—think young Paul Newman—that was Brock, tall and lean and effortlessly smooth, with rich silky brown hair neatly parted and swept to one side, a few strands always in his eyes, a brilliant, dazzling smile and warm brown eyes.

Baxter was the complete opposite, rough around the edges, blunt, hysterical, vulgar, but still sweet, and sexy in his own way—bulky, brawny, heavy with massive muscles, physically intimidating and yet easy and fun to be around; Bax was nearly as tall as Brock, but half as broad and very muscular, with the same dazzling white grin and brown eyes, although Bax's gaze was always on the move, and glittering with humor. His hair was the same rich brown as Zane's, but Bax kept his clipped close on the sides and long and messy up top, wavy and tangled in a permanent just-fucked look.

When Bax slipped into the booth the first time,

he did so affecting a dramatic limp. I snickered as he grabbed his thigh and pretended to have to haul his leg in after him, as if his entire leg was game.

"Oh, stop," I said, laughing. "It wasn't *that* bad of an injury."

He faked a shocked expression. "I'm barely able to walk, doc. I may never be the same again."

I rolled my eyes. "Oh, please. It was, what, thirty stitches? You'll be fine."

"Thirty-one, actually, and I've got orders from the doctor to take it easy for a while." He lifted his chin at me. "I never got a chance to properly thank you, though. You jumped in and saved the day, and possibly my football career. So...thanks."

I shrugged. "I was a combat medic. It's second nature."

"Still, thank you."

I smiled at him. "Of course, Bax." A moment of silence passes between us. "So, for real though, will the injury affect your career?"

He shrugged. "Probably not. I'm staying in Ketchikan for at least the year, so I'm not sure what I'm going to do about football long term, anyway. But physically, I'll be okay. It'll take time to heal, but time is one thing I've got, I guess." He stayed to chat with me for a few more minutes and then left, and I was alone in the booth again...at least until the next twins slid in.

The twins were a force of nature. Like all the Badd brothers, they were tall, standing six-three, but the twins were built more like Brock, Xavier, and Lucian, tall and lean rather than tall and built like Greek gods. Canaan had shoulder length hair, the same rich brown as all the brothers. When he was working, Canaan kept his hair in a ponytail, but the rest of the time he left it down and loose, usually hanging in his eyes and half-obscuring his features. Corin was edgy, more hipster-punk-rock star, he wore his hair with buzzed sides and the long, wavy top dyed neon blue at the tips. Canaan wore a beard, which made him look a little older, while Corin was clean-shaven. They both had the same vivid brown Badd eyes, and had a tendency to finish each other's sentences and speak in unison.

They dressed like rock stars, too, even while working, with tight, low-slung jeans stuffed into half-unlaced combat boots and obscure band concert T-shirts, full sleeve tattoos, lots of heavy silver rings, pierced ears, and Canaan had a ring through the center of his lower lip while Corin had a septum piercing and gauged earlobes.

They never showed up alone, always together, and they were fiercely energetic, voluble, prone to rapid-fire, back-and-forth spats of wildly eclectic conversation. They'd bicker over best 70s-era bassists, and weird indie art movies and then get into an argument over Britney versus Madonna versus Beyoncé, all within the space of fifteen minutes, and you just had to kind of try to keep up.

Lucian was the hardest to read and, for me, the most impossible to understand. Taciturn would be a generous term, and that's putting it lightly. He spent as much time in my booth that week as the rest of the brothers, but he was silent for the most part, content to sip beer and share cheesy french fries and read his book while I read mine. I once got him to list his five favorite books: *The Foundation Trilogy* by Isaac Asimov—he counted that as a single favorite rather than three books; *A Brief History of Time* by Stephen Hawking, *Fahrenheit 451* by Ray Bradbury; *A Farewell to Arms* by Ernest Hemingway; and *Jubal Sackett* by Louis L'Amour. I'd asked him what his favorite book was, and he'd stared over my shoulder in thought for a solid five minutes, and then listed those books in that order, with no explanation, and then had gone back to reading an Anne Rice novel.

Lucian was like the twins and Xavier, built like a razor blade, tall, lean, hard, and rangy. If Canaan's hair was long at shoulder-length, Lucian's was something else entirely, bound low at his nape and dangling past mid-spine in a thick brown queue; Lucian had a habit of wrapping the long ponytail in his fist while he read and yanking on it absently, and I'd never once seen him with it unbound.

And then there was Xavier. Possibly my favorite brother—except for Zane, obviously. Xavier was sweet, quirky, cute, and eclectic in the extreme. He'd set up at the booth across from me, a stack of thick textbooks in front of him, his laptop beside them, and a bin of assorted robotics parts on the seat next to him, each part organized by type in little compartments. He'd read and build his robots, and then take a few minutes to talk to me, usually about whatever he was reading at the time.

Mostly I had no clue what he was going on about, but he was fascinating to listen to, being articulate to the point of eloquence, and given to using archaic turns of phrase. He could wax on easily and at length on just about any subject, literature, physics, philosophy, sociology, history...anything except pop culture, about which he was hopelessly and comically uninformed. He didn't look the part of a robot building, super-science, math-wizard über-genius, though. He was tall and lean, and he looked the least like the rest of his brothers, with brown hair that was nearly black, and was the only Badd brother with bright green eyes. He had triple-pierced ears and an intricate series of geometric, math symbols tattooed on his forearms.

His hair was cut a lot like Corin's and Bax's, short on the sides and long and wavy and loose on top. He had an air about him that said he had no idea how sexy or gorgeous he was, and even less of a clue about how endearing his eccentricity and intelligence was.

If I learned one thing over the week, it was that I could definitely understand why the Badd brothers had a reputation in this town, because they were all stupidly, absurdly, incredibly gorgeous men, each with their own unique, vibrant, potent personalities and styles. They were rough and sometimes vulgar, always entertaining, always warm and welcoming, and always sweet toward me.

No wonder the bar was as busy as it was, since at any given time there would be at least two of the delicious Badd brothers at work, one behind the bar and one on the floor, and another one, usually Xavier or Lucian, in the kitchen, with Zane, Brock, the twins, taking turns working the bar and waiting tables, with Bax usually set up in a chair by the entrance acting as a bouncer and ID-checker, since he was supposed to stay off his feet as much as possible.

The clientele was predominantly female, whether young and looking to party, or single women in their thirties on the prowl, or married women just there for the fun, good drinks, and eye-candy. The men in attendance were almost exclusively single

men hoping to take advantage of the unending parade of single women—all of this meant the bar was
raking in cash hand over fist from open to close.

When Zane wasn't working, we spent a lot of
time hiking the trails outside Ketchikan, an activity
I'd had no idea I would enjoy as much as I did. He'd
pack a bunch of food in his rucksack, and we'd take
the truck the brothers owned up to a trailhead—Zane
had convinced his brothers to all chip in on a new
Silverado 2500 that they could all share, as they rarely
needed to be anywhere they couldn't walk to.

When we weren't hiking or at the bar, we were
at my room in the B&B, fucking like teenagers who'd
just discovered sex. And, except that one time in his
bed, we always used protection. I couldn't bring myself to regret that indiscretion, though, because it was
a memory seared deep into my soul. We'd created
something, that morning, with each other. Crossed
some boundary where union of body became union
of soul. Sex after that was always emotionally intense,
almost always fierce and wild, sometimes slow and
gentle. I discovered that he liked it best when we started out missionary and switched to me riding him for
the finish, and that I liked it best when we started out
reverse cowgirl and finished doggy style, so he could
let go with all the full and furious force of his powerful body. Whatever the position, though, there was

always an element of vulnerability, a sense of depth between us.

And we…talked. A lot. About everything. Those day-long hikes were always spent talking to each other, taking selfies, laughing, teasing each other…I think I learned more about Zane in that week than I knew about everyone else in my life combined. And I learned about myself. He had a way of getting me to talk, getting me to open up in ways I'd never thought possible.

And then, all too soon, it was Wednesday night and I was dreading the morning in a way I'd never felt before. My flight for San Francisco left at ten, and I had to check out of the B&B by nine, since the Kingsley's had a couple arriving who wanted to check in early. I opted to check out Wednesday night, and had Zane bring the truck so I could haul my suitcases to the bar, and leave them stacked just inside the stairwell.

I'd already done an online check-in for my return flight and had the boarding pass loaded into the browser on my cell phone. I also had a change of clothes for the morning folded into my carry-on…

And I was full out panicking.

Zane was working until nine p.m., which only gave us a handful of hours left together. I was sitting in my booth near the service bar, sipping a pint of stout and nibbling on some nachos. The twins were on the floor serving tables and doing their best singing waiter impressions, getting the crowd howling along as they sang bar band favorites like "Sweet Caroline", "Free Bird", and "What Do You Do With a Drunken Sailor", going back and forth on the verses and singing in harmony for the chorus, all while dancing around the floor with trays full of drinks or punching in orders at the computer.

Lucian was in the kitchen with Xavier, and Zane was behind the bar, with Bax carding at the front door.

And me, alone in the booth, hopelessly watching Zane shake martinis and cosmos, pull pints, pour shots, uncork wine, and sling mixers. Wishing I didn't have to go. Wishing he'd ask me to stay. Wishing I knew what the fuck to do. Because, god, it'd be crazy if I just stayed, right? Like, I've known the guy a week. It's infatuation. And even if it was something more, I've known him *a week*. Seven days. Seven magical, glorious days. Six nights—and five mornings—of the most incredible sex of my entire life. One week, and I was gaga on this guy.

But I had a job back in SF, and a possible new job lined up in Seattle working with Claire, not to mention an apartment with a lease through October. My life was in San Francisco. I had friends there. I had memories there. Dad had visited me there before he got busted and sent to the federal penitentiary in

Terra Haute, Indiana. Mom spent every Christmas with me in San Francisco. It was home.

Although, lately the idea of moving to Seattle sounded nice, being with Claire again, a new job, a new city….

But Ketchikan?

Fuck. Ketchikan had Zane. Ketchikan had the mountains and the hiking trails, and the cute bars and seafood places Zane and I had frequented. It also had Brock and Bax, the twins, Lucian, and Xavier. And Zane.

Did I mention Ketchikan had Zane?

But…who just upends their entire life for a guy they met a week ago?

And if Zane didn't ask me to stay, it's not like I could bust out with, "So hey, um, I was thinking I could just stay here with you in Ketchikan…forever." Yeah, that'd work.

We'd agreed on a week. We'd agreed this was practice, that we'd spend this week together, and then I'd go home and find another man to have a real relationship with, and he'd find a woman to have a real relationship with, and we'd never see each other again.

But…god, the thought of Zane with another woman in that bed, another woman with her hands on him? Gah, no. I couldn't even think about it, or I'd go crazy. Just thinking about it right now made me want to throw the salt and pepper shakers at Zane for cheating on me in my own head, or start crying, or run out of here so fast I'd leave a Mara-shaped hole in the wall, Looney Toons style.

And the thought of being with another man? That wasn't any more appealing. I tried to picture someone else kissing me, someone else stripping my clothes off, someone else sinking into me…and my stomach revolted and my brain insisted on replacing the mental image of the mystery man with one of Zane, as he'd kissed me, as he'd stripped me naked, as he'd sunk into me.

I was desperately trying to create some semblance of mental and emotional stability inside myself, when a body slumped into the booth opposite me. Lucian, smelling of restaurant kitchen, his hair braided, folded in half, and tied off into a thick club between his shoulder blades, wearing a black T-shirt stained and spotted and smeared with kitchen yuck. He had a bowl of stew in one hand and a pint of beer in the other.

I sniffled. "Hi, Luce."

He eyed me warily, hearing the sniffle. "Hey." He spooned some stew into his mouth and chewed, still eying me thoughtfully. "Leaving tomorrow?"

I nodded. "Yep."

"Well, speaking for at least five of us, we'll miss

you. It's been nice having you around."

"It's been great meeting you all." I swirled my beer at the bottom of the glass, watched bubbles form a scrim on the surface. "But why only five of you?"

"Well, Bast isn't here, and I can't speak for Zane."

"Why wouldn't Zane miss me?"

Lucian ate a few bites before responding. "Not what I meant."

"Then what did you mean?"

He chewed, swallowed, and washed it down with beer. "Maybe he doesn't want to have to miss you."

"Oh." I finished my beer. "Think he'll…say something?"

Lucian shrugged. "Dunno. Might, might not." He poked at the stew with his spoon. "You're better off talking to him about this than me, though."

"It's not that simple," I said.

Lucian shrugged. "Usually things are exactly that simple." He finally met my eyes, his own dark and intense and unreadable. "Simple and easy aren't the same thing, though."

At that moment, Zane slid into the booth beside me, reached out and snagged Lucian's bowl of stew and devoured half of it in three bites, then washed it down with a long pull on Lucian's beer. "You boring her with your mystic nonsense, Luce?"

Lucian just lifted a wry eyebrow. "By all means,

help yourself." He took his bowl and beer back and continued eating as if nothing had happened, then eyed his brother. "What mystic nonsense?"

"Your sparsely-worded nuggets of wisdom."

"That's hardly mystic nonsense."

Zane laughed. "Sure it is."

Lucian just shook his head, and went back to eating in silence.

I found Zane's hand under the table and threaded my fingers through his. "No mysticism, just..."

"Lucian being Lucian?" Zane supplied. "Knocking apart whatever you think you know about life in a dozen words or less?"

I bobbed my head to one side. "Kind of."

"I'm convinced he's an ancient Eastern mystic disguised in the body of a sullen teenager," Zane said. "It's the only possible explanation for how he knows half the shit he does."

"I watch, and I listen, and I ask questions. I pay attention. I read." Lucian finished his stew and knocked his beer back. "It's not mysticism, it's called being a keen observer of human nature."

"Yeah, whatever, Confucius." Zane leaned back in the booth and slung his arm around me. "Get back in the kitchen, you slacker."

Lucian shook his head again, a small but genuine grin on his lips, and then flipped Zane the bird.

"Shouldn't *you* be behind the bar?"

"Brock got bored being by himself upstairs, so he came down to relieve me."

Lucian just nodded and went back into the kitchen, whistling the theme to *Kung Fu*.

Zane watched him, and then grinned at me. "That kid is something else."

"How old is he?" I asked.

"Nineteen, almost twenty."

"He's not really a kid, though, is he?"

Zane shook his head. "No, you're right, he's not. But then, he never has been. Even when he was a little kid he was quiet to the point of silence. He didn't speak until he was more than two, but then he was speaking full sentences. Mom thought he might have developmental problems, but the doctor said he was physically capable of speech, fully capable mentally, and developing normally, he just…didn't want to speak for whatever reason."

"Huh. Well, he's a wise young man."

Zane laughed, nodding. "No shit. You forget he's there, and you'll be having this conversation or whatever, and then he'll just bust out with a sentence or two that's so…insightful, I guess, that it makes everyone just go, 'Huh, he's right. I'll be damned.'"

I leaned against Zane's shoulder. "Want to, um, go upstairs? Or downtown? Something?"

He eyed me. "When's your flight out, again?"

I blinked back some kind of weird, hot, salty wetness that was gathering in the corners of my eyes. Not sure what it was about, but I didn't like it very much. "Ten tomorrow morning."

"This week went by way too fast, didn't it?" His arm, slung around my shoulders, tightened. "I'm kind of just feeling one more night together in my bed. Whatcha say, babe?"

I nodded. "I'd like that."

He threaded his fingers into mine, swung his legs out of the booth, stood up, and then bent to lift me bodily out of the booth. Effortlessly, he carried me to the stairs leading up to the apartment, pausing to let me open the door for him. Before ascending the stairs, he kissed me.

Right there in full view of the entire, packed bar, eliciting a chorus of wolf whistles and cat calls from his brothers and several of the bar patrons. I laughed though the kiss, unable to keep a grin from spreading across my lips, despite my melancholy.

To his room, then.

And his bed.

Clothes came off, and he settled above me, kissing me breathless, kissing me senseless, kissing me into teary-eyed oblivion. He backed away, his thumb brushing under my eyes.

"Hey, none of that," he murmured.

Ask me to stay, ask me to stay, ask me to stay—the plea rang through my mind, but didn't pass my lips. I wouldn't beg, couldn't.

"This has just…it's been the most amazing week of my life," I whispered.

He slid into me, bare, his erection hot and hard inside me. "It has been for me, too."

I wrapped my legs around his waist, my arms around his neck, and I kissed him as we began moving together in perfect synchronicity. Our hips met, our tongues tangled, our breaths mated, and I couldn't help another tear from sliding down my cheek. Zane didn't wipe that one away, even though he saw it. His eyes locked on mine as we moved together. He didn't shush me as I began moaning, a sound lost somewhere between a groan of rapture and a sob of sorrow.

His eyes reflected his own deep well of intense emotion, none of which he expressed verbally. He showed me, though, in the desperate fervor of his thrusting, in the tremble of his lips as he held off his climax, in the clench of his jaw and lowering of his brow, in the rippling of his arms on either side of my face like solid iron-hard bars of flesh and muscle.

I pressed my face into his shoulder and ground up against him, whimpering.

We came together, his face buried between my

breasts, his hair soft against my cheek. I let a few tears drip into his hair as I came, clinging to him, shuddering beneath him, still silently begging him to ask me to stay.

He never did.

Not before we fell asleep.

Not when we woke in the small dark hours of the morning to make love again, bare once more.

Not when my alarm went off at seven-thirty, and we found each other one last time, skin sliding against skin, breathing shuddering in the new light of dawn. We didn't speak a word as we reached climax together faster than we ever had, coming more desperately than ever before, eyes locked, knowing it was the last time.

My heartbeat pounded in my chest as I rested on Zane's shoulder—*stay—stay—stay—stay*—the beat of my heart said.

But I couldn't.

My life wasn't here.

Zane wasn't mine.

How can I upend my entire life for a man I've known a week? It would be the height of foolishness, no matter how intensely I may feel. Emotions change, feelings change, desires change. This was temporary, a fleeting thing created in the vacuum of a vacation. It wasn't real. It wasn't meant to be.

Minutes passed, and the digital red numerals on Zane's alarm clock ticked over from 7:30 to 7:45, and then to 8:00.

Finally, I knew I had to go or risk losing my tenuous grip on my stupid, ridiculous, nonsensical emotions.

I had to go.

I forced myself to move, to roll away from Zane. I tugged on Zane's T-shirt and brought my carry-on bag across the hall to the bathroom, took a quick shower and dressed in clean clothes. Brushed my teeth, combed through my hair and bound it up still damp in a tight bun at back of my head.

When I emerged, it was twenty after eight and Zane was dressed in white gym shorts, a blue SEALs hoodie, and a white ball cap bearing the outline of an assault rifle with the letters HK in red. He had the truck keys in one hand, and two paper cups of coffee in the other.

"I've got your bags loaded into the truck," he said, handing me the coffee.

"Okay," I said, my voice barely a whisper.

The drive to the airport was quiet.

He accompanied me to the security checkpoint, and then handed me my carry-on.

"So." He sipped his coffee, his dark brown eyes opaque and unreadable to me, now. "This is it."

I nodded, hating the sudden, painful awkward-ness between us. "Guess so."

One tense moment, then another. It was 8:50 a.m., and I still had to go through security and find my gate. But how could I leave without any kind of goodbye? This wasn't goodbye; this was an awkward, tense, uncomfortable parting.

"Zane, I—"

He kissed me. Hard, intense, one hand on the back of my head, his huge hard body pressed against mine. His tongue swept my mouth again and again, and I delved into the kiss, drowned in it, reveled in it, hoped hoped hoped it meant he'd—

He pulled away, stumbling backward a step. "Bye, Mara."

I blinked hard. "See ya, Zane."

Fucking awkward. Fucking painful. Fucking stupid.

I went through security and stopped on the oth-er side, turning back. Zane was still standing where I'd left him, one hand on the back of his neck, brows drawn, shoulders rising and falling heavily, his jaw tensing and releasing. He forced a smile when I turned back, waved at me, and then abruptly pivoted on his heel and left the airport, almost angrily.

I didn't cry on the flight home.

Nope, nope, nope.

TWELVE

Zane

IT HAD BEEN ALMOST TWO MONTHS SINCE MARA LEFT, AND I was still fucking miserable. I was a complete bastard to my brothers and a jackass to the customers, to the point that when Bast and Dru got back from their honeymoon, Bast told me to cut the bullshit attitude or find a new job. So I dug deep, and pretended like shit was hunky fucking dory.

But it wasn't.

I shouldn't have let Mara leave like that. I knew it in my heart, in my soul. But how could I have asked her to stay? What would she do? You can't base an entire life, a whole new relationship on knowing someone for a week. That's stupid. I may not know dick about relationships, but I know they don't work like that.

They just don't.

To make matters worse, after the first month of misery, I finally broke down at three a.m. and drunk texted Mara. Spent a fucking hour composing that message, deleting and starting over, reading and re-reading a thousand times, tweaking it until it felt right.

Me: **I miss you. What if I said I regret letting you leave?**

When I finally hit the blue send arrow, the message popped up in the thread in the blue bubble; "Delivered."

I stared at the screen for twenty fucking minutes, and it never changed to "read." I passed out, and when I woke up, it was still delivered but not read.

Two days later, still unread.

A week, two weeks, and she never read the fucking message.

I called her, right on the two-month mark. The phone rang and rang and rang.

"Hey, this is Mara. Leave a message and I'll get back to you."

I let out a sigh right as the voicemail beeped.

"Hey. Um, this is Zane. I—just call me back, okay? Please?"

I threw my phone across the living room of the apartment so hard it smashed against the wall. Bast, in the kitchen pouring a mug of coffee, glared at me.

"What the fuck is your goddamn problem, Zane? You've been a complete shithead for two months. What happened?"

"She left, and I let her. And now she's not returning texts or answering calls."

"Then it's done, man. I'm sorry." He came into the living room and handed me a mug. "Can't really say much to make you feel better or to fix it. Other fish in the sea, time heals all wounds, all that is just bullshit. Hurt is hurt, man."

"Fuck the other fish, I want *her*," I growled.

"Then go get her?"

"How? I don't know where she lives, I don't have her address, and she's not answering her phone."

Bast snorted. "Did you forget about your youngest brother? You know, the one who was recruited by the NSA?"

"Oh. Right." I stood up and kicked at Xavier's door. He opened the door and blinked at me sleepily. "Xavier, I need you to—"

He turned away from me without a word, rummaged through some papers on his desk, and returned with a printout bearing Mara's full name—Amarantha Lucille Quinn—and a San Francisco address.

"About time, you pussy," Xavier groused, shoving the paper at me. "Printed this two and a half weeks ago."

And then he shut the door in my face.

Bast was smirking over his coffee. "He may not need much sleep, but when he *is* sleeping, he really doesn't like being woken up."

"Clearly," I said, reading the address over and over again, compulsively, as if I could conjure the woman out of the words.

"Suggestion?" Bast said.

"What?"

He pointed at the window, indicating the docks, where the sound of an airplane's propeller could be heard coughing into life. "Go catch Brock. He's headed to Seattle to see that mystery girl of his. He'd probably take you to San Francisco if you asked him really nicely."

Barefoot, shirtless, wearing nothing but a pair of gym shorts, I jogged outside into a cold early fall rain. Brock was in the pilot's seat of a single engine seaplane, flicking switches and glancing at a clipboard, a headset over his ears. I jumped onto the float and threw myself into the passenger seat.

Brock didn't look up, didn't miss a beat. "Need a

ride to Frisco?"

I nodded. "I can chip in on the gas."

He flipped another switch. "Might I suggest a shirt and shoes, at least?" He shot a grin at me. "I promise I won't leave without you."

I ran back home, changed into jeans, a T-shirt, hoodie, and combat boots, and stuffed a few things into a backpack and then ran back to the seaplane. When I was seated, Brock indicated to the second headset and then backed the aircraft away from the dock.

When we were airborne, I glanced at Brock. "So...your girl lives in Seattle, huh?"

He nodded. "Still not talking about her. I don't want to jinx it. This is my first visit to her. Maybe if this goes well, I'll share. Until then, I'm keeping her to myself."

I shrugged. "I get that. You been talking to her?

He nodded. "We FaceTime every night."

"So would you call that...sex-timing?" I said, smirking.

He rolled his eyes at me. "It's not like that."

"Isn't this the girl you fucked six times in one night?"

"Yeah," he said, grinning, but then quickly sobered. "But we decided that if we were doing a long distance relationship, sexting or whatever, even via

FaceTime, would be cheapening what we had, so we're waiting until we see each other. We're trying to do this right, since it's new for both of us."

I made a surprised face. "Wow. That's…impressive, actually. Respect, brother." I held out my fist, and he tapped his knuckles to mine.

He shot a look at me. "So, what are you gonna say to Mara when you see her?"

I sighed. "I've been scripting it out in my head, and I can't come with anything good."

Brock snorted. "How about the truth? 'Hi, Mara. I was a dumbass for letting you leave. Will you please move to Ketchikan to be with me?'"

"But how can I ask that of her? We barely know each other."

Brock shrugged. "Yeah, well, sometimes you don't need to know each other to know each other, know what I mean?"

"As stupid as that sounds, it does make sense."

"Just play it as it comes, dude. Don't over think it, and don't let your head get in the way. Sometimes what we think we know is true or right or possible has little or no relevance to what really *is* true or right or possible." He adjusted one of the dials, and then glanced at me again. "Arthur C. Clarke stipulated that the only way to discover the limits of what is possible is to venture a little way past them into the impossible."

"And there's the pithy quote I've been waiting for," I joked.

"Hey, don't knock my storehouse of pithy quotes," Brock said. "If you think about it, it makes a lot of sense."

"Sure, but how does that help me know what to say to Mara?"

"It doesn't. It just means you never know what she'll say unless you ask."

"Oh." I frowned. "And if she says no?"

"Then you get shitfaced in Frisco and I'll pick you up before I go back to Ketchikan."

"I kind of smashed my phone," I said.

"How very mature of you," he deadpanned.

"Shut up."

"*You* shut up," he shot back. "You're a big boy, you can figure it out."

Going through BUD/S all over again seemed like an easier prospect than this, but I wasn't one to back down from a challenge, especially not when it involved a woman like Amarantha Quinn.

I felt stupid. I had a dozen roses gripped in one fist, and a stomach full of butterflies. Stepping off the elevator, I resisted the impulse to turn and run, which was dumb as fuck, since I hadn't turned and run from anything in my life.

I made my way slowly down the hallway to apartment 14B, and knocked on the door.

"MOMMY! SOMEBODY'S HERE!" I heard a small female voice say.

"I'll get it, sweetie. Keep eating your lunch," I heard a woman say.

There was the rattle of a chain lock and then the door opened, revealing a pretty young woman of maybe thirty, wearing stained black yoga pants and a white tank top, braless, her breasts heavy and her nipples prominent behind the thin cotton. She had a baby on one hip, her hair in a messy ponytail, and she glared at me angrily.

This was *not* Mara.

"If those are from Harry, tell him to shove them up his ass," the woman snapped. "He wants to talk to me or see me, he has to crawl his slimy ass here himself."

I blinked at her venom. "Uh, sorry. I'm not from Harry."

The woman sagged. "Oh. My bad. How can I help you?"

I struggled to figure out what was going on. "This is apartment 14B, right?" I rattled off the rest of the address. "Do I have the right place?"

The woman nodded, glancing down as a curious young girl of three or four peeked from behind her. "That's us."

"So…obviously Mara Quinn doesn't live here anymore."

The woman shook her head, her expression sympathetic. "Sorry, no." She winked at me. "But give me those roses and come on in, and I can pretend to be Mara for…oh, twenty minutes. You're hot."

"Thanks, but…no."

She nodded, understanding. "Sorry, honey. We've lived here for a little over two weeks now. I think the previous tenant, your Mara, must have moved unexpectedly because I'm still getting a lot of her mail."

I sighed in defeat, rubbing the back of my neck. "Gotcha. Well, sorry to have bothered you."

"Sorry I couldn't help more."

I nodded and turned away, still carrying the flowers. I stopped, hesitated, and then jogged back to 14B, just as the woman was closing the door.

"Here," I said. "Take 'em."

She smiled, and I saw a vibrant, beautiful woman, one I'd have been interested in had Mara not consumed my attention.

"Thanks," she said, happiness suffusing her features as she accepted the roses. "My dick of an ex-husband never gave me flowers even once."

"You're really beautiful, you know," I said. "Your ex is an idiot."

She blinked at me. "Sure you don't want to come in? It's almost nap time in here."

I laughed. "No, but thanks. I'm flattered."

"Mama? What's a dick?" The little girl said.

Her mother didn't miss a beat. "Your father. And you can tell him I said so, next time you see him, assuming he shows up for his visitation."

I backed away. "If things don't work out for me, maybe I'll be back."

The woman sighed wistfully, hiking the baby higher on her hip. "I'll be here, dreaming of it."

I left, phone-less, Mara-less, and hopeless. Brock had said he'd be back in three days, which gave me three days alone in San Francisco. Would have been fun at one point, but now?

All I wanted was to see Mara. Which, clearly, wasn't going to happen.

I booked a one-way trip back to Ketchikan. Row 16D, window seat, alone.

Flying commercial sucked.

THIRTEEN

Mara

I STAGGERED THROUGH THE FRONT DOOR OF THE SEATTLE apartment I shared with Claire, barely standing on my feet. It was just past eleven in the morning on a Friday, and I'd just left work. I'd been battling bouts of extreme nausea all week, and then this morning I'd barely made it to the bathroom before spewing all over a toilet—*on*, more than *in*, unfortunately, and I considered myself fortunate that I'd even made it to the bathroom. I fought it as best I could for another few hours, but my new boss had finally sent me home. I caught a cab, even though Claire and I only lived three blocks from work, because I'd known I wouldn't be able to make the walk.

I made it through the door, crashing back against it, sweating, gasping, and moaning in pain. My whole body was screaming at me to lie down, sit down, anything. Sleep. I dropped my purse on the floor at my feet and staggered toward my bedroom.

Slowly, exhaustedly, I swiveled my head on my neck to peer blearily at my best friend. I blinked through the dizziness, and then blinked some more, because I wasn't sure what I was seeing; I was feverish, after all, so maybe it was a fever dream?

Claire, home from work early, or, considering the scene in front of me, not having gone in at all.

Claire was on the couch.

Completely naked.

Sitting reverse cowgirl on top of a man. His hands were on her breasts, his thighs on either side of hers. Claire's hands were on his thighs, and she was leaning forward, staring at me like a deer caught in headlights.

"Hi, Mara," she said, feigning a pretense of casualness.

"Claire. What—um. What are you doing home?"

"Having sex with my boyfriend, obviously." She eyed me. "What are you doing home?"

"Sick," I said, clutching at the wall to stay upright.

The guy Claire was riding had stayed silent so far, and being hidden behind Claire from this angle, I couldn't see his face. But then he tilted to one side, and I slumped fully against the wall.

It was Brock.

As in, Zane's brother.

"Hi, Brock."

He lifted his chin at me. "Hey, Mara."

I stared for another moment, because I was sick enough and heartbroken enough and confused enough that it hadn't fully registered yet. "So...you're the guy? Claire's mysterious local from Ketchikan? Sex six times in one night guy? The pilot?"

Claire blinked at me. "You two know each other?"

I nodded heavily. "He's—Brock is Zane's brother."

Claire blinked owlishly. "He...what?" She twisted to glance at Brock. "You are? You're Zane's brother? As in...the guy Mara spent a week with? The reason she's been moping around for the last two months?"

Brock hesitated a moment, glancing at me, then at Claire. "Um. I feel like maybe we need to have this conversation when Claire and I aren't...you know... mid-coitus?"

"Good point," I said, and continued stumbling toward my room. "Wake me up when you're done fucking."

I closed my door, collapsed on my bed, and

tugged the pillow over my head, because I could hear Claire and Brock slamming the couch back against the wall, and Claire moaning, and Brock groaning, and I didn't need to hear Zane's brother having sex.

I fell asleep, fighting memories of Zane.

I was woken by Claire shaking my shoulder. "Mara, wake up."

"Hnnnggg."

"We need to talk."

"Sick."

"I know." She smoothed my hair away from my face, tugging a strand out of my mouth. "But I think you're gonna wanna hear what Brock has to say."

"No."

"Mara." She slid to kneel on the floor so her face was in front of mine. "I really, really, *really* think you want to hear Brock out."

"Fine," I groaned. "But in here. Sick. Can't move."

"Okay. Stay here. Be right back."

"Claire." I forced one eye open, and Claire stopped with her hand on my doorknob. "Brock is a great guy."

She smiled at me. "I know."

A few minutes later, Claire came back in, Brock in tow. She sat on the bed beside me, pulled me so my head was lying on her lap, and Brock took a seat on my desk chair.

Brock started to talk, stopped, sighed, and then started over. "So, Zane has been a fucking mess without you."

"And you've been a fucking mess without him," Claire said.

"So?" I mumbled, my stomach roiling.

"So, I kind of made a detour to San Francisco on the way here," Brock said.

I frowned. "San Francisco is, like, not even remotely on the way to Seattle from Alaska. It's way, way, way out of the way, in fact."

He nodded. "Yeah, obviously, but Zane asked me to fly him to San Francisco. So I did."

I blinked, my heart managing to skip a beat at the same time that my stomach lurched into my heart. "But I'm here."

"He texted you, and then called you, but you didn't answer."

I swallowed hard. "I lost my phone, and my contract was up anyway, so I got a new phone and a new number with a different provider when I moved up here."

"Well, Zane is in San Francisco, looking for you."

"But…I'm here."

"And Zane was so upset when you didn't answer your phone that he threw his against the wall and smashed it."

"Zane went to San Francisco? To find me?" I asked again.

Brock nodded. "Sure did."

My shoulders shook, and I blinked back tears, and then sobbed. And the sob shook something loose in my stomach, and I had to lurch off the bed and stumble-run to the bathroom to puke. But I'd already puked up everything I'd eaten, so all I could do was dry heave bile.

I felt Claire beside me, holding my hair back. "You've been sick a lot lately," she remarked.

I nodded. "It sucks. It won't go away. I think I've beaten it and then it comes back."

A beat of silence. And then Claire, her voice oddly tense and quiet. "I just had a thought. You're not gonna like it, and it's probably stupid and crazy and dumb."

I heaved again, and then felt the nausea subside enough that I could sit up and wipe my mouth. "What?"

"You've been getting sick pretty much every day for the last week, right?"

"Off and on for longer than that."

"And correct me if I'm wrong, but for the most part you've only been getting sick…in the mornings."

I slumped sideways against the tub. "Ohmygod."

"Right?"

Tears trickled down my face. "No. No-no-no. *No.* No no no no no no."

"When was your last period, honey?" Claire asked, her voice soft and sympathetic.

"I had one right after I got back from Ketchikan, and then this month…" I thought back. "I just had a period. It was light and spotty, but—"

"The one right after Ketchikan, was it normal?"

I twisted to pillow my head on my forearms on the edge of the tub. "No," I moaned. "It was light and spotty too."

Claire patted my shoulder. "I'll run to the corner store for a couple tests."

"What the fuck do I do, Claire?" I sobbed.

"Take a test, first."

"Or seven."

"Or seven," Claire agreed. "And then you take a breath, and think, and then you go see Zane."

"But…but—"

Claire smoothed her hand in circles on my back. "You know I'll be here with you every step of the way, right? No matter what."

I couldn't answer, on account of being too busy bawling my eyes out.

FOURTEEN

Zane

SIX HOURS AND THREE STOPOVERS LATER, I DRAGGED MY ass into Badd's Bar and Grill. It was ten p.m. on a Friday, so the bar was packed and chaotic. The twins were set up in a corner, jamming, Canaan on an acoustic guitar, Corin on one of those drums that was a box he sat on and slapped with his hands, each with his own mic. Bax and Bast were tending bar, Lucian and Dru serving tables, Xavier bussing.

They all saw me shuffle through the door, and Bast immediately flipped a rocks glass in the air, set it on the service bar, and poured a hefty measure of

Bulleit, nudging it in my direction. I made my way through the crowded floor to the service bar and slammed back the bourbon.

"Brock texted me," Bast said, leaning close to be heard over the hubbub.

"She wasn't there," I said, ignoring his statement.

"I know." Bast grabbed me by the shirt and hauled me so we were nose-to-nose. "She moved to Seattle."

I shrugged. "Okay."

"Which is where Brock is." He let me go and smoothed out my shirt, a weird, shit-eating grin on his face.

"Okay."

Bast shoved my shoulder. "*Think*, dumbfuck."

I scowled at him, exhausted from a long day of travel and even more exhausted from disappointment. "If you've got something to say, then fucking say it, Sebastian. I'm in no mood for bullshit games."

"Brock is in Seattle, because his new girlfriend is in Seattle." He paused. "And Mara is in Seattle."

"And what's your point?"

Bast hissed in disgust. "How do you think *Brock* knows *Mara* is in Seattle?"

I stared at him for a moment, and then it sunk in. "Oh. *Ohhhhh*. He *saw* her?"

Bast tugged his phone out of his back pocket,

unlocked it, and handed it to me.

In a gray bubble was a message from Brock: **So my girlfriend is Mara's best friend, Claire. Mara is in Seattle. I'm in her living room with her right now.**

I groaned, handing the phone back. "Fuck me. Of *course* Brock's new girlfriend is Mara's best friend."

Bast grinned. "So now you can go see her."

I shook my head. "If she wanted to see me, she would have answered my text. She would have answered my call, or returned it. She would have fucking mentioned she was moving." I trudged, depressed, upstairs, ignoring Bast's attempts to call me back, to talk sense into me.

I wasn't interested in sense.

A fist pounding on my bedroom door woke me up the next morning; I peered at my clock: 9:08 a.m.

"What?" I snarled.

"Get your mopey ass out of bed, you stupid lazy motherfucker," I heard Bax shout. "Someone's here to see you."

"Unless it's Jack Daniels himself with a barrel of bourbon, tell them to go away." I rolled over and pulled the blankets higher.

"You really don't want that," Bax answered.

"The fuck do you know about what I want?" I growled.

"In this case, more than you," Bax said.

"Zane, get out of bed and come out here." That was Brock.

"Thought you were in Seattle with *Claire*."

"I was. And now I'm here, and I didn't come alone."

"Tell Claire I said hi," I said. "Now shut the fuck up and leave me the fuck alone."

"Open the door in the next three seconds or I kick it in and drag you out of bed," Bax shouted.

I didn't bother sitting up. "I'll break your god-damn kneecaps if you come in here."

"One."

"I'm serious, Bax. Don't do it. You'll just hurt yourself worse, and then *I'll* hurt you even more."

"Two."

"I'm fucking serious, asshole."

"Three." There was a pause. "Okay, I'm kicking the door down."

I heard a loud thud, and a splintering sound.

"Ow." I heard Bax groaning in pain. "Ow, my leg, ow, ow, ow, fuck my leg—fuck, my leg, ow."

I ignored it.

Another kick, more of Bax shouting in pain, and

I laughed despite myself. "Can't even kick down a flimsy door in one kick?" I taunted. "Pussy."

And then I heard another voice. A softer one. A more feminine one. A sweet, familiar voice. "Bax, stop. You'll reopen your injury. I'll go in there. This is a private conversation anyway." I heard my doorknob rattle. "Zane? It's me…it's Mara. Open up, please."

"Fuck," I mumbled under my breath. "Fine, I'm coming," I said, louder.

I rolled out of bed, tugged on a pair of shorts, and unlocked my door, sighing in frustration at the splintered area below the doorknob. I opened the door.

"You gotta kick just to the side of the knob," I said to Bax, pointing at the door. "The latch is the weakest spot."

Mara was standing there, stunning, breathtaking, and looking just as miserable as I felt. She was dressed in tight black yoga pants and a pink crewneck sweatshirt with the word "PINK" across the chest, a pair of leopard print TOMS on her feet.

"Hi." She whispered the word, staring at her feet.

I stood frozen, unsure what to say, how to feel, what to think. "Hey."

She finally raised her eyes to mine, and I saw that her beautiful green/brown/gray eyes were red-rimmed from crying. "We need to talk, Zane."

I really didn't like the tone in her voice, or that phrasing. "Okay. Come on in."

She slipped past me into my bedroom and sat on the edge of my bed. She had a small black purse in her hands, and was twisting the strap between her fingers and thumb. "About, uh, the reason I didn't answer your text or call—"

"I figured you didn't want to see me."

She reached out and took my hand. "No, Zane. No. I lost my phone, and then got a new contract and a new number. I just...I figured you wouldn't be calling me anyway, since you didn't for like a month and a half."

"So you would have answered my call?"

She nodded. "Of course. I was a complete mess for the first month, waiting for you to call or text."

I growled. "Shit."

She leaned against me, her head on my shoulder. "You went to San Francisco to find me?"

"Yeah, I did."

A long, awkward, tense silence, and then Mara sat up straight, unzipped her purse, and pulled something out, a white stick inside a Ziploc bag. "So, we have to talk."

My heart lurched. "So you said. What...um, what do we have to talk about?" I glanced at her hands, at the thing she was holding. "This isn't about us being together, is it?"

She bobbled her head from side to side. "Yes, and no."

"What's that mean, Mara?"

She opened her hands, and extended the baggie and the object inside it to me. "Look."

It was a white plastic stick with a small oval opening in the middle and a tab on one end covered by a pink lid. To the left of the oval opening was the word "pregnant" with two vertical lines beside it, and then beneath that the words "not pregnant" with a single vertical line.

I stared at the stick, blinking. Processing.

The stick had two pink vertical lines in the opening.

I turned my head to look at Mara. "Um. Am I... am I—is this what I think it is?"

She nodded. "I'm pregnant, Zane."

Everything inside me twisted, lurched, sank, and leapt all at once. "You're pregnant."

She nodded again. "Yes. That's the eighth test I've taken, and I had a blood test at a doctor's office."

I swallowed hard. "You're pregnant. With my— with *our* child."

She eyed me, and then turned her gaze to her feet, pulling away from me. "Yes. I'm—I'm sorry."

There was so much going on inside me, in my

head, in my heart, that I almost missed what she'd
said. "Wait. Why are you sorry?"

She lifted one shoulder, a tiny, miserable gesture.
"I—you...I mean, how does this work?"

I felt emotions rise up, fierce, sudden, and intense. I lifted her so she was sitting on my lap, cradled
in my arms. "Mara. I flew to San Francisco to find
you, because I wanted to be with you."

She sniffled and looked up at me. "You did?"

"Well, yeah, of course." I smiled down at her. "I
want to be with you. I don't know how this works,
Mara, but I want us to try and figure it out. I want—I
want *us*. I want *you*."

"You let me leave."

I let out a harsh breath. "I was an idiot. I...I'm
still not sure if I'm...if I'm good enough for you, but
I'll try. I can't help but need you. I tried living without
you, and I can't do it."

"Why wouldn't you be good enough, Zane?"
Mara asked.

I couldn't quite look at her as I admitted to
her what I'd barely admitted to myself. "I shouldn't
be here. I shouldn't be alive. The bullet that killed
Marco...should have killed me. He should be alive
with his wife and son, but he's not, and I'm here, and I
know logically it doesn't make any sense, but I just...I
feel—god*dammit*. I feel like I'm...like I'm not good

enough for you. Like I don't deserve to be alive, much less deserve someone like you."

She took my face in her hands. "I know I can't erase how you feel just by saying something wise or whatever, Zane. But...I'm glad you're here. I'm sorry your best friend died, and I know that's a scar you'll bear forever, that's pain you'll never get over. You don't have to, and you shouldn't. He died, and you're allowed to mourn him and miss him. But you're not at fault. You don't deserve to die just because he had a wife and kid to take care of. You're alive, and I need you, Zane. I'm so, so glad you're alive, that you're... that there's a chance for us. For this to work. I want—I *need* this to work, Zane."

I held her gaze. "And all I can say right now is that...I'll try."

"But I'm pregnant, Zane. I'm going to have a baby." She slid off my lap and sat turned toward me, her gaze on mine wary but fierce. "I'm keeping it, Zane. That was never a question. I hope you understand that."

"Nothing else even entered my mind, Mara." I took her hands in mine. "We'll just have to figure this out together."

"I just moved to Seattle."

"And I can't leave Ketchikan."

"So...how does this work?"

I shook my head. "I don't know, honey. I'm still in shock, but I know we can figure something out."

"You're not mad? You're not…upset with me?"

I frowned. "We created a life together, Mara. That week with you, it…it *meant* something. Shit— it meant *everything*. Every time I was with you, they were the most incredible moments of my entire life. Some people might say what we did was irresponsible and reckless, but I can't make myself care." I palmed her cheek, my thumb brushing over her cheekbone. "You're pregnant. With *my* child. We made that child in the most incredible week of our lives. How could I be mad or upset about that?"

She sniffled. "I was…I was so scared, Zane. I'm still scared. I don't know how to do this! I don't know how to…I don't know how to be a mother. Hell, I don't even know how to be a *girlfriend*." She twisted, buried her face in my bare chest, and her shoulders began to heave. "I thought you'd be mad at me. I thought…I was afraid you'd resent me."

"Why the hell would I be mad?"

She shrugged, speaking to my chest, her words muffled. "I don't know. Because I was tying you down. Burdening you with a kid you don't want. Trapping you, somehow. And…when you let me leave, and didn't call or text…I guess I just figured you were done with me, with us."

"*Let* you leave?"

"Yes, *let* me leave. I spent that whole night hoping you'd ask me to stay. I knew it was stupid and crazy, but if you'd told me you wanted me to stay here with you, I would have. I mean, I didn't dare say anything because I knew exactly how stupid the idea was, but…it's what I wanted. Right up until I went through security, I kept hoping you'd be like 'Mara, wait!' But you left, and then I never heard from you again. So I knew it was stupid. That I'd been stupid to think what we had was something worth—shit, I don't know…something worth having, I guess. Like, why would you want me? Why would you want to tie yourself down to one woman forever when you can have as many as you want, any day of the week?"

"Mara, that's not—"

She kept going, ignoring my outburst. "And then…and then I was feeling sick, and I thought it was just a weird flu or something. But then I left work early because I'd been puking and I walked into Claire's and my apartment and she was there with Brock, on the couch, having sex. With *Brock*. Your brother. My best friend. Having sex on my couch." She shuddered. "And then it turned out I didn't have the flu, I was fucking *pregnant*. So I had to come here. I had to see you, I had to—I had to tell you in person. Because I…I owed it to you to tell you in person."

I cradled her as she cried, then. I just let her cry, holding her, running my hands through her hair. Eventually, her crying quieted and she pushed away from my chest.

"Thanks for letting me be a baby."

I snorted. "Mara, crying about all this doesn't make you a baby. I'm a dude so I don't cry, but ask any of my brothers…I've been a miserable bastard for the last two months."

"Part of me is sorry that you've been miserable, but part of me is glad that you've been as upset as I have. Is that weird of me?"

"That makes complete sense."

She craned her neck to stare up at me. "I can't tell if you're making fun of me or not."

"I'd never make fun of you, Mara."

"I don't mind being teased, but I'm just so…emotional and hormonal right now, and sometimes I don't make any sense to myself. Like, the thoughts I have, the emotions that go through me…is this what it's going to be like for the next seven or eight months?"

I shrugged. "I have no idea, Mara. I know absolutely nothing about pregnancy." I leaned her backward to lay her on the bed, pushing her sweatshirt up to look at her belly. "I mean, how far along are you?"

She watched me, bemused, as I touched her belly with my hand. "I don't think you can see or feel anything yet," she said. "I'm eight weeks. I mean, obviously it was one of those times we didn't use a condom."

"I thought you were on the Depo shot or whatever it's called."

Mara let out a shuddering breath. "I *was*. But no pill or shot is ever one hundred percent effective. There's always a minute chance you can still get pregnant. I mean, I've heard stories about girls getting pregnant when they were on birth control *and* the guy was wearing a condom."

"Life always finds a way," I said.

She rolled her eyes at me. "Okay, Ian Malcom."

I laughed. "It's true, though, right?"

Now that she was lying down, Mara looked absolutely exhausted. She had dark circles under her eyes, and her eyelids were sliding closed and then opening again, looking heavy. I went to pull her sweatshirt down, but she latched onto my wrist, holding my palm against her belly.

"You're not upset?" she whispered, peering at me through half-closed eyes.

I shook my head. "No, Mara. Not at all." I curled up on the edge of the bed beside her. "I'm a little scared and nervous, and I have no idea how to be a boyfriend or a father or anything, but...I'm in this. I'm in it with you."

"Just promise me…" she trailed off and started over. "Just promise me if you're not…if you don't really want this, or me, that you won't pretend and you won't lie to me, and you won't stick around just because you think you should. I'd rather never be with you than have you walk out on me…on me and the baby…"

I pulled the blankets up over her. "Sweetheart, I have a lot of faults. But I'm not a faker, and I'm not a liar. And I'll *never* abandon you. I'll *never* walk out on you." I palmed her belly under the blankets. "Either of you. Never. Okay? I never leave anyone behind, and I have the medal to prove it."

She cracked one eyelid open. "What? What are you talking about? What medal?"

I sighed. "I don't make a big deal of it, but…I was awarded a bronze star."

She opened both eyes then. "And you're just now mentioning it?"

"It was…when Marco died, um…he and I were cut off from our unit, and I did some crazy shit and got a bronze star out of it. But Marco died, so it was kind of…I don't want to say meaningless, but it's hard for me to feel proud of it. I dunno. Can we talk about it another time?"

"Of course." Mara offered me a sleepy, tender smile. "Thanks for telling me."

I leaned over her and kissed her lips softly. "You should rest."

She nodded. "I haven't really slept much the last couple days."

I curled around her as she faded into sleep. When she was snoring softly—that fucking ridiculously adorable snore of hers that made my heart melt and pitter-patter all at once, her mouth open slightly, the cute little button nose, her long eyelashes dark against her cheek, her thick blonde hair sweeping over her face.

I brushed her hair away from her eyes and mouth with my index finger, feeling a deep, sharp, intense protectiveness toward her, a fierce need to never let her out of my sight again. To keep her safe. To make sure she never felt such fear again, to make sure she knew she was take care of.

Loved.

I slid off the bed and crept out of the room, closing the door behind me, finding literally all of my brothers in the apartment, nonchalantly sipping coffee. Xavier was in the kitchen, scrambling a giant pan of eggs and tending to a giant skillet of bacon, using his left and right hands at the same time to do totally separate things. The twins were playing Xbox, of course, and Lucian was reading a paperback book as thick as a dictionary; Brock was on the loveseat with

Claire—Mara's diminutive but stunning blonde best friend—on his lap, chatting in low tones to each other; Bax was standing behind the couch watching the twins play a first person shooter game, and Bast had Dru on his lap on the couch beside the twins, watching them play as well.

When I entered the living room, clad in nothing but a pair of shorts, everything stopped. Corin paused their game, and all eyes turned to me.

I looked from brother to brother in turn, and then to Dru and then Claire—Brock obviously knew what was going on, judging by the wary but hopeful expression on his face, and Claire just looked unreadable, fearful if nothing else.

"What?" I demanded.

"So? What's going on?" Brock asked.

I scrubbed my hand over my scalp in irritation. "Can I get a cup of fucking coffee before we start the interrogation?"

"Where's Mara?" Claire asked.

"Sleeping." I gestured at my room. "She was exhausted."

Claire sighed. "She was a mess. She's barely slept in days."

Dru appeared in front of me with a huge mug of coffee in one hand and a plate heaped high with bacon and eggs in the other.

"Thanks, Dru," I said, and sat on the floor in front of the coffee table, digging into the food.

The room was silent then except for the clink of forks on plates and the occasional slurp of coffee. Finally finished, I leaned back against the couch between Bast's and Dru's legs.

"So, um. Brock and Claire, I'm guessing you two already know, but, uh, Mara—" I swallowed hard, because saying it like this, in this setting, was a lot harder than I thought it'd be. "Mara's pregnant."

There was a stunned silence.

"Holy shit," Bax said, eying me. "So...is this a congratulations thing, or is this a disaster mitigation planning thing?"

"I think it's a congratulations thing," I answered. "I think I'm still sort of—"

"In shock?" Canaan suggested.

"Stupefied?" Corin said at the same time.

"Gobsmacked?" Canaan.

"Stunned stupid?" Corin.

"Blindsided?" Canaan.

"Flabbergasted?" Corin.

"Enough, you two!" I shouted. "Yes, it's safe to say I'm a little surprised."

Dru set her feet on the coffee table, ankles crossed, her calves resting against my shoulder. "Does this mean I get a sister?"

"I'm not sure what it means, yet." I patted her legs. "But I'm hoping so, yes."

"Well...you're going to be together, right?" Claire asked, her tone sharp.

"That's the idea, yes," I said between sips of coffee. "I just...we're not quite sure of the logistics yet."

"What's the hang up?" Bax asked. "You like her, she likes you, you made a kid together...what is there to figure out?"

I snorted a laugh. "Everything, you big dumb lummox. She just got a brand new job in Seattle, and I can't exactly just pick up and move down there. Dad's will stipulations won't let me, and I don't think I could leave you guys right now anyway."

"Awww, he really likes us," Bax quipped. "But for real, though, it's not like you can do a long distance thing seeing as she's gonna pop out a kid in a few months."

"Now you see the issue," I said. "It's not exactly simple."

Brock shot me a look. "I'm gonna be going back and forth to Seattle pretty frequently to see Claire and to bring her here, so you're welcome to come along, and I'll bring Mara up whenever, too. It'd be helpful to have some help with the cost of the fuel since that shit ain't cheap."

"That'll work in the interim," I said, "but we

gotta figure out a way to be together full time. I don't know shit about pregnancy, but I do know there's a lot of appointments and stuff, and I'm not gonna miss those."

"Meaning, she has to find a way to move up here," Bax said.

I nodded. "Yeah, but I can't expect her to just… uproot herself."

"And, just saying, since I know Mara best, she can't not work," Claire said. "She's way too restless for that. She's taken care of herself her whole life, so she's not gonna just sit around eating bon bons. And nothing against you guys or your bar, but there's not a snowball's chance in hell she's gonna work here. She had to wait tables in high school and she absolutely hated it."

Lucian piped up for the first time. "What's her degree and experience in?"

Claire glanced at Lucian. "Her degree is in business, with a minor in communications, plus she has a military nursing license, but I'm not sure how that transfers into civilian licensing, since neither of us were interested in the medical field once we got our walking papers. Most of her civilian experience is in HR." She crinkled her forehead. "Why do you ask?"

Lucian shrugged, setting his book face down on his thigh. "One of the regulars was telling me that he was thinking about putting an ad out for a position at his firm."

"What's his firm do?" Claire asked. "And what's the position?"

"It's a marketing firm," Lucian said. "I guess it's new and it's expanding fast. He's in dire need of someone to run his office so he can focus on the actual accounts. Right now it's just him and his cousin, who's also his business partner. They're trying to run the accounts and manage the office at the same time."

"She's third from the top in the HR department at a *huge* tech company, and making close to six figures," Claire said. "It'd be a massive step backward for her to take a job as the office manager of some rinky-dink marketing firm in Ketchikan, Alaska."

Lucian didn't answer immediately. "It was just a thought," he said, his voice quiet.

Claire sighed. "I'm sorry, I didn't mean to insult you or your friend's company, or Ketchikan. I love it here, honestly. But what I said is true. I mean, I can't speak for Mara, but—"

"We're all kind of trying to speak for Mara and make plans for her," I said. "I think we need to just take this one step at a time. Lucian, thank you for the suggestion. I'll pass it on to Mara."

Lucian nodded and went back to his book.

I glanced around the room, realizing everyone

was still eyeing me expectantly. "I'm done talking about this for now. I need to process things. I literally just found out my entire life is changing, and I'm not really ready to hash it all out right here, right now." I reached up and snatched a controller from Corin. "Now, how do you play this game?"

It was eleven thirty that night, and I was behind the bar with Bast, slinging booze to a crowded bar. We'd been slammed all evening, to the point that there really wasn't much opportunity for anything but work. I'd seen Mara briefly a couple hours before, but she'd been on the way out the door with Claire and Dru. She'd given me a quick kiss and explained that they were going to find somewhere quiet to have girl talk.

Now, though, the bar was starting to die down a little, leaving Bast and I time to lean back and breathe. Time for Bast to give me a look that hinted at questions to follow.

"Never in a million years did I think you'd be the first of us to be a daddy," he said.

I laughed. "Never in a million years did I think *any* of us would be parents."

"But yet here you are, with a pregnant girlfriend."

I poured a shot of bourbon for each of us. "Here

I am, with a pregnant girlfriend."

Bast clinked his glass against mine, downed his shot, and poured another for us both. "So."

I took my glass, eyeing my older brother. "So."

"You love her?"

I slammed back the shot and then tossed the shot glass into the sink. "Yes."

"You're sure?" He crossed his arms over his chest and glared hard at me. "Don't hook into this because you think you have to. You can take care of your responsibility to her and the kid without trying to make something work neither of you are sure about."

I nodded. "I'm sure. I mean, I have no clue what the fuck I'm gonna do, but I'm sure I love her. It's not just about the kid. I haven't even really processed that as a reality yet. Right now, I'm just trying to figure out how to be in a relationship."

A trio of young girls angled up to the bar and Sebastian leaned forward on his forearms, shooting them his trademark sexy bartender grin. They tittered and bent over to offer him a look down their low-cut blouses, but he didn't even glance that way. Getting the message, they ordered chocolate martinis and left a nice cash tip when he handed them their drinks.

He wiped the stupid grin off his face, stuffing the tip into the jar. "It's complicated, being in a relationship. But it's also a lot easier than you'd think."

I eyed him. "That makes *no* sense."

He shrugged. "It does, though. You gotta be thinking about her all the time. It takes some adjustment. Like, you wanna go somewhere, go hit up a bar for drinks, or take a ride, or sleep in, or hit up downtown for breakfast, you gotta think about her. Everything you do affects her. It's not just you anymore. She'll want you to do shit you won't want to do, tell you what to wear, nag about the fuckin' toilet seat, all that bullshit, and it's all exactly that, just bullshit. Being around someone all day, every day, putting her first, in everything…that's the part that's harder."

I snickered. "Been married two months and suddenly you're a relationship expert?"

"We've been living together for six months, so I'm farther ahead than you, asshole."

I acceded his point with a shrug and a nod. "I guess you're right. You make it sound like it's…easy, though. Like, what the fuck have I been afraid of all this time?"

He bobbed his head side to side. "I was as committed to casual, no-strings sex same as you, if not more. That shit was my *life*, Zane. But then Dru appeared and everything just…changed. It's not like suddenly I understood relationships or had this come to Jesus moment about the sanctity of sex or some shit. The change was *Dru*. I can't fathom being in a relationship with anyone else. I didn't want one in the first place, but I couldn't *not* be with her. It was just this…it's a *need*, man. Remember when I said the only way you'll know is if you *know*? Well, if what I just said makes any sense to you at all, then you *know*." He hissed in frustration. "Shit, I don't know how to put it any better than that."

"No, dude, that makes perfect sense, now."

He grinned at me. "But once you're in it for a while, there is this moment like holy shit, what was I so scared about? This relationship shit ain't so bad after all."

"How so?"

"I grew up taking care of you guys and myself, right? So I can cook, I can clean, I can do laundry, all that shit. I did it for all of you guys *and* Dad after Mom died, and I kept doing it until Xavier left for Stanford, and I kept doing it for myself. So, I'm not this asshole gorilla who thinks women belong in the kitchen. But having a woman around all the time? It's amazing. I mean, the shit she thinks of, it's just all this stuff I'd have never even considered."

"Like the way she organized the kitchen?" I said, thinking about how much more neat and organized and sensible the kitchen was, now that Dru lived with us.

"Or the laundry? I mean you and Xavier do your

own, but she folds my things different, and I don't even know how or why, but the clothes are just...*softer*, and smell better."

I laughed. "That's called better detergent and fabric softener, doofus."

He rolled his eyes. "You know what I'm talking about, fucker."

"I've gotta admit, I love the food she buys. Like, I'd have never even thought about it, but she stocks all this food for actual meals, not just, like, fuckin' burgers and cold cuts and mac 'n cheese and shit. Like, we can make fuckin' chili and pasta and baked chicken and shit."

"That's what I'm saying! She just makes things better, and she's not even trying. It's just how she does life." He nudged me. "And getting to go to bed at night with her? And waking up next to her every morning? I'm not even talking about sex, I just mean going to bed and waking up with her. I wake up happier every single morning just because she's there, because I get to have my arms around her all night."

I nodded. "A few months ago I would have ripped you to pieces for that mushy bullshit, but now?" I tapped the bar, thinking of the nights I'd spent with Mara. "I get it, now."

"There's nothing like it, is there?"

I shook my head. "There really isn't."

The women came back at that moment, all three with their arms linked together, cackling like a pack of hyenas. Brock, who was on the floor tonight, stood at the service bar, staring at the women just like Bast and I were.

"That's a hell of a sight, ain't it boys?" he asked.

Bast and I glanced at him.

"You got that right, brother," I said, and then laughed as a thought hit me. "You know, guys, if things keep going like this, we're gonna have to think about expanding our living situation. There ain't no way eight couples are all gonna fit into two little apartments."

Brock gave me a look. "Damn, son, you might be on to something." He grinned. "Especially you, with a baby on the way."

I nodded. "That's what I'm saying." I jerked a thumb at Bast. "I can't imagine it'll be too much longer before this guy is making his own announcement."

Bast held up his hands. "Whoa, man, don't go jinxing me. I just got married, I'm not ready for that yet."

"Yeah, neither am I, but here I am."

Brock snickered at me. "What, didn't Bast give you the talk about how babies are made? You see, when a man and woman *really* like each other—"

I threw a lime slice at his face, nailing him dead

center between the eyes. "Shut up, fucker. And besides, I wouldn't mock too much, since you could be next on the surprise-I'm-a-daddy-train."

Brock's eyes widened. "Hey, don't jinx me either. Just because *you* rode bareback doesn't mean *I'm* going to."

"You can't try and tell me you guys haven't been tempted." I looked at him and then Bast.

"He has a point, Brock," Bast said.

Brock groaned. "I know, I know. And actually, if you want real honesty, we have. Once. The first time I went up to see her, after like a week without her? We couldn't wait, and neither of us had anything, so we just…"

I lifted an eyebrow. "And *that*, brother, is how babies are made."

Brock rubbed the back of his neck. "Yeah, no shit. Bareback is damned addictive."

"Sure as hell is," Bast agreed.

When we both glanced at him in surprise, he just stared back at us.

"What? We're married. We may not be actively trying for one, but if Dru does get pregnant…honestly, I'd be happy. Scared shitless, but happy." He shrugged. "We had a moment a few months ago where we thought she was pregnant, but it was a false alarm. That made me think about things, though, and

I realized I wouldn't mind if she got pregnant."

The women had clustered around us at that point, and Dru reached across the bar, grabbed her husband by shirt and hauled him in for a kiss. "You'd be happier than a pig in shit if I was to get pregnant, you big macho fuckstick," she said. "You know you want a baby girl."

"Yeah, true," Bast said as she released him. "But, babe, I've never even *held* a baby before," he said.

Dru tapped his nose. "It's easy. You just don't drop it and don't squeeze too hard."

Bast chuckled. "Well, yeah, that much I know. It's the rest I'm not sure about. Changing diapers and making bottles and all that shit? And what about when the kid starts talking back? I mean, how do you go about raising a human being so they're not a complete fuckup?"

My heart was racing as Bast talked. "Those are all pretty pertinent questions, I'd say." I eyed my older brother. "You took care of us all, so you've got some experience."

Bast shrugged. "I kept you from starving and made sure you went to school. Barely counts."

I shook my head. "No, man, it was more than that. You took care of us. None of us have forgotten that."

Mara cut in, quietly. "None of you boys have

anything to worry about. You're sweet, caring men. You'll take care of us, and when you become fathers, you'll be amazing at that, too." She kept her gaze on me. "All of us are proof that life isn't ever perfect, and parents aren't perfect, and things happen. My dad wasn't necessarily a good father or even a good person, but he did his best to love me, and I think I turned out okay. Same with my mom. Just do your best. That's all there really is, I'd say."

"Now *that's* damn truth," Claire said. "Love is all you need."

Canaan and Corin, who'd snuck up at some point, started singing The Beatles song Claire had un-wittingly referenced, getting laughter from everyone.

Bast slugged my shoulder. "I've got closing. Get out of here. Be with your girl."

I glanced at him. "You're sure?"

He snorted at me. "Bitch, I worked open to close by myself every single day for years. I *got* this."

I ducked under the service bar and went upstairs with Mara. We didn't talk. We didn't say a word, in fact. The second we got into my room, we closed the door, locked it, and stripped each other naked in re-cord time.

We didn't say a word as I lowered her to the bed, kissed every inch of her body, and then slowly slid bare inside her. Nor did we speak as we moved together in perfect synch, breathing mated, lips touching now and again, hips meeting and parting in a slow, fierce rhythm.

We drew it out, held off our climax until we couldn't wait any longer. Mara trembled beneath me, her thighs wrapped around my waist, her hands cupped around the back of my head to pull me closer, to clutch me into a kiss.

I felt her orgasm burst through her, felt it in the trembling grip of her fingers, in the crushing squeeze of her thighs, in the clamping tightness of her channel around me, and I lost myself then, giving in to the climax, pouring myself into her.

We came together, our eyes locked, groaning in unison.

"God, I love you, Amarantha," I whispered as I quaked and thrusted through my climax.

She sobbed against my shoulder, clinging tightly to me. "Zane...god, Zane. I love you."

I lost track, then, of how many times we breathed that phrase to each other, over and over and over again that night, into dawn, until we collapsed together, exhausted and sated and deliriously happy.

FIFTEEN

Mara

"ARE YOU SURE THIS IS WHAT YOU WANT TO DO?" Claire asked, for the tenth time. "I mean, I know you love the man and all, but this is a big step."

For the second time in three months, I was packing my life into boxes. I had ten full size moving boxes already packed and taped, and was working on the last one. My clothes were in suitcases and giant black contractor bags and I was leaving Claire all my furniture, so everything should fit nicely into the cargo hold of Brock's seaplane.

I sighed and stuffed the last newspaper wrapped

mug into the box. "Yes, Claire. For the ninety-five thousandth time. I'm absolutely, positively, unequivocally *sure* I'm ready to move in with Zane. It's long past time. This past month has been hellish, only seeing him on the weekends or whenever Brock can make it down here." I folded the flaps in and rolled the packing tape across the middle of the box and then along the opposite edges. "And besides, Seattle never really felt like home. I mean, *you* feel like home, but Seattle doesn't. That job wasn't right for me either. They would have wanted me to advance, and eventually I would've been a department head or something, and maybe once upon a time that would have been what I wanted, but it's just not anymore."

"So what are you going to do in Ketchikan? Play housewife?"

I shrugged, not quite able to look at Claire. "Yeah, I guess."

Claire sighed and slumped down to sit cross-legged next to me. "I'm sorry, honey. That was a bitchy thing to say." She sniffled. "It's just that...I just got you back. And this whole thing with Zane feels fast, and—I'm gonna miss you, and..."

I hugged her to me. "Listen, whore. You're gonna see me like every week. You're dating Zane's brother, remember? Who also lives in Ketchikan? Something tells me we'll see each other more this way than if we lived together, especially with the weird-ass hours you keep."

"I know, I know." She sighed. "I've actually been thinking about doing some telecommuting from Ketchikan myself, just so I can see him more."

"That bar, those boys, the city…it all has a way of growing on you, doesn't it?"

"It sure does. Like fucking tentacles."

I laughed. "Exactly. But in this case, the tentacles are attached to a really hot, sexy, amazing man."

"And a beautiful city," Claire added.

"And a really kickass bar."

"And a shitload of sexy, funny, loyal brothers."

"It's kind of ridiculous, isn't it?" I leaned my head on Claire's shoulder. "How much awesomeness one little town in Alaska can hold?"

"For real, though," Claire tugged on my hair. "You're not really going to sit around and twiddle your thumbs all day, are you?"

"No, I'm gonna make him sandwiches and shuffle around the house in fuzzy pink slippers vacuuming with my Hoover." I slapped her shoulder. "No, dumbass. I'm gonna work at that marketing firm. I can manage the office in my sleep, and then I'll have the baby, and eventually I'll go back to work. Maybe eventually I'll buy in as a partner. For now, it's something to keep me busy until the baby gets here, and then I can take some time off. I'll need to learn how to be a mommy, and besides, the whole HR thing was just how things happened. It was never something I really wanted to do as a career for my whole life. I never really *did* know, to be honest. It was a job I could do, and it paid the bills, but it wasn't, like, my dream."

"That makes sense, I guess."

I labeled the box with a Sharpie, and then toyed with the cap, trying to formulate my thoughts. "But what's funny is, I *can* see myself being a stay-at-home mom and wife. It's weird, because I never *ever* thought that would be me, but I've been thinking about this a lot, and it doesn't sound so bad."

Claire stared at me. "Who are you and what have you done with my best friend?"

I rolled my eyes at her. "Oh, shut up. I know I'm not some, like, domestic goddess or whatever, but...I can learn. I'm not gonna force myself into a career I don't love just because society says that's what the modern woman is supposed to want. What if I'm discovering that I *want* to stay home and take care of my husband and baby? What's wrong with that?"

Claire stood up, carried the box to the stack of boxes near the door, and then sat back down beside me on the floor. "There's nothing *wrong* with it, but I just...I can't fathom it for myself, that's all."

"You don't have to want the same thing I want.

You just have to keep being my best friend, even if I never lose the baby weight and start watching daytime talk shows."

"I draw the line at *The View*, Mare. You start watching that, we're through."

I surreptitiously removed the Sharpie's cap, reached out, and swiped the black tip across the back of her hand. "You're stuck with me for life, ho. If you marry Brock, we'll be sisters."

"Hey now, I'm still getting used to the idea of *dating* him," she said, taking the Sharpie from me and turning my errant line into an interesting design.

"It's been three months, you lunatic."

"And it's still fucking weird."

"What's weird about it?"

She shrugged. "I don't know, everything. When I'm not around him, I miss him, but then sometimes I get the urge to do something impulsive, like I used to. But then I remember Brock, and I don't do it, but I'm still thinking about it. Like, I see a hot guy at the bar or something, and the instinct is to hook up with him, or do a bathroom B-J or something, just for fun. But then I remember Brock, and I don't. When I'm with him, I can't imagine life without him. And that's weird enough as it is. And sometimes we just…want totally different things, and I don't know how to reconcile the differences."

"Like what?"

She lay down on the floor and stared at the ceiling. "Sex, for one thing. When we're fucking, it's literally mind-blowing. But I like...other stuff, and he doesn't. He says he's willing to try new things, but never actually ends up trying anything with me. Or family, we just have different ideas about family. I'm estranged from my parents, mainly my dad, and Brock just doesn't understand how I won't take the first step to reconciliation. I get that he lost both his parents and would do anything to have them back, but that's not my situation. And he's always harping on it. It drives me nuts, because I didn't do anything wrong, so I'm not going to apologize, and that's what Brock keeps telling me I should do."

"If Brock is worth it, then you'll figure it out."

"It's not about him being worth it or not, it's just...in some ways we're completely different types of people and I don't know if we can bridge those differences." She sniffled, swiped a finger underneath her eyelid. "Which just sucks, because I really, *really* like Brock."

I hugged her. "Remember what you told me about keeping an open mind?" I squeezed her hard. "Time to take your own advice."

"I know. But advice is easy to give and hard to follow."

"Just take things one day at a time, and don't be a chicken."

"I'm not a chicken, I just—"

"*Bock*," I clucked, imitating a chicken, bobbing my head forward. "*Bock, bock…bockbockbock.*"

"Shut up, stupid. That doesn't even sound like a fucking chicken."

"*Bock-bock, bock-bock.*"

She swiped at me with the Sharpie, and I ducked out of the way, but then she was chasing me around the apartment, trying to draw on me with the marker. So I grabbed another Sharpie and chased her back, which turned into a Sharpie war…

When Brock showed up a few minutes later, both Claire and I were covered from fingertips to elbows in black Sharpie marks, with a few on our faces. He stood in the doorway watching as we chased each other around, cackling.

"Did I come at a bad time?" he asked.

Claire stopped, capping the marker. "Nope. Just having a little marker war."

He frowned. "You two know that's permanent marker, right? It's not going to come off for days."

Claire kept the marker behind her back, approaching Brock as if for a kiss. "It's just a little fun. It'll wash off."

"Eventually." Brock said, eyeing her suspiciously.

He should have been suspicious, too, because she was sneakily working the cap off as she sidled closer to him. And then, right as he was millimeters from her lips, she flashed her hand up and stamped a dot right on the tip of his nose.

"Gotcha!" she shouted, and then shrieked as Brock swept her off her feet in a snakebite fast movement.

He snatched the marker from her, pinned her arms to her sides with one arm, and bent her backward over his knee. "My turn," he said, his voice a deep, hot rumble.

"What are you doing?" Claire demanded, wriggling.

He tugged her shirt down, baring her tits. "Marking my territory," he explained. He signed his name with a flourish across the slope of one breast, and then the other. "There. Now it's official. Your tits are mine."

She glared at him, trying desperately to hold on to her stern, angry face. "You didn't need to write your name on them for that to be official, douchebag."

"No, but now every time you look at them, you'll be reminded."

She blinked up at him. "How much time do you think I spend staring at my tits, Brock?"

He shrugged. "It's hard for me to be objective

being a guy, and one who's ridiculously attracted to your tits."

"You're an idiot," she murmured, clearly meaning it as an endearment.

"Yes, but I'm *your* idiot." Brock kissed her, and then stood her up on her feet, tugging her shirt back into place. "Now, let's get these boxes down to the truck."

He suited action to words, propping open the door, lifting two boxes, and carrying them out the apartment and down the stairs.

I couldn't help laughing as Claire stood in front of the mirror by the front door, and pulled her shirt down to stare at Brock's handiwork. "I can't believe he signed *both* of them. And he's not even famous!"

"I think he's pretty perfect for you, Claire," I said. "You may have some differences to work out, but from where I'm standing, I'd say it'd be damn well worth it."

She glanced at me in the mirror, letting her shirt slide back into place. "Like I said before, some things are easier said than done."

Let me just say, moving is a hell of a lot easier when there are eight burly men around to help. My things were moved from the seaplane to the apartment over the bar in less than thirty minutes. Zane and I had agreed it'd make the most sense for me to live with him above the bar until we found a place of our own, so for now most of my things would go into storage in the basement beneath the bar, which was a tight, cramped space they only used for storing extra cases of liquor and as a workout room. My boxes filled it to overflowing, but it was only temporary, so Bast had said it would be fine.

Zane had condensed his clothes and stacked some in a few laundry baskets to give me room for my clothes, which was a sweet gesture, but fairly pointless, given the amount of clothing I owned. I would be able to fill the drawers with the essentials, hang up my favorite jeans and blouses and dresses in the half of the closet he'd given me, and I still had three contractor bags and two suitcases left over.

Zane pointed at the bags. "So, what's in those?"

I hung my favorite sweater in the closet. "More clothes."

He pointed at the suitcases. "And those?"

"Clothes."

He scratched his scalp. "Then…what's in all the boxes down in the basement?"

"Stuff? My snow globe collection, my mugs, pho- to albums, folders of paperwork, my coffeemaker, books, DVDs. Just...stuff." I looked around at his room, which I just now was realizing contained very little by way of personal effects. "You really don't have anything but what's in this room?"

He lifted a hand. "I was a Navy SEAL, Mara. I was either on assignment or on base, so everything I owned all fit into a footlocker and a duffel. Never got in the habit of acquiring knickknacks."

I eyed the open drawers, and then the closet. "And those are all the clothes you own?" I did a quick tally. "Six pairs of jeans, eight long sleeve shirts, ten undershirts, three button-downs, a dozen pairs of underwear, the same amount of socks, one leather jacket, and two sweaters?"

He followed my gaze. "Um, yeah?"

"We need to go shopping. You don't even have one pair of jeans for every day of the week!"

He gestured around at the tiny room. "And where are we gonna put it, babe? Not even all your clothes are gonna fit in here, much less more of mine."

"Well then, we'll just have to start apartment hunting soon, won't we?"

He sighed. "I guess so. But, just so you know, I've never done that."

I glanced at him as I refolded underwear and stacked them in the top drawer. "Done what?"

"Bought an apartment."

I laughed. "You don't buy apartments, usually, you rent them." I tilted my head. "And you've never once lived in an apartment?"

He shook his head. "Nah. I grew up here, and then joined the Navy. I lived on an aircraft carrier for a couple years, and then on bases wherever I was stationed."

"Oh, I guess that makes sense," I said. "Well, it'll be fun. We'll pick something nice together."

He eyed my leftover clothes. "Something with a lot of closet space?"

I laughed. "The kitchen can be so tiny it's nonexistent, as long as there's a lot of closet space."

He nodded, musing as he sat on the bed, watching me toss my thongs into the drawer. "I did some poking around the area while you were packing. I have a few ideas."

I abandoned the unpacking for the moment and pushed Zane onto his back on the bed. "Honestly, babe, I'm not in a hurry. I lived with Claire for three months and I never fully unpacked. I can live out of bags and laundry baskets for a while."

He curled an arm around my neck and rolled me so I was beneath him. "We're gonna need space when the baby gets here, and we're not gonna want to feel like we just moved in, either. We're gonna want to be settled. And if I'm gonna follow through on this idea

I've got, then I'm gonna have to get started."

"What's your idea?"

He kissed me slowly, and then backed off a little. "You trust me?"

I nodded. "Yeah, why?"

"Because I'd like it to be a surprise, for now."

I giggled breathily as his fingers stole under the waistband of my yoga pants. "Just…just so you know, I've been doing some reading on pregnancy, and I'm going to start nesting before too long."

"What, you're gonna turn into a bird?" He teased, sliding a finger into me.

"No, dumbass. I'm gonna start wanting to make my home ready for the baby. Decorating, organizing, things like that. It's some kind of maternal drive we get, apparently." I had to gasp then, because those talented, sorcerous fingers were doing their dark, hot, dirty magic to me, making my hips writhe.

He slid his other hand under my shirt, scraping my nipples over the fabric of my bra. "Can you give me…three months?"

"Probably?" I breathed. "Oh…oh god. Right there…"

"I'll be like six months pregnant by then, so probably getting pretty big. Not sure I'll be much help moving."

"There are eight of us, remember?"

"And I'll need help decorating."

"Dru and Claire would love that, I'm sure."

"We'll need a nursery," I said. "A little one, at least."

"When do we find out the gender?" Zane asked, now tugging my pants off completely.

"Um…between sixteen and twenty weeks, I think?"

"So another month or two?"

"Yeah…" I reached between us, finding him naked for me, bare, ready. "Why?"

"Well, if I can make this work, you'll be able to decorate the nursery right around then."

He slid into me then, and I clung to him.

"I'm gonna get a nursery?"

"And a huge closet, and everything else I can give you."

"What are you planning?" I demanded, palming his face and gazing into his deep, liquid, expressive brown eyes—he'd learned to let me see his emotions in his eyes, and I loved him for that all the more. "Tell me!"

He ignored my demand for a few minutes, and then grinned down at me as we both neared climax. "You'll see, babe. You'll see. Just trust me."

I came around him, then, biting his shoulder to muffle my screams. When I could breathe, when I could speak, I whispered in his ear. "I trust you, Zane."

He kissed me through his own climax, which came hard on the heels of mine. "You won't regret it, babe. I promise."

I clung to him as we shuddered together in the afterglow. "I know," I whispered. "I know."

EPILOGUE

Brock

IT WAS SIX IN THE MORNING, IT WAS MID-DECEMBER, AND I was sandwiched in the back seat of the Silverado between Xavier and Lucian, with Bax up front. The bed of the truck was full of power tools, tool boxes, sheets of drywall, buckets of drywalling mud, piles of two-by-fours, boxes of nails and screws, screw guns and charger packs, enough building materials to build...well, a house.

Zane was driving, an XM hard rock station on low. At least we had coffee in hand, although I still maintained it was too damn early for this shit.

"How far is this place, Zane?" I asked.

"Not far."

"And does that mean two minutes or ten minutes? My legs are going numb."

He swiveled his head to glare at me. "Three minutes, pussy."

"Shut up," I snapped. "I didn't sleep much last night and I'm too tall to be sitting in the bitch seat." I tried to adjust my legs, but they were wedged in so tight I couldn't even flex them.

"No shit, you didn't sleep much last night," Bax said with a derisive laugh. "You and Claire were up all night banging." He slammed his fist against the door of the truck, mimicking a high, breathy groan. "Oh, oh, oh, oh, Brock, oh my god Brock!"

I reached forward and slugged him on the shoulder. "Shut the fuck up, dickhead."

"What? That's what she sounds like," he said, twisting in his seat to slug me back. "Not my fault you guys are loud as fuck when you're fucking."

"Yeah, well, I haven't heard much noise coming from *your* room, I notice," I taunted.

Bax just smirked. "Maybe I do my playing *else*where."

"Yeah, like in the bathroom with Pornhub and a family size bottle of Jergens," I said.

Bax just laughed. "Hell yeah. I saw this video the

other day, man…this chick took a cock so fucking big it was a miracle she didn't pop her jaw out of socket." He dug his phone out and brought up the video he'd mentioned. "Check that shit out."

"Thanks, but no thanks," I said. "Don't need to see that."

He frowned at me. "When'd you turn into a prude? We used to text each other porn links all the time."

I shrugged. "I'm just not into that as much anymore."

"Since you met Claire, you mean," Bax said.

I nodded. "Yeah, exactly. I don't want it, and I don't need it. I get everything I could possibly want from her."

Bax handed the phone to Xavier, who watched the video with a slightly horrified expression on his face. "Good for you, I guess." He laughed when Xavier handed off the phone with a queasy expression on his face. "Speaking for myself, I don't know what I'd do without porn."

Zane laughed. "Find the right girl, and you'll understand."

Bax snorted. "Not likely. It's not like I'm going through a dry spell, I get laid plenty. I just don't bring girls back to the apartment."

"So constant sex isn't enough for you?" Xavier

asked. "You need pornography as well?"

Bax shrugged. "Need? No, I don't *need* it. I just really *like* it. And just because I get laid a lot doesn't mean I don't also need to jerk the turkey, if you know what I mean." He winked at Xavier. "You know what I'm talking about, don't you, bro?"

Xavier blushed furiously. "I am familiar with the meaning of your vulgar colloquialism, yes."

"What kinda porn do you watch? Vanilla shit? Straight fucking? Or are you into kinky shit like bukkake?"

Xavier shifted in his seat uncomfortably. "Bukkake? Is that an anime thing?"

Zane choked on his laughter, while Bax guffawed loudly.

"No, kiddo, it's not an anime thing." Bax tapped at his phone, selected a video, and handed it to Xavier. "*That* is bukkake."

Xavier watched, his expression growing increasingly disgusted. "What the…? What's the purpose of that? I genuinely do not understand."

Bax laughed again. "Different strokes for different folks. Or, in this case, a lot strokes for one person." He took the phone back. "Not your thing, huh?"

Xavier shook his head in renewed disgust. "I could have gone my whole life without seeing that. No, Baxter, that is assuredly *not* my thing."

"What *is* your thing, then?" Bax asked. "I'm just curious."

"Do I have to have a *thing*? Maybe I'm not into any of that stuff at all." Xavier said this while pretending to be absorbed in picking at a string on his jeans.

"So you're not into *any*thing?" Bax pushed. "No porn, nothing? Not even, like, *Playboy*?"

Xavier sighed. "No, if you must know. Obviously you're all aware that I'm a virgin. I'm keeping all of that for when I find the right person to share those things with." His voice strengthened, and he met Bax's curious gaze. "It's a conscious choice, I should point out. I've had plenty of...offers, both here and at school. I've even been on a few dates, but I'm just not willing to invest my time in someone I'm not immediately drawn to. And I don't believe that pornography is an accurate representation of sexual relations, nor are the practices depicted in pornography healthy mentally or physically, nor are they emotionally satisfying. It's a drug, if you ask me. Harmless fun at first, but increasingly damaging and addicting. My roommate last year was a prime example."

Bax blinked at Xavier for a moment. "Wow. Um, well...that's your opinion, I guess."

"I'm certainly not attempting to foist my opinion on you, Baxter. It's just my feelings on the subject, based on my observance of my roommate's struggles with pornography addiction."

"Pornography addiction? Really?" Bax demanded, skeptical.

"Yes, really," Xavier answered. "It was all he did. He skipped class to watch it, flaked out on studying for exams, ditched his friends. He always had other excuses, but that's what he was doing. It negatively affected his life, and he was both unwilling and unable to curtail his usage of it, which by any definition is addiction, only mental rather than chemical."

"Huh." Bax stuffed his phone in his pocket as Zane pulled up outside a warehouse. "That's not me, though. It's just something I enjoy, and I don't see the harm in it."

He slid out of the cab and slammed the door, tugging the hood of his sweatshirt up against the icy early morning wind as he trudged to the entrance of the warehouse with an armload of supplies.

I patted Xavier's chest. "I think you made him think harder than he cares to, little brother."

Xavier searched me. "Am I wrong?"

I shook my head. "No, not at all. You've got a great point, actually, which is something I realized myself. I was never as into it as Bax, but when I started seeing Claire, it became something I just...didn't want anymore."

"Even though you don't see her all the time?"

I nodded. "That's definitely part of it. Things... build up, I guess, and then when we see each other it's more intense." I patted him again. "Don't ever let anyone give you shit about your choice, Xavier. I think it's admirable."

He sighed. "It's hard sometimes. I mean, it can be extremely difficult to not feel embarrassed about still being a virgin, especially having overly-virile sex machines for brothers." He rolled his shoulders, rubbing his chest where'd I'd patted him, leaning as far away from me as he could get; he disliked physical contact, and we'd been squeezed together for several minutes now. "I need air."

He got out and shut the door, joining Bax in the warehouse, leaving Lucian and me in the truck with Zane.

I glanced at Lucian. "You got anything to add, Luce?"

Lucian lifted a shoulder. "Nope." And then he was out of the truck too.

"Heavy conversation for six in the morning," Zane said, shutting off the truck.

"Yeah, well, if you didn't drag us out of bed at five-fucking-thirty..."

"You're really not a morning person, are you?" Zane asked, laughing.

We both got out and hauled supplies into the warehouse.

"I'm really not," I said. "There's absolutely no reason to be awake before seven."

"Don't you ever get up early to fly?" Zane asked. "Like for airshows?"

"Sure, obviously. But I hate it. And everyone I fly with knows to leave me alone if it's early, especially before coffee." I followed Zane into the warehouse and set my load of drywall on the floor just inside.

Zane had purchased the warehouse for a relatively cheap price, considering the size of it and its decent condition; I hadn't realized Zane had as much money saved as he had, and when I asked, he just said he wasn't much of a spender, so he'd saved almost all of his earnings over his ten years in the Navy, which, apparently, equalled a sizeable chunk of change. Obviously so, if he could afford to buy the place outright *and* the supplies necessary to renovate. The warehouse wasn't abandoned; the company that owned it had gone out of business and needed to unload it. It was, as Zane had claimed, a three-minute drive from the bar, so it was a convenient location. The interior had been set up for production of some kind of metal product, with offices in a loft area over the production floor. The company had removed and sold all the equipment and supplies in an auction before selling the building itself, so there was very little to do by way of clean up and demolition.

Zane, Xavier, and Bax had already spent most of the preceding week in here, knocking down all non-load bearing walls, and getting the interior ready for construction. Apparently Xavier had done some dabbling in architecture and design—because of course he had; only Xavier could "dabble" in something like architecture—so, he already had a CAD program on his laptop and the basic skills necessary to redesign the interior. Apparently Bax had moonlighted at a house building company during the offseason over in Canada, so he was actually a skilled builder, and the rest of us were all fairly handy naturally; Dad had renovated the upstairs apartment himself, so we came by it honestly.

Thus, I found myself roped into helping Zane turn the interior of a ten thousand square foot, one hundred year old warehouse into a liveable home. Despite my complaining, though, it was going to be a fun project. The outside of the warehouse was in excellent condition. Being an early twentieth century design, it was built to last, constructed of deep red brick, two stories, with a row of windows on each level. Inside, the front half of the interior was open from floor to ceiling, and then the back half was split into two levels. It had its own water tower on the flat roof, and a massive and fairly new central heating and A/C system. Zane had already had the electrical and plumbing inspected, so all we had to do was put in walls where he wanted them upstairs, build the kitchen, put down flooring, have some extra insulation blown in where necessary...

Yeah, that was it. No big deal. And, oh yeah, he wanted it done before the baby came, sometime in May. Which meant he was planning on spending every available moment here, and was hoping the rest of us would too. And us being the brothers we were, he knew he could count on us. We'd helped the twins build their studio, we'd all helped each other move, and we'd all pitched in to help both Dru and Mara move as well. If one of us asked for help, he got it, no matter what—and Badd brothers didn't do anything half-assed.

We went to work, Xavier guiding our efforts. The day went pretty fast, and we made decent progress. A quick break for lunch, and then we worked through until four. Bast had requested we all put in a few hours at the bar tonight, since he expected a busy crowd and the twins were playing a couple sets and thus couldn't work the floor, which meant I put in five hours behind the bar before Bast told me I could cut out.

I found Claire by herself up in the living room

over the bar, staring at her phone, sniffling, dabbing at her eyes with a Kleenex. I took a seat next to her and drew her close.

"What's wrong, babe?" I asked.

She showed me her phone; she had received a text message from an unknown number, the sender's bubble in green rather than blue.

Them: **Claire, this is Hayley. Texting you from my friend's phone. Dad is sick. Stage 3 cancer. Come home soon.**

I read the message several times. "I'm probably latching onto the totally wrong thing here, but why is Hayley texting you from a friend's phone?" I read the message again. "And...why would she *text* you this, rather than calling you? And why her and not your mom, or your dad?"

"I told you my family situation was complicated," Claire said, wiping at her nose.

"Yeah, you said your dad and you haven't spoken in, what, six years?"

She nodded. "And I told you why."

"You got pregnant out of wedlock, then had a miscarriage."

Claire took the phone back, staring at it; she hadn't responded, I noticed, and she'd received the message more than an hour earlier. "It's not that we don't *talk*, Brock. We didn't have a little falling out; he *disowned* me. I don't exist to him. If you asked him, he'd tell you he only has two daughters, even though Mom bore him three. He took me out of his will, retook all the family photos, deleted me from all contacts lists in his phone, in Mom's, in Hayley's, and in Tab's." She clicked the side button to put her phone to sleep, and then immediately woke it back up again. "I...do...not...*exist* to him."

I hesitated; Claire seemed more fragile than usual, on edge, and I wasn't sure how to proceed without hurting her more. "And, um...because your dad disowned you, that means your mom and sisters can't contact you?"

She nodded heavily. "Right. They're not allowed to talk to me, see me, email me, nothing. I'm not in the family."

"So your sister felt like you should at least know that your dad is sick, so she texted you from a friend's phone."

"What do I do, Brock? He's my dad and he's dying, but...he *hates* me. It wasn't just the pregnancy and miscarriage, that was just... the last straw. That would have been enough, don't get me wrong, that alone would have gotten me kicked out of the house at the very least. But I'd been...stubborn. Rebellious. I hated my dad's rules, hated the church, hated religion, hated being controlled and told what to do. So

I did what I wanted. Drank a lot, stayed out for days at a time, did drugs, messed around with boys, and I didn't try to hide any of it.

Dad tried to corral me, but I refused to listen, refused to capitulate to his fucking rules, so then when I had the miscarriage that was it. I mean, I hadn't told them I was pregnant. I'd been hiding it, because I had no clue what the fuck I was going to do about it. I couldn't afford an abortion, and I didn't think I could go through with that anyway, so…I didn't tell anyone. Not my friends, not my sisters, not the guy who knocked me up, no one. And then my family came home from mass one day and found me on the bathroom floor in a pool of blood. They knew right away what it meant, and once I'd recovered, they kicked me out, told me not to come back." Claire wiped under her eyes with the Kleenex again. "Well, not *they*, just my dad. Mom wanted to talk about it, wanted to give me another chance, but Dad had made up his mind."

I struggled for something useful to say. "I—shit, Claire. I have no clue what to say."

She laughed and sniffled. "I don't expect you to say anything. There's nothing *to* say." Another sniffling laugh, but this one was bitter. "My dad is dying of cancer, and I find out via text message from my baby sister. And there's not a damn thing I can do. I can't even fucking *see* him.

"You're not going back?" I asked, shocked.

She shrugged miserably. "Why? What's the point? He'll just ignore me until I go away. You don't understand my father, Brock."

I hauled her onto my lap. "Claire, honey, listen. I don't claim to understand your situation, but you know how I feel about this. I'd give anything to see my mom and dad one more time, literally *anything*. I'd give up flying, and that's...flying is my fucking life, it's who I *am*." I cupped her cheeks and forced her to look at me. "You can*not* just sit here and pretend it's not happening, Claire. You *have* to go back. You have to at least make the effort. If your dad dies and you don't at least make an attempt to see him one last time, you'll never forgive yourself."

She ripped her face out of my hands and buried herself in my shirt. "It hurts too much. I act tough, but...it hurts. I miss my family. I never did any of those things because I don't care about them, I just..." she shuddered, shook. "I can't do it."

"I know it's gonna hurt, but you have to try. You'll regret it the rest of your life if you don't."

She nuzzled closer, and I held her as tight as I could. When she spoke again, her voice was muffled against my shirt. "I tried to go back, once. Right before I joined the Army."

"What happened?" I asked.

She sighed. "He slammed the door in my face." Another sigh. "I'd just broken up with this guy. We'd been dating a few months, and—I was homeless at the time, right? So I was couch hopping. My lease had run out and I'd lost my job, and I only had a few friends, and most of them were druggies. I was fucking...I was lost, a complete mess. No job, no family, no real friends, nowhere to live. So I'd hooked up with this guy, a decent guy, not a bad guy at all. Just... average. I was living with him, but then he broke up with me and...I had nowhere to go. I'd worn out my welcome with most of my so-called friends...so I went back to Mom and Dad's. Thought I could beg them to let me stay with them for a while, get my feet under me."

"And he turned you away?" I couldn't believe it.

She nodded. "Yep. He answered the door when I rang the bell, took one look at me, and slammed the door in my face without a fucking word. Mom came out, gave me forty dollars, and told me to give him some time. My dad started shouting for my mom to stop consorting with a prostitute, and I realized then that..." Claire had to pause for breath, and start over. "I realized that he'd never get over it. No amount of time would change his mind. I'd actually considered prostitution, honestly. Before I got the courage to go home to Mom and Dad's. I was on the streets, hungry, cold, broke...it seemed like a way to put a roof over my head and food in my stomach. I'd have been able to find a john easily enough, I figured. I didn't end up doing it, but I thought about it, and the fact that I even considered it was the reason I ended up going back there at all."

"Jesus," I breathed. "I didn't grow up religious, but isn't there something in the Bible about, like, having compassion and forgiving people seventy times seven times?"

She laughed bitterly. "Yeah, but apparently that doesn't apply to wayward daughters." Another long silence, and then she continued. "I walked away from Mom and Dad's house with that forty bucks in my pocket. I bought a Happy Meal, a bottle of Popov, and a bottle of Aspirin." She let out a shuddering breath. "I meant to kill myself, and I probably would have succeeded, too. Some skinny teenager vomiting in an alley? Who's gonna give a shit? Well, on the way to find somewhere I could chase the Aspirin with the vodka, I passed by an Armed Forces recruiter. He got me to go inside and listen to his spiel, and I ended up joining the Army right then and there. His name was First Sergeant Tim Troyer, and he saved my life, very literally. I got into computers while I was in the Army, met Mara in our Sixty-Eight Whiskey unit, and then I met you..." another pause. "But I can't go back, Brock. I won't be turned away again."

I let the silence linger, until I could keep it in no longer. "He's your *father*, Claire." I spoke this in a low murmur.

"He's no one."

"Claire—"

"NO!" She shouted, lurching off of me. "Stop trying to push this! He can fucking croak for all I fucking care. He's a goddamn bastard and I hate him and I don't fucking care if he dies!"

I stood up and grabbed her, hauled her close, and she readily collapsed against me. "You're going back, Claire, but you won't be alone this time. I'll go with you. I won't leave your side, not for a second."

She leaned against me, crying, for several minutes. "I hate you."

"That's not how the word 'love' is pronounced, babe. But I know what you mean."

She laughed, despite herself. "You're so annoying."

"If by annoying you mean practically perfect in every way, then yes."

She glanced up at me. "Isn't that from *Mary Poppins*?"

I shrugged. "So?"

She shook her head, rolling her eyes. "You're really weird, you know that?"

"I do know that." I tipped her face up to mine. "So. Where are we headed?"

She rested her cheek on my chest, staring out the window. "Huntington Woods, Michigan."

Jasinda Wilder

Visit me at my website: **www.jasindawilder.com**
Email me: **jasindawilder@gmail.com**

If you enjoyed this book, you can help others enjoy it as well by recommending it to friends and family, or by mentioning it in reading and discussion groups and online forums. You can also review it on the site from which you purchased it. But, whether you recommend it to anyone else or not, thank you *so much* for taking the time to read my book! Your support means the world to me!

My other titles:

The Preacher's Son:
Unbound
Unleashed
Unbroken

Biker Billionaire:
Wild Ride

Big Girls Do It:
Better (#1), Wetter (#2), Wilder (#3), On Top (#4)
Married (#5)
On Christmas (#5.5)
Pregnant (#6)
Boxed Set

Rock Stars Do It:
Harder
Dirty
Forever
Boxed Set

From the world of Big Girls and Rock Stars:
Big Love Abroad

Delilah's Diary:
A Sexy Journey
La Vita Sexy
A Sexy Surrender

The Falling Series:
Falling Into You
Falling Into Us
Falling Under
Falling Away
Falling for Colton

The Ever Trilogy:

Forever & Always

After Forever

Saving Forever

The world of Alpha:

Alpha

Beta

Omega

Harris: Alpha One Security Book 1

Thresh: Alpha One Security Book 2

The world of Stripped:

Stripped

Trashed

The world of Wounded:

Wounded

Captured

The Houri Legends:

Jack and Djinn

Djinn and Tonic

The Madame X Series:

Madame X

Exposed

Exiled

Badd Brothers:
Badd Motherf*cker

The Black Room
(With Jade London):
Door One
Door Two
Door Three
Door Four
Door Five
Door Six
Door Seven
Door Eight

Standalone titles:
Yours

Non-Fiction titles:
Big Girls Do It Running

Jack Wilder Titles:
The Missionary

To be informed of new releases, special offers, and other Jasinda news, sign up for Jasinda's email newsletter.

61425766R00207

Made in the USA
Lexington, KY
10 March 2017